EVEN THE BIRDS

GUERNICA PRIZE 8

Canada Council for the Arts / Conseil des arts du Canada

ONTARIO ARTS COUNCIL
CONSEIL DES ARTS DE L'ONTARIO
an Ontario government agency
un organisme du gouvernement de l'Ontario

Ontario

Canada

Guernica Editions Inc. acknowledges the support of the Canada Council for the Arts and the Ontario Arts Council. The Ontario Arts Council is an agency of the Government of Ontario.

We acknowledge the financial support of the Government of Canada.

EVEN THE BIRDS

RUTH TAYLOR

GUERNICA
EDITIONS
TORONTO • CHICAGO • BUFFALO • LANCASTER (U.K.)
2026

Michael Mirolla, editor
David Moratto, cover and interior design

Guernica Editions Inc.
1241 Marble Rock Rd., Gananoque, (ON), Canada K7G 2V4
2250 Military Road, Tonawanda, N.Y. 14150-6000 U.S.A.
www.guernicaeditions.com

Distributors:
Independent Publishers Group (IPG)
600 North Pulaski Road, Chicago IL 60624
University of Toronto Press Distribution (UTP)
5201 Dufferin Street, Toronto (ON), Canada M3H 5T8

First edition.
Printed in Canada.

Legal Deposit—Third Quarter
Library of Congress Catalog Card Number: 2026936245
Library and Archives Canada Cataloguing in Publication
Title: Even the birds / Ruth Taylor.
Names: Taylor, Ruth (Journalist), author.
Description: Series statement: Guernica Prize ; 8
Identifiers: Canadiana (print) 20260153176 | Canadiana (ebook) 20260156833 | ISBN 9781778491429 (softcover) | ISBN 9781778491436 (EPUB)
Subjects: LCGFT: Novels.
Classification: LCC PS8639.A9566 E94 2026 | DDC C813/.6—dc23

Let yours be the first,
the first to be honoured by the daughters
born in light, by the sons born in light.
Your names will not be forgotten.
—*Popol Wuj, c. 1558*

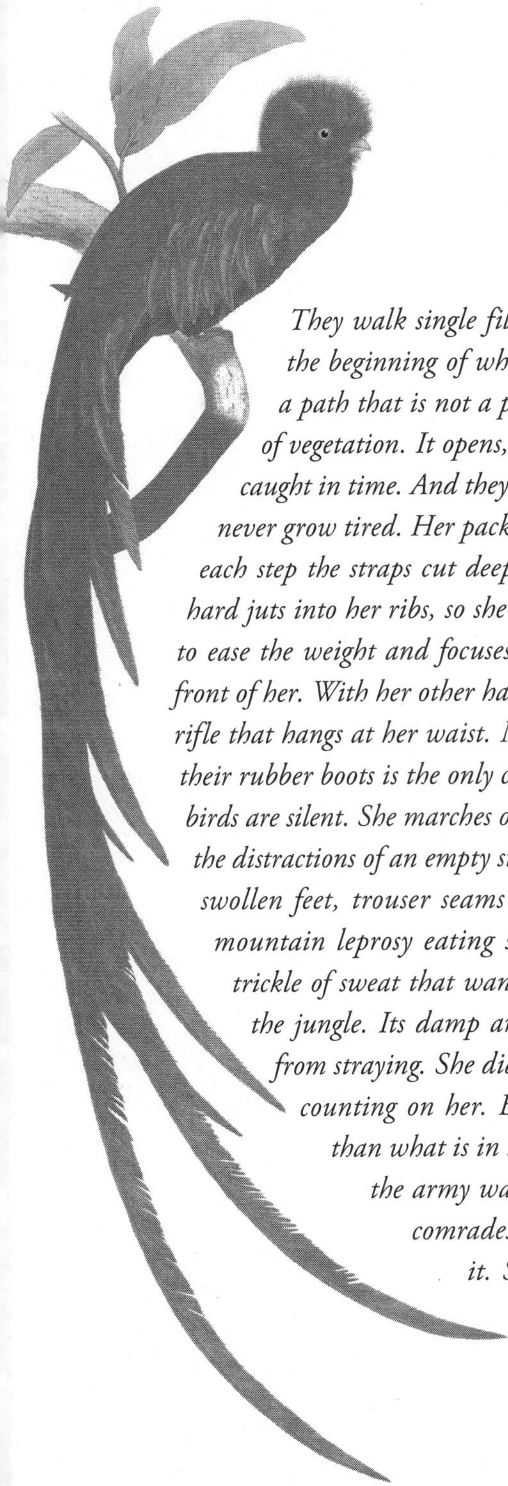

PART I

q'aq' (fire)

They walk single file through an endless green tunnel, the beginning of which they no longer recall, following a path that is not a path but a mere parting in the wall of vegetation. It opens, closes, opens, closes, as if they were caught in time. And they would never grow old. They would never grow tired. Her pack is heavy on her shoulders and with each step the straps cut deeper. She shifts the pack. Something hard juts into her ribs, so she wedges her thumb under one strap to ease the weight and focuses on the pack of the young man in front of her. With her other hand, she clasps the grip of the assault rifle that hangs at her waist. No one speaks: the muffled tread of their rubber boots is the only communication they need. Even the birds are silent. She marches on, resisting the earth's pull, refusing the distractions of an empty stomach, aching muscles, sodden and swollen feet, trouser seams chafing against her inner thighs, mountain leprosy eating sores into her arms and legs. The trickle of sweat that wanders down her spine. The steam of the jungle. Its damp aroma. She shakes her head to keep from straying. She did stray. And she mustn't. People are counting on her. Because nothing is more important than what is in her pack. And somewhere out there, the army waits in ambush. For her and for her comrades. For their secret cargo. She knows it. She has known it her whole young life, though all she can see is green.

CHAPTER 1

It was early morning, the hour when people in some parts of Guatemala City would be turning in their wide white beds, smiling at a tender moment from the movie channel that had infiltrated their dreams, dreaming perhaps of what the world would give them on waking. Nothing in their cool urban fortresses challenged their slumber. Not the movements and whispers of maids and house staff as they pressed shirts and school uniforms, checked the car's oil and tires and tank, and prepared the family breakfast. Not the parade of workers beyond the wrought-iron bars and high stucco walls topped by shards of broken glass, who arrived on foot, tossing their boasts, their entreaties, their prayers to the sky. Not the blossoming April heat. Not one breached the sleepers' peace.

Here in Eighteenth Street, on this ordinary Saturday in 1997, everybody was up: shopkeepers, market vendors, prostitutes, thieves. On every corner, down every alley, along block after block of broken sidewalk, in doorways, at open windows, people yelled to be heard above the gnarl of intercity buses, idling delivery vans, and their own neighbours. The exception was a handful of men who'd drunk their way to early dawn, only to sink into sleep wherever they happened to be—propped against a urine-stained wall or sprawled atop a small mountain of discarded corn husks. A scrawny patio rooster, its head feathers sticking out at odd angles, squawked to life with an ear-piercing crow, yet the men slept on.

In her small apartment behind the shops, Soraida, too, was up before dawn, pulling on a faded housecoat and blue flipflops and padding her way from bedroom to bathroom to kitchen. She made her bed, brushed her teeth, showered, boiled an egg and ate it. She filled one side of the outdoor laundry sink with water and began to fill a large rubber trash can as well. She tapped on the door of her grandniece's bedroom, and then opened, to see whether Yasmin had crept in unobserved, whether the girl had kept her word and returned home in time for the morning's work. She lay out yesterday's tortillas on a cloth serviette to dry. She put a pound of black beans in water and set them on the stove to boil. She looked into Yasmin's room again. She swept and mopped the kitchen, changed into a simple floral dress and slip-on flats, tied an apron across her thick belly, raked a comb through her short, greying hair, checked her watch, and greeted Byron when he knocked on her door, as promised, at seven o'clock.

"Good boy. We've no time to lose."

Byron trailed her down the long hallway, across Soraida's small open-air courtyard and into the shop. He was a tall, slim youth of sixteen, with burnished skin and a head of dark lazy curls. Dressed in the uniform of youth—a T-shirt and jeans—he was the sort of boy who kept the cities' shops and markets in assistants, porters and messengers. But unlike many, he was still in school. His mother, a woman Soraida knew only through the inherited scraps of wisdom and warnings her son regularly invoked, insisted on it.

"You get the pine needles and I'll bring the machete," Soraida said. She pulled a set of keys from her apron pocket and handed them to him. "And get that overhead door up an inch so we can breathe. Just a smidgen, mind you. Nobody gets in till we're ready."

Byron did as he was told, removing the padlocks at the door's base and returning the keys to Soraida, who dropped them into her apron pocket. Then he hefted the door an inch, its metal wheels screeching. Sunlight shot across the polished cement floor. At its centre sat an enormous blue bundle. They could hear people gathering outside.

Soraida approached the bundle, machete in hand. "She should be here," she said as Byron circled past her, strewing pine needles over the floor. Their scent rose to greet her like an embrace.

"Yasmin?" he asked.

"Of course, Yasmin."

"It'll be all right." He drew another handful from the garbage bag he was dragging behind him. The needles fell, silent, barely visible until the early morning light that slid under the overhead door caught them like a spotlight. "We'll do okay."

We've done it before, he might have added. But he didn't. He was too well mannered for that. In the four years he'd worked for Soraida, he'd never let her down.

Soraida checked her watch again, adjusting the strap as she did so. "She said she'd be back in time." The voices outside were growing stronger, and now and then somebody banged on the metal door or tried to peek under. "Hold on, ladies," Soraida shouted. To Byron she said, "You about ready?"

Byron hauled the half-empty garbage bag out to the courtyard.

Soraida breathed deep, slipped the machete blade between one nylon cord and the blue tarp that held the bundle together and severed it. She loved this moment, tugging at the covering and watching the wonders hidden within tumble forth: bright toddler outfits, designer jeans, big label shirts. A leather jacket! Skimpy dresses, trousers from the Gap, J.C. Penney, Urban Jungle—some of them had probably been stitched together in Guatemala and then, like virtually everything else the country produced, exported. Exported, sold, used, discarded, and sent back to Guatemala to be resold by Soraida and hundreds of shops like hers. Of course, the bale contained an equal number of clunkers. She lifted one now, an oversized T-shirt with an indecipherable slogan scribbled across the chest. The face of some celebrity with long blonde hair and pouting red lips. People and products unknown in these lands. And books—fat paperbacks in English that she deposited in a pile by the door in case anybody wanted them, but nobody ever did.

Occasionally there was treasure. Once she'd found a fifty-dollar bill in the pocket of a pair of jeans. Another time it was a watch—a Casio, the one she now wore on her left wrist. They were small gifts that surfaced without rhyme or reason, too rare to hunt for. Nonetheless, Soraida felt blessed when they did appear.

She dug her thick arms into the mass and extracted a heap, carried it over to a spot in the middle of the floor and dropped it. Older stock occupied the narrow shelves that lined three of the shop's four walls. A wooden table, two white plastic chairs and a counter completed the furnishings.

"Just make piles," she said to Byron. "Three should be enough."

He obeyed without comment, walking to and from the bale with armloads of clothing to make one pile, then another.

"Farther back," Soraida said. "Farther from the entrance."

Byron moved the pile.

When they'd finished unpacking the bale, they folded up the tarp and carried it out to the courtyard. Then Byron walked to the overhead door and raised it.

Women rushed in, elbows working, manoeuvring for the best spot, their voices a battery of giggles and oaths. Most of them were middle-aged matrons, like Soraida, and most were ladina, as she was. But some Indigenous women from the market had joined the throng, bent to the task like the others, the neon oranges, pinks, turquoises, purples of their huipiles clashing above deep indigo cortes. Three crowds formed around the three mountains of fabric, articles of clothing rising into the air and falling as the women picked expertly through them. They leaned in, squeezed closer, one as thin and sturdy as iron rods, another solid as a sack of corn, another rosy and plump. Brown faces eager, glistening; their chatter raucous and relentless despite the heat of the room and its smells—cheap perfumes and budding perspiration that soon overpowered the scent of pine.

Soraida found comfort in the ritual, in the way nothing about the shop ever changed: not the people, not the clothing, not even the gossip. Somebody's man had left her, somebody else was the man-stealing tart, somebody's daughter was pregnant, somebody miscarried—aborted, the knowing ones said—somebody died, and somebody lived, against all odds. Most of it wasn't good news, admittedly, but none of it was out of the ordinary. She knew where she stood when she was at work. Names and dates ticked by, but life—her life—kept to its well-worn track.

What the Indigenous women talked about in their languages of clicks and whispers, she didn't know. As ever-present and unremarkable as the horizon, they elicited in her neither ill will nor curiosity. To each his own was her philosophy.

As her customers rummaged, Soraida joined Byron at the shop entrance, surveying the street in the slender hope that Yasmin might yet appear. A few doors down, Doña Estela was hoisting a giant Pikachu to the awning above the entrance of her piñata shop. Other favourites—Scooby-doo, Power Puff Girls, Spider-man—crowded above her. Soraida called out in greeting and Estela waved back. At the other end of the block, where Eighteenth Street crossed the city's main avenue, Otto sat on his step wedging a retreaded tire into its rim. A stack of tires marked his repair shop out to passersby in the same way a red light posted outside a house on Saturday meant they had tamales for sale. On Thursdays, the same bulb swaddled in red acetate meant the house sold paches, a tamal-like dish made from potatoes. Or the way the American flags painted on either side of Soraida's entrance advertised the articles of second-hand clothing within.

From somewhere above, the roar of a jet plane shook the air.

Soraida turned once more to Byron. "She had a sleepover but she said she'd be back early."

"We'll do okay," he said again, his gaze drifting up and down the street.

Perhaps his eyes, so much sharper than her own, would see what she could not.

On the plaza opposite, separated by nothing more than the dirty street and a ribbon of blue sky, the market buzzed. Porters of all sizes, doubled over from bundles that were twice as big as they were, darted along its shaded aisles, in and out of narrow metal stands. Under plastic tarps and fabric canopies that would protect them from the blistering midday sun, vendors shouted instructions back and forth as they batted off flies, kicked away dogs and set out their wares: tapes and video cassettes, baseball caps and nylon children's costumes, backpacks—hundreds of them—cameras and lenses, electronic gadgets the names of which Soraida could barely keep track. An endless parade of pirated and stolen goods. Every morning they set up and before dusk they tore down. Eighteenth Street was famous for its contraband market. And for the smell. Exhaust, rotted fruit, urine. Soraida wrinkled her nose. She considered herself a cut above the market vendors and two cuts—at least—above the poorest inhabitants of the zone. Tidy, clean, more practical than elegant, she had long since given up makeup, nylons, and heels. Petit bourgeoisie, Yasmin liked to say in a mocking tone, as if there was some kind of shame in it. But Soraida was not one for airs. She did nothing to distinguish herself from most of her neighbours, shopkeepers like herself.

"I had to take my sister to hospital this morning," Byron said.

"No! You should have told me. Is she all right?"

"She was having pains, but the doctor says it's too soon. It's just her body getting ready." He grinned. "They let me listen. I heard the baby's heart!"

And he'd still made it to work on time. The boy was right as rain. If only the same could be said about Yasmin. Where that child got her ways . . . ? Not from Soraida. That was certain. Yasmin was as unlike her great-aunt as a person could be. Taciturn, headstrong, rude. Fifteen. Yesterday she'd arrived home from school in a sulk and spent most of dinner glaring at her beans. Yet as soon as Soraida cleared her bowl, she was bouncing up and down, pleading to meet a girlfriend for ice cream. Soraida chuckled to herself. She adored Yasmin. Perhaps that indulgence was part of the problem. It was hard to say no to a girl whose mother was little more than a ghost in her life—floating in unbidden, gone again before daybreak—whose father ... Soraida didn't even know who the father was.

"I'm glad you're taking good care of her," she said to Byron. "Family is the most important thing we have. And children." She watched a skinny, shoeless boy race another along one of the market aisles, laughing so hard he could barely keep upright. Yasmin had been happy like that, springing into fast and easy friendships with the market children or indeed with any child who visited the shop. They'd play dress-up and outfit their dolls with items from Soraida's stock. They'd skip rope and toss pennies. Once Yasmin swallowed one and Soraida had to turf the other children from the shop, close up and find Don Julio's taxi so they could get her to a hospital. Time and again Yasmin would try to sneak out to join her pals across the street. Until Soraida told her she could do better. No doubt Isabel, too, had been carefree and happy at one time. Soraida certainly hoped so. By the time she first met her niece, Isabel was already grown, pregnant with Yasmin, and well along a path Soraida rejected out of principle and plain good sense, any trace of childhood long gone. No, Isabel was not a ghost; she was all too real. And despite her faults, which were many, Soraida adored her too.

"Seño!" A customer was calling.

"Twenty quetzales for everything," Soraida said after she'd reviewed the articles of clothing the woman laid out one by one across the counter: a skirt, two blouses, a pair of shorts. As Soraida collected the garments, the woman plucked the cash from inside her brassiere. More customers, ready to purchase, formed a queue behind her that coiled inside the shop like the spring of a clock.

Soraida motioned to Byron. "Help fold these while I make change."

The women weren't pushy or impatient although some of them wanted to haggle. Soraida strove to dispatch them promptly without giving in, from time to time patting her forehead with the pale green handkerchief she kept in her apron pocket. The room was baking now. If Yasmin had been here, they'd have done the work in half the time. Not because Yasmin was particularly adept with customers—she was all business, no chitchat—but she made quick work of them, if only so she could brandish her Walkman and tune out.

When the rush was finally over, clothing dotted the shop from one end to the other. Soraida began to return the strays to one of the large piles while Byron swept up the pine needles. With their movement, a strong foresty scent drifted again through the space Soraida's customers and their many smells had just vacated. Soraida flexed her back. She was getting too old for this.

Just then a boy of ten or eleven hopped up the front step waving a piece of paper. "Soraida Barrios Ibargüen?" he asked.

Soraida went to him to receive what turned out to be a telegram. She tipped him twenty-five centavos for his trouble and then, in the light of the shop entrance, held it at arm's length. "Home tonight" was all it said.

Soraida stared at the fragile page, the fuzzy black type, the pinpricks of searing white light that pierced the holes cut by the two o's. The street quivered with heat.

"Anything wrong?" Byron asked.

She'd just been thinking about Isabel. And now a telegram. She fanned her face, blinking to clear the tears that pricked at the corners of her eyes. Isabel. Here. In the flesh. Her flesh. Her own flesh and blood. She tried to smile. "All good news. I'm just surprised."

Byron remained where he was, broom in hand. He observed her with concern.

Soraida re-entered the shop, folded the telegram with care, and placed it beneath the ledger she kept on a shelf behind the counter. "I think, perhaps, I've never talked about Yasmin's mother."

Byron shook his head.

"She's coming to work for me." At least, that's what she'd assumed would happen.

"I always thought ..." He didn't finish.

Soraida stooped to rescue a grey cardigan that lay abandoned near her feet, mindful of a new ache in her bones. There were things—political things—you didn't talk about, except to family, and even then, you had to be careful.

"She's coming back. That's what's important," she said.

Byron nodded. "Yasmin will be happy."

Soraida straightened her apron, smoothing it with both hands. Yasmin hadn't seen her mother in more than a year, a visit—like all of them—arranged in secret, at a location far from the shop and anybody they knew. They'd ridden the 81 to a Pollo Campero on Simón Bolívar and waited forty minutes before Isabel appeared. Half an hour more to order and eat three pieces of overpriced fried chicken and then a twenty-minute stroll among the boulevard's furniture stores and carpentry shops. That was it. No word since then to tell them whether she was alive or dead. In its absence, Soraida had clung to the belief that bad news travels faster than good. Now here was a telegram to prove it. And Isabel was returning.

"Happy?" she said to Byron. "I don't know if I'd say that. Or perhaps she will be, but she won't want me to know it." She breathed deeply in an attempt to settle the flutter in her stomach. "Yasmin's never been too happy with me, either. She's just not a very happy girl."

"She's had a hard time." Byron moved the broom in a wide arc to gather needles and dust he'd missed on the first pass.

"And haven't you had a hard time? All the work you do to care for your mother, your sister?"

"They're my family."

"Exactly. They're family. There's no liking or not liking about it. You're a good boy. You study hard. You work hard. It's not like it's been easy, but you do it. You don't go mouthing off to your mother, do you?"

Byron looked as though the thought alone would strike him dead.

Soraida sighed. It shouldn't be difficult to speak about your own niece. Your only niece. But Isabel had made it difficult. More than difficult. Dangerous. What would she do once she was back? "I just don't understand this country of ours," she said.

"Maybe things will get better now. It's good if Yasmin's mother comes back. You'll have more help."

She'd said *home.* "What if she takes Yasmin away?"

Byron stopped sweeping. He looked uncomfortable.

"Yasmin's mother—she has the right," Soraida said. How to explain things without really explaining them? She shouldn't have said anything at all. "Her mother and I haven't always seen eye to eye. We see the world very differently."

The bouncy rhythm of the latest pop hit reached them from one of the stands across the street.

"Maybe you'll get a chance to make up," Byron said.

Soraida laughed. How could a boy like that exist in a place like this, or worse, in the place he lived. La Limonada made Eighteenth Street look like the Zona Rosa: sixty thousand people wedged into a ravine half a kilometre long. Yet he was sweeter than sugar cane. She fished in her apron pocket and drew out a crumpled five-quetzal note. "Go get some champurradas from the bakery."

Once Byron had gone, she took two mismatched porcelain mugs and a small jar of Nescafé from behind the counter and dumped a spoonful of the chocolate-coloured grains into each cup. Then she pulled the stopper—a dried-out corn cob wrapped in a plastic bag—from the large checkered thermos she kept there and filled each cup with hot water. Now to face the rest of the day: Yasmin and her excuses, Isabel … Soraida added sugar and stirred. Keeping order in her shop, in her home, wasn't easy but surely it wasn't impossible. Small and simple rituals, like sharing a cup of coffee and a sweet bun at eleven o'clock, were the stuff that held the world together. It was something she firmly believed.

CHAPTER 2

THE OLD BUS swayed from side to side as it rumbled over the potholes and joined the long line of vehicles inching across the bridge that separated Ciudad Hidalgo, Mexico, from Tecún Umán, Guatemala. In the other lane, a string of cars, buses and trucks crept under the blazing sun in the opposite direction, to Mexico. Yellow bicycle taxis weaved in and out among them, carrying travellers between the border control points on either side of the river. The bus was full, but not overstuffed, with men and a handful of women, most of them dressed in collared plaid shirts or simple blouses, and jeans or dress pants. Most of them underfed. Moments earlier they'd been animated, chatting nervously or getting up to visit their fellow travellers, but as they moved onto the bridge they fell silent.

Like the others, she pressed her face against the window to get a better look. Sunlight bleached the world outside. On the river far below, not ten metres from the bridge's shadow, another line of migrants moved across the water. Men and women, children even, were wading to the other side, their belongings balanced on top of their heads. Larger parties ferried across on inner tubes strung together by enterprising locals. So this is peace, she thought.

"I've gone that route before," Danilo said from his seat beside her. "There's usually a cop waiting on the other side, but if you tip him, he lets you pass. You wonder why anybody bothers with the bridge . . . or the border." He smiled. "You excited?"

"Anxious, more like." She rubbed her hands against her face to calm her nerves and loosen the whisper of a headache that had settled around her eyes.

"But it's good to be back home, isn't it?"

She tried to clean the window with the heel of her fist. "Does it look any different to you?"

Danilo leaned across her and peered through the grubby pane. He was a small man, though larger than she was, with an overgrown mop of straight brown hair, thick beard, and large round glasses.

"Not as green," he said.

They heard a voice from the front of the bus, and she raised herself from her seat to see. Eduardo, the captain in charge of this busload of demobilizing guerrilla fighters, stood tall and gaunt, an arm looped over each of the baggage racks that ran above the seats.

"Listen up!" he shouted. "We're arriving at the checkpoint. I need everybody to get off the bus, line up and show whatever papers you have—if you have papers—to the U.N. official. Tell him your name and he'll check it off the list. If anybody has trouble, I'll be there to sort it out."

Somebody at the back let out a whoop and several others joined in.

Danilo eased a half-empty pack of Rubios from his shirt pocket and tapped it until it produced a lighter and a cigarette.

"Will Yasmin be meeting you?"

"I'll meet them at the house. Soraida's not really a fan."

Danilo nodded.

They rolled past the border guard, who waved them on with one hand while shielding his eyes from the sun with the other. She watched Mexico recede.

"We did what we had to," Danilo said. He had a knack for stating the obvious. Or it might have been an attempt at humour. Jokester was his natural state. And fighter. He was an ace combatant.

She poked him in the ribs.

"You're just an old kiss-ass. Lost the habit of thinking for yourself?"

"Careful now. Talk like that'll get you shot."

She shook her head, but she was grinning.

All around them their compañeros were talking and laughing. For some reason the sound made her lonely.

The bus jerked to a halt and Eduardo was shouting again. "All right, follow me!"

When it was her turn, she showed her identity card to the burly man in a blue beret and watched him search his list and write a check mark next to her name. Beside him gleamed a large white pickup with a U.N. insignia on its door. Huddled at a short distance, a ragged group of barefooted children stared as the strangers filed past. A small boy trotted across the barren plaza driving a metal hoop before him with a stick.

Guatemala in plain daylight. No more coded messages or secret rendezvous. No more roll call or military manoeuvres. No more chain of command. No more criticism and self-criticism. No more marches, no camps, no firefights. No more hiding. No more pretending. Four months before, a final peace accord between the state and the URNG rebel forces had put an end to thirty-six years of war. Many promises had been made on both sides, but the main ones were: the guerrillas would hand over their weapons and the government would not kill them. And now? Now they had to look for work, find a place to live, reconnect with family and friends. Now it was safe, so they'd been promised, to fight for change without a gun in your hands. That pledge was all they had to protect them from whatever lay ahead.

"So what's your name again?" Danilo asked, sucking at his cigarette to finish it before they climbed back on the bus. It was an inside joke. They knew each other only by their pseudonyms.

"Isabel Martina Barrios Cun." For *eighteen* years, she'd hardly uttered it.

"That's a mouthful." He extended his hand in greeting. "How do you do? I'm Danilo."

He was sticking to his pseudonym.

The bus left Tecún Umán, twisting through the rugged highland provinces of San Marcos and Quetzaltenango, down to the steamy South Coast. The immense plantations of the Guatemalan oligarchy stretched in all directions, as flat and fertile as the highway that served them was smooth and straight. One steaming transport after another wheeled by in the oncoming lane, each stacked high with charred stalks of sugar cane. Long green living cane nodded from both sides of the road, but up ahead smoke billowed from the fields and the air above the highway rippled with heat. Indigenous farmworkers, flashing torches held aloft, were setting fire to the fields to reduce the cane's weight and concentrate the sugar.

Isabel's head began to throb. She knew this place. She knew the scorched syrup smell, the deafening crackle of burning cane. Like hell come to earth, great black clouds erupting from its core, chasing the blue from the sky. A wall of flame. A barricade of machine-gun fire. Her chest constricted, squeezing the air from her lungs, her skin prickled, she couldn't breathe. The flames reared and roared, a mammoth, punishing beast, impossible to slay. Grasping the chrome handrail across the top of the seat in front of her, she strained to see a way out. Then, as the bus pulled past the worst of the smoke, leaving the blazes farther and farther behind, whatever phantom had seized her released her again.

Her skin was damp, as if the fear that had filled her had escaped through her pores and lay now in a film of moisture, evaporating in the breeze that wafted through the bus windows. Around her, low voices murmured. In her mind's eye, her daughter hovered like a promise. *Yasmin, it's been so long. Will you still have me?*

Danilo was flipping through the pages of a newspaper he'd bought at the border.

"I keep having this dream," she said. "At least it feels like the same dream over and over, even though different things happen each time.

I've always got my pack and we're marching and the army's somewhere watching. But my pack is too heavy, and I can't carry it anymore—"

"Not too subtle."

"So I leave it in a clearing. I'm thinking it's just my supplies I'm carrying. I figure it will distract the army."

Danilo nodded, as if all of this had really happened.

"It does distract them. They all run to my pack and circle round it, and then they open it."

"What's in it? Can I guess?"

"No! It's a baby. But not always a baby. Sometimes it's other things. Once it was a storm, a howling wind that blew everything away."

"And you don't know what this is about?"

"Yeah, I do, I think, but that doesn't stop the dream." She stared at the fragment of her reflection caught and distorted by the chrome railing.

"You'll be seeing your baby soon," Danilo said. "Maybe that'll help."

"Maybe." But Isabel wasn't persuaded. There was more to the dream than a mother's longing, and there was more in the pack than Yasmin. It might be endless, what was in there. Wasn't that why she'd wanted to leave it behind?

Soraida sat with her coffee at the counter, drawing quetzal bills from her apron, smoothing them, and sorting them into piles before counting. She'd sent Byron home, with pay and regards to his mother. The day's take was modest, equivalent nonetheless to about two weeks of regular business. Most of the revenue from the sales they held when a new bale of clothing arrived went straight into an empty powdered milk tin. Day-to-day foot traffic was what kept them in groceries and school supplies.

As Soraida placed the last bill on the counter, Yasmin arrived at the back door, lolling against the jamb. Her black hair was long and straight, her limbs smooth and brown beneath white shorts and a white tank top, headphones looped around her neck, a Walkman clipped to her waist.

"Auntie?" she called, peering into the space through dark glasses.

Soraida gathered the stacks of bills, folded them and returned them to her apron pocket. "I'm right here, child. Where have you been?"

"Sorry I'm late. I overslept. Oh lord, my head feels like a melon."

Soraida knew she should scold Yasmin—give her a good talking to—but she didn't have the heart. Not today. Not any day. She never had the heart. "You missed the whole morning. You knew it was the big day."

Yasmin strode into the room, hands on hips, surveying the piles of clothing. "How did it go?"

The managerial pose made her seem even younger than she was. A child playing dress-up.

Soraida fetched the ledger and a pen, which failed to write on the first try. She poked at the tip with her tongue and tried again. "I think people are buying less every day. They're nervous. They don't know where things are headed, and they don't want to take a chance."

Yasmin snorted. "Nonsense." It sounded out of place on a fifteen-year-old. "You're talking about the peace accords, right? They're not worried. They don't even know. They don't even care." She collapsed into one of the plastic chairs and stretched. "Ooh, are those champurradas?"

Soraida frowned at her grandniece. "Go ahead, but then it's to work. There's still plenty to do. We need to sort and fold all those clothes there into the stands."

"Oh, my head."

"Now who's talking nonsense." Soraida got up and dug behind the counter. She drew out an embroidered blouse. Calvin Klein. "I saved something for you."

Yasmin turned, her face brightening. She went to the counter and examined the blouse. "Oh, Auntie," she said as she threw her arms around Soraida and rocked with her from side to side.

"Silly girl."

Yasmin kissed her great-aunt's cheek. "To work," she said.

"Hold up. I've got something else for you." Soraida retrieved the telegram from between the pages of the ledger, unfolded it gingerly and passed it to her grandniece. She'd played this moment, or ones like it, in her mind on more occasions than she could remember. But it hadn't helped. She felt completely unprepared for whatever might happen next. Eyes fixed on the telegram, Yasmin returned to her chair, her face flushed, her mouth half-open, the girl Soraida knew and loved better than anybody as silent and inscrutable as a sphynx. The Calvin Klein blouse had fallen to the floor.

After three hours on the South Coast, the bus rocked up the steep slope past Villa Nueva and into the commotion of Guatemala City. Their driver leaned on the horn like everybody else in the jam of traffic and bullied his way into one lane and then another until he swung onto the Periférico. Isabel thought she saw the first house she'd ever lived in whizz past. She pointed it out to Danilo.

"I used to work all over these parts," he said. "I was what you might call *lumpen*."

Isabel knew a bit of Danilo's history: petty thievery and confidence scams, the gang life of the poor urban teen before the Salvatrucha and the M18 arrived from the United States. "I heard you're going into the security business," she said.

"Did Claudia tell you? They're putting me in with the trainees for the new police force."

"So you'll be taking classes with the roaches."

"Now, Isabel, you won't be able to talk like that anymore." He wagged his finger at her.

"Yeah, yeah. But nobody's going to be able to stop what I think."

"And I'm very glad of it." He smiled, and Isabel suddenly missed him terribly. It didn't make sense—he wasn't hers to miss.

This life has warped me, she thought. I'm never going to be able to see things straight again.

"If you need work," he said, "I'm sure Claudia could get you in with the Foundation. There'll be lots to do. Housing projects, building the party—tons to do."

"My aunt will want me in her shop."

"Is that what you want?"

They crossed a long narrow bridge over one of many vast ravines that cut through the city. Houses, from cinderblock to zinc to cardboard, sprouted like vegetation down its banks.

She'd wanted revolution. "I owe her. And Yasmin loves her. She may not even love me anymore."

"You obviously know nothing about children."

Isabel winced. It was easy to feel angry and hurt. And just as easy to feel guilty. Either way, it was selfish. She had to be the best person she could be for Yasmin. Nothing else mattered.

When they got to the Toriello Foundation, set up by the URNG rebels to support their fighters in their return to civilian life, they pulled belongings from the rack overhead and stepped from the bus. Isabel shouldered her pack and looked about. The Foundation's pale blue walls glowed in the late afternoon sunlight.

"Danilo, I'm heading out," she called to him.

Danilo hurried over, an unlit cigarette dangling from his lip. "Why don't you stay here tonight. The compas are fixing up a big meal."

"Yasmin's waiting."

"You're not armed. Maybe I should go with you."

"It's still light out. I'm going to have to get used to this sooner or later." As Danilo lit his cigarette, she watched her compañeros unloading parcels and baskets from the top of the bus, searching through bags and backpacks, greeting other compas who'd arrived sometime before.

It wasn't easy to leave, even though leaving at a moment's notice was something she'd done many times in her thirty-five years.

"Walk me to the corner," she said.

As it turned out, Isabel wasn't the only one taking the city bus. She rode with a compa from Suchitepéquez and another from Petén, but the camaraderie of their trip from the border was gone. Accustomed to the role of appearing to be what they were not, they smiled at each other and eyed the other passengers with a mixture of curiosity and caution. "See you around," Isabel said as she got off.

She walked a block along Eighteenth Street to the intersection with Sixth Avenue and then across the empty plaza until she reached a black metal door. She'd never been in the house, though her aunt had lived here since before Yasmin was born.

Isabel knocked. After a moment she heard footsteps and the door opened.

Her aunt looked at her in stunned silence before she embraced Isabel briskly and kissed her cheek. She squeezed Isabel's arm tenderly, as if she were choosing fruit. "Goodness girl, when was the last time they fed you?" Then she called to the back of the house. "Yasmi!"

Yasmin peeked around the corner of the long hallway and grinned. "Mami!" she shouted and ran to throw herself into Isabel's arms.

Soraida reached for Isabel's backpack. "Is this all you've brought?"

Nudging Soraida aside, Yasmin tugged at her mother's waist. "Come, Mami. You'll sleep with me."

They showed Isabel her bedroom: cream walls, yellowing in spots, empty but for two posters—one of Pocahontas, a cartoon Indigenous maiden surrounded by cartoon animals, and one of Selena, all hips and lips and gold lamé—a dresser topped by a tape deck and a stack of blue-papered exercise books, a small, barred window of frosted glass above twin beds. When had they found time to add a second bed?, Isabel wondered. Or had it always been there, awaiting her return? Isabel placed her hand against the cement wall, half-thinking it might dissolve at her touch. Its cool hard surface steadied her. Before she could ask anything, they led her back to the kitchen, Yasmin still gripping her hand as though to keep her from running away.

"There's food on the stove if you're hungry now," Soraida said. "Or if you want to wash up first?"

Isabel was trying to take it all in: the small, clean apartment, the kitchen brimming with warmth and the smells of home cooking. Her daughter, bright with health and youthful vigour. "I'll sit here with you first." She was holding back tears.

Soraida brought a steaming bowl of pepián and placed it on the table before her. She inhaled its rich aroma of toasted sesame and pumpkin seeds.

Yasmin sat, too. "Auntie killed a turkey," she said.

Isabel smiled at her aunt, who stood by the table, hands clasped across her apron, waiting for Isabel to begin eating.

"Soraida, join us," Isabel said.

"Oh, I've already eaten. I always have something as soon as I'm done at the shop." As she spoke she fiddled with her apron, brushed a crumb from the tablecloth, replaced the clean fork with a cleaner one, and returned to her post, where she shifted from foot to foot as if she couldn't find the right stance, her eyes never parting from Isabel's. "Do you want some Nescafé? Or Maizena?" she asked, looking Isabel over critically. "You really need to put some meat on you!"

Isabel smiled and reached for her daughter's hand. She felt like she was melting.

CHAPTER 3

Soraida opened her eyes. A cry from the next room had awakened her. She waited, blinking in the half-light, to see whether the dreamer would call out again or the danger had passed. After a few minutes of silence, she turned to the wall and went back to sleep.

Near dawn she was roused again by the explosion of machine-gun firecrackers on the street outside. When the last of the belt was spent, the crackle of a phonograph playing "Las Mañanitas" started up. It was somebody's birthday.

With Isabel and Yasmin still sleeping and the shop closed, Soraida set out to prepare the neighbourhood for her niece's arrival. Her first stop was Estela's piñata shop.

"She wasn't deported," Soraida told her neighbour as she took a seat at the worktable. "She just thought it was time to come home."

Estela was slicing up sheets of purple tissue paper for a giant Barney dinosaur.

"Besides she'd finally earned enough money there in Arizona to put Yasmin through school."

Estela made quick short snips into the translucent paper's edge, her scissors clacking to the beat of a tune on the radio. "Well, hold on to her if you can." She motioned to the glass jar of watered-down glue at the other end of the table, and Soraida passed it to her. "Maybe the peace will bring us something new, eh, Soraida?"

Soraida remembered then that Estela's son was in the United States and it had been months without word of him. She felt ashamed she'd let her own fears blind her to her neighbour's pain. "If Raúl hasn't returned it's because he's doing well. That's what we want for them, isn't it?"

Estela sniffed.

"Or have you heard something?"

Estela carried the delicate tissue frills that would form Barney's purple hide to the naked Barney base and pasted them one by one against the cream-coloured shell. She smoothed them with her hand. "I haven't heard anything at all."

"You will," Soraida said, though she didn't believe it herself. Good wishes didn't change anything. "I'm sure of it."

After taking her leave of Estela she proceeded to Otto's tire repair shop, at the other end of the block, watching her footing for places where the pavement was broken or uneven. As she passed the shoe store, open shoe boxes displaying the range of styles and sizes, more boxes filling the back wall, she heard muffled clanging from La Victoria bakery around the corner and thought she smelled a trace of rising bread in the air. It occurred to her that perhaps Raúl wasn't in the States at all. Perhaps, like Isabel, he'd been in the jungle all this time. She imagined an invisible, parallel world percolating beneath the one she knew: an illegal printing press hidden behind the ovens in La Victoria's back room, the bus driver's helper sneaking out at night to plant explosives at the base of a transmission tower, cash or hand grenades or ammunition delivered in shoe boxes to urban guerrillas posing as customers, the middle grade teacher recruiting students for clandestine Saturday meetings. People always said that the grubby men who offered to keep an eye on the cars that parked down by Don Julio's taxi stand doubled as army spies. But who were they spying on? Soraida shook her head. What a game of mirrors. One world—the one that slapped you in the face every time you stepped out your door—was more than enough to deal with.

She skirted the couple who sat on the sidewalk—always sat there—between Estela's and Otto's, getting in the way of passersby. The woman, barefoot in a long shapeless dress, stooped over her companion, a soot-faced man with thick black hair that stuck out in all directions. As the woman straightened and arranged her dress to sit beside him, a smooth lump showed beneath her ribcage. It was small—not more than five months, Soraida wagered—but already it had dropped into her pelvis, ready to slide from between her legs at any moment. Soraida knew the couple, though not by name. They'd occupied that square of the sidewalk for years, disappearing occasionally for short periods but always reappearing at the same spot. They didn't beg and they didn't look capable of assault. It was a wonder they survived at all.

A screech of tires made her turn. Something red, a pickup, spun around the corner of the next street. A red roar tearing by. A flash. Something popping, the echo thudding inside her chest. Pedestrians, shoppers, vendors scattered in an expanding wave, but Soraida just stared, unable to move. The transvestites worked that corner. They'd been standing there when the pickup passed. Soraida held her breath. Between two parked sedans, somebody lay sprawled on the ground, legs akimbo, convulsing. One foot, still in its glossy black pump, slapped against the asphalt. She was sure she'd seen those legs before, wriggling from the rear seat of the cars that would stop there, stepping to the sidewalk, tall, poised, statuesque, in a tight, sequined dress—blue or purple or green. But the face? Her head pounded as she strained to recall it.

By then the expanding wave of bystanders had reversed direction and a swarm was gathering at the spot across the street, blocking the victim from view. Gone. Just like that. As if she were emerging from a deep well, or from a nightmare that refused to release her, Soraida gasped for air and rushed past Otto's garage and up the steps into his office.

Otto, drawn by the sound of gunfire, was leaving just as Soraida was trying to enter.

"What is it? What happened?" he asked as she pushed her way past him. He was a short, dark-skinned man with straight, tidy hair, and his coveralls, though stained in grease, were in good repair. He paused at the open door, craning to get a better look outside, before he stepped back into his office, shut and bolted the door and turned to Soraida, who stood there quaking.

"Somebody get shot?"

Soraida couldn't speak.

"You see what happened?" He brought his face close to hers, examining her as he might a punctured tire. "You're safe now," he said too loudly as he parted the curtain of the front window and peeked out. "Have a seat. I'll get you some water."

Soraida nodded her thanks but remained standing. Her hands shook as she accepted the glass of water Otto poured from a large plastic jug that rocked in its metal cradle on the counter. She took a small sip. Her head was buzzing. After a few more sips, she felt calmer. Otto had left, no doubt to find answers to his questions, since Soraida was unable to provide any. She splashed a little water from her glass onto her handkerchief and wiped her face with it. She blinked. What *had* happened?

Otto was back. "They popped one of those faggots," he announced as he took Soraida's glass, stopping to peer at her a moment, perhaps to see if his comment had registered. "Nothing to worry about, Soraida. Nothing to do with us." He went to the window again. "As far as I'm concerned, they're doing us a favour."

Soraida coughed. She remembered now why she didn't like Otto. Still she ventured, "Are they … ?"

"Just one. I don't know which. Can't say I've ever got close enough to distinguish." He shuddered like a bad actor.

Idiot. Soraida was feeling stronger and eager to be going. She was embarrassed to have been so easily disarmed before such a man. She didn't know any of the transvestites either. Like her good neighbour, she'd walked past them countless times, pretending not to see. Now she had no face to recall, no name to add to her prayers—prayers she realized she would only offer now that it was too late to do anything else. She handed Otto the empty glass, straightened her dress, and patted her forehead again with her handkerchief. "Thank you, Otto. I'm sorry to have put you out."

"Do you want me to walk you home?"

But she was already out the door, taking the steps with care because her legs were still unstable. The street had returned to normal—shoppers squeezing by the market stalls, leaning in to examine products, jostling each other good-naturedly—except for the paramedic truck that had arrived across the square and a small group of onlookers around it. The homeless couple had disappeared. Not so stupid after all.

When Soraida got home, Isabel and Yasmin were sitting in the kitchen, hands clasped, the smallest of smiles upon their lips, immersed in some shared, sweet dream from which they were reluctant to wake. Soraida ducked into the bathroom to check her face in the mirror. She pinched her cheeks to bring out some colour.

"How did my angels sleep?" she asked as she entered the kitchen. They seemed unaware of the commotion outside and Soraida hoped to keep it that way. Two mugs of Nescafé, still full, sat on the table between them. She said to Isabel, "When you're done here, why don't we show you the shop?"

Soraida led the way, and mother and daughter followed like sleepwalkers.

The shop sat in sombre shadow, stacks of clothing filling the pine frame stands. The sleeve of a man's shirt hung from one in forlorn greeting. Soraida flipped the light switch and went ahead of them into the room.

"It looks like you've done well," Isabel said from the doorway.

"These days there's clothing to spare and people can't get enough of it," Soraida said. "Not like in my mother's day. People who couldn't afford a tailor would patch and mend the same outfit over and over, wear it every day and wash it once a week. Until they looked like a quilt of everything they'd ever owned." She waved Isabel forward. "If you need anything, just help yourself."

Yasmin trotted behind her mother. The previous night, the girl had flitted about like a butterfly, as if she were six years old again. Soraida, who had often heard Yasmin curse her mother roundly, wasn't sure the show was all for Isabel. She was fairly sure some of it was directed at her.

Isabel began sorting through the pile of trousers, Yasmin at her side. They could pass for sisters, Soraida thought, almost identical, both in jeans and faded T-shirts. Twin dimples whenever they smiled or frowned. But Yasmin's flesh was smooth and soft, her features gently rounded. Isabel's face had grown angular over the years, her hair cropped to a simple shoulder-length bob. She held up a pair of camouflage pants. "Do you really have to sell these?"

Soraida shrugged. "People pick out what they want to wear. It's not up to me."

"It's not up to them either. It's not like they choose what gets sent."

"They're just clothes, Mami. Besides camouflage is in." Yasmin looked her mother over: pants hiked to her waist, a thick leather belt holding them in place, ankles exposed at the ends of the pant legs. "Maybe I'd better help you pick something," she said.

Soraida said nothing. Isabel had her prickly side—she'd met it before. Nonetheless, it hurt to see her dear brother's only child still so distant, even when she was standing right there in front of her. The shooting that morning came to her again in a jolt: a red blur, the air exploding, one foot slapping. She leaned against the counter for support as she felt the air ripple and bend. A plane. It was just a plane passing overhead.

Her vision cleared and the room returned. Isabel was still picking through trousers and blouses as Yasmin, her expression stern, eyed first the garments and then her mother before selecting something she thought Isabel should try. Soraida had spent her life steering clear of people who caused trouble, but fate had contrived against her. Her neighbourhood was a haven for misfits and delinquents, and now she had a political outlaw—pardoned outlaw, if that made any difference—under her roof.

Yasmin was pulling her mother towards the door.

Soraida felt a chill in her stomach. "Where are you off to?"

"I'm going to show Mami the neighbourhood."

Soraida searched her mind for a reason to stop them, but without success. Perhaps she was overreacting. Heartless as it was, Otto was right. The shooters had targeted the transvestites. Tragic, yes, but it had nothing to do with them.

"Let me give you some money and you can buy what I need for dinner." She went back into the house and returned with a shopping bag and a cloth serviette. "And you should know, I've told the neighbours you've been in Arizona."

Isabel looked puzzled.

"That's what we always say if anybody asks," Yasmin said. Then she turned to her great-aunt. "But why should we have to now?"

Soraida didn't answer. It hadn't occurred to her that they could just tell the truth.

Isabel spoke. "Soraida's right. It's better this way. Safer." But she didn't look happy and Soraida couldn't think why.

She dug in her apron pocket and handed Isabel twenty quetzales. "Cousin Quique is coming for dinner."

Isabel followed as Yasmin sprang ahead of her along the sidewalk, leading the way. The sun was full overhead, beating down upon the market tarps. Shoppers, vendors and transients flowed past her unperturbed, dressed as they always dressed, whatever the weather. And Isabel looked like any one of them. There could be among their number another or several, like her, just come from the dark and steamy heat of the jungle to this urban oven. Just come from war to this thing called peace. She studied the crowd filing through the market. There was no way to tell, and nobody who would ever tell her.

"Hurry up!" Yasmin called.

But she didn't hurry. She stopped to exchange greetings with a couple who sat in the middle of the sidewalk, the young man with his arm around a woman who slumped against him, asleep, her limbs folded around her belly. The man showed her a toothless grin and made signs with his hands.

She caught up with her daughter at a stand selling music tapes.

"I have a player if you want to find something you like," Yasmin said. "What is it? marimba? rancheras? Los Guaraguaos?" She tittered at the last one, an iconic revolutionary trova band.

Isabel's glance slid over the endless cassette cases spread before them. She didn't know yet what she wanted or didn't want. She didn't even know what to ask, what she might want to know. Her mind was busy taking everything in, recording, cataloguing. As if she were on some sort of recognizance, stowing the details and the questions away for later, for a safe place where she could take them out, turn them over and decide what they meant. "I think I'll just look around for today, honey." She looped her arm through her daughter's. "Tell me about things. How is school?"

"It's okay," Yasmin said with a grimace as she detached herself and ran her finger along the backs of the cassettes. She selected one and began reading the liner notes. Suddenly she brightened. "I know who you should meet!"

She dragged Isabel across the plaza, past stand after stand bursting with exactly the same merchandise as the stands they had just left —tapes, blankets, backpacks, plastic tubs, soccer jerseys, flowers— aiming for the corner where the market ended. Isabel, who had no desire to rush anywhere, resisted until Yasmin, too, slowed and then stopped, looking left and right as if she didn't know where she was or how she'd gotten there.

"Never mind," Yasmin said. "Let's get the groceries."

As she followed Yasmin again, Isabel looked back to see what might have stopped her daughter. Pedestrians were milling past as they were everywhere else. Whoever it was wasn't there today.

After buying the meat and vegetables Soraida would need, they stopped at a narrow tortillería erected in a laneway between the shops. As they entered, the attendants—two women—were talking in hushed tones in Kaqchikel. From what Isabel could make out, somebody had been shot. They stopped as soon as Isabel addressed them in their language, which was her language, too, although Spanish had overtaken as the one she spoke most often.

"Where did you learn?" the elder of the two women asked as she tossed a round disc of corn masa back and forth between her palms. "You don't wear the clothing."

"My mother was from a village in Jilotepeque. I grew up there."

The woman nodded to her younger partner, who stretched out her hand to receive the serviette. They both wore their town's distinctive red *po't*, its embroidered yoke reminiscent of a Mayan calendar. In Isabel's village, the *po't* the women wore buzzed with densely packed zigzags in purples, turquoises and blues. Isabel had not seen or worn those colours for years.

"A beautiful place," the elder woman said. She continued to shape the tortilla and then placed it on the hot comal.

The Kaqchikel words bubbled inside Isabel like water flowing over stone, lifting her and carrying her back, to the swish and thud of machetes, the snap, snap, snap of a backstrap loom, the hiss and pop of the family hearth, as if the things of her childhood lived inside the language, embedded in its vowels and consonants. "I haven't been to my village in a long time. My father was ladino. We're living with his family now."

This confession drew no comment from the women. The younger of the pair was turning the tortillas on the comal and stacking the ones that were ready on top of the open serviette in her hand. When she had counted ten, she spoke up. "Is she your daughter?" She jutted her chin toward Yasmin, who had not said a word during the exchange.

Isabel nodded.

"You haven't taught her?" the elder said.

"I must." Isabel remembered that she'd intended to find out about the shooting, but she couldn't think of a way to ask without arousing suspicion.

The elder woman addressed Yasmin now, in Spanish. "You like to learn lengua? Maybe come make tortilla?" The women laughed at the thought.

Yasmin ducked behind her mother.

The younger woman wrapped the serviette around the steaming tortillas and passed it to Isabel. Isabel paid and picked up the bag of groceries at her feet. They left the wooden hut and headed into bright sunshine.

Yasmin still hadn't spoken.

"Is there something wrong?" Isabel asked. She switched the woven nylon bag to the other shoulder.

"Will you teach me Kaqchikel?"

Isabel smiled, relieved. "I'll try. Maybe we can spend some time up there, in *Öch äj*—that's what we call San Martín Jilotepeque in Kaqchikel. Find some of your relatives."

"I thought there was nothing left."

Isabel shaded her eyes from the sun's glare which seemed suddenly to magnify, zeroing in on the dusty lane that led from the tortillería. She felt lightheaded. "I . . . I don't know what's left, but there must be something." She looked at her feet and tried to see the countryside of Öch äj again, its green hills, its golden corn, her grandparents' village tended by a slender chalum tree. She didn't know what she would find there now. A thin man ran toward them, his shadow bouncing over the street and walls. Isabel flinched as he passed. "Yasmi, would you mind carrying these groceries? I'm feeling the sun a bit."

Yasmin took the bag.

Back at Soraida's they unloaded their purchases and set to peeling the potatoes and yucca and washing and chopping up the other vegetables. Isabel observed her aunt as she dropped the soup bones into a large pot of water, at each step explaining why her method was better than either Doña Estela's or Doña Martita's. If Soraida knew something of what had happened in the plaza that morning, she wasn't letting on. Or perhaps it was an everyday occurrence. The thought made Isabel's heart sink.

"Enrique always comes by on Sundays," Soraida said.

As if on cue, Isabel heard a voice bellowing down the front corridor. Yasmin rushed to open the door. Enrique turned out to be a stocky, energetic man, his skin neither as pale and yellowish as Soraida's nor as dark as Isabel's. He had an arm around Yasmin as he entered, but on seeing Isabel he released the girl. "Am I seeing double?" he asked.

"For goodness sake, Quique," Soraida said as she poked at the soup cauldron. "Stop sputtering and give your niece a hug."

Enrique threw an embrace around Isabel. "Welcome, niece, and God bless you." His breath was warm with liquor.

Soraida kissed her cousin on the cheek and steered him to a wooden chair at the kitchen table. Then she sent Yasmin to fetch a litre of Gallo from Doña Maritza. Since Soraida didn't seem to need her help, Isabel took a seat, too.

Enrique gazed at her, a smile fixed to his face. "Now I know where Yasmin gets her good looks. Eh, Soraida?" He turned in his chair to find her.

Soraida ignored him. She was ladling out the soup into earthenware bowls. "Enrique lives in zone seven, just this side of the bridge, not far from your parents' old house," she told Isabel.

"My house, too," Isabel said. She remembered that house. She'd seen it whizz by when they entered the city.

"He's a tailor, so if you ever want anything made to fit—"

"Was a tailor," Enrique said, "until second-hand clothing from Gringolandia came and put me out of business. How can you compete with clothes that cost less than the fabric it takes to make them?"

Yasmin returned and plonked a large cold bottle of beer in front of Enrique. Soraida placed two glasses on the table. Then she brought the first bowl of soup and laid it before her cousin. "This is Enrique's constant refrain," she told Isabel. "You'll get used to it."

"Reduced to hemming pants and taking in waistbands," he said.

"And don't forget school uniforms," Yasmin said, having taken a chair next to him.

"Until all I can see is navy blue." Enrique reached for a tortilla. "But I forgive Soraida because she makes such damn good beef soup."

Yasmin laughed. Isabel laughed, too, but more in imitation than because she saw the humour. The role of polite guest, she supposed, was the only one open to her until she better understood the workings of this strange new world.

"Mami speaks lengua," Yasmin said between mouthfuls, once they were all seated. "She was talking to the tortilla lady."

"Kaqchikel," Soraida said. "The name of your mother's language is Kaqchikel."

"They couldn't believe it. A ladina talking to them in their own tongue. I mean, what is the world coming to?" Yasmin was dabbing the end of a tortilla in her soup. "Now they won't be able to gossip about their customers because they can't be sure others don't speak it too."

Isabel was tempted to ask Yasmin whether she, too, thought of her mother as ladina. But she resisted the urge. She wanted to hear what else Yasmin would say.

"If you say *lengua* it makes it sound like they're all the same," Soraida went on. "That there's just one big Indigenous language."

Enrique was eyeing her. He looked amused.

Soraida turned to Isabel, presumably for confirmation.

"Yes, okay," Isabel said. "They're not all the same: Kaqchikel, K'iche', Mam, Ixil, Tz'utujil and so on. They're full-blown languages, just like Spanish." She smiled at her daughter, but Yasmin looked hurt.

"Oh, I know all that," she said. "You guys are such drips. It was *funny*."

Soraida patted Isabel's arm. "Well, it does make me think we could make better use of you than in the shop. I've long been wanting to get some clothing out to the village markets. Borrow a pickup and take a load out on the weekend. Yasmin could go with you"—Yasmin made a face—"or Byron. He's free weekends. But Yasmin"—she turned to her grandniece—"it would be a wonderful way to spend time with your mother, get to know the country a bit. You could learn a lot."

Isabel nodded. She was willing to do whatever was needed. "I'd have to get a driver's license."

"I know somebody who can help with that," Enrique said.

Soraida shushed him. "She doesn't need your help. She can get it through the proper channels, can't you, Isabel?'

The only piece of identification Isabel still had was her cédula. Yasmin's birth, too, was undocumented. "I don't know. Updating my cédula would be a start. And I should get Yasmin registered. There's new legislation to help with cases like ours . . . uh, people who've been away."

"No need," Soraida said. "Enrique took care of that way back. You're down as the mother. No father. She's got only the one surname."

Isabel glanced at Yasmin, who was staring dully at the table. "It's only me, then," she said.

Yasmin straightened from her slouch. "And another thing," she said as if she'd been talking all the while. "The transvestites weren't there today. Did anybody notice? What was that about?"

Isabel didn't know what she was talking about. She looked to Soraida for clarification, but her aunt just sat there, pressing her handkerchief to her mouth.

"Auntie could set her watch by them. Conchita, the tall one, arrives at seven and is gone by six. Menche—"

Soraida coughed softly. She looked pale.

Still bent over his soup, Quique burped and served himself another glass of beer before digging back in.

"I'm afraid there was a shooting this morning," Soraida said at last. "One of those people—"

"You knew about this?" Isabel felt her voice go tight.

"I didn't want to upset you."

Isabel's arms and legs began to tingle. Her face was hot. "You can't keep things like that to yourself."

"But we're fine . . ." Soraida, her voice like silk, inclined her head in Yasmin's direction. Yasmin was staring at her great-aunt, mouth agape. Were those tears in her eyes?

"I need to know things like this," Isabel said again, her voice sharp. She felt on edge—on alert, like she did before combat. She needed to move. "Anything that happens in this neighbourhood. Who the spies are—they're there, believe me." She remembered, too late, that Enrique was at the table. He was Soraida's family and, therefore, hers. But that was all she knew about him.

"But it's not like that, Isabel." Soraida's voice was coaxing. "It's terrible what happened but it's nothing to do with us. They're transvestites. People like that . . ."

Isabel got to her feet. "People like what? People who *deserve* to die? She was beginning to shake, the fire that had started in her head seeking the rest of her body. "That's the sort of thing people said when my grandparents were killed. Their entire village wiped out. Or my parents? *Your* brother? That's what they said when we buried their bodies. They got what was coming. We're better off without people like that." She glared at Soraida, trembling, her heart thumping against her chest. "*You* ought to know better."

The last time Isabel had seen her parents alive, they were about to leave for an appointment in the capital, smiles on their faces and bright kisses for their daughter as they said goodbye. Three days later, she'd watched her neighbours lower their bodies from the bed of a pickup her grandfather had borrowed to bring them back from the city morgue. She was six years old.

Yasmin had slouched farther down her chair. She was swallowing hard. Enrique was gazing at the bottle in front of him. Soraida's mouth was open but nothing came out. She looked very small.

"I'm sorry," Isabel stammered. She scanned the room, its dull white walls, the stove, the television, the rack of dishes, trying to recall where she was. "That wasn't justified."

Yasmin, Soraida, Quique—they were still seated around her, but at the same time they seemed to be somewhere else, somewhere she could not reach. If one of them were to speak, she wasn't sure she would hear them, as if they were on the other side of an enormous and thick pane of glass. Isabel inhaled, exhaled, willing time to slow down, to allow her to catch up. Then she reached, carefully, for her half-empty bowl, concentrating hard to control the tremor that lurked just under her skin, and began to stack it with the others. "I haven't been sleeping well. I'm sorry."

She carried the bowls to the cement sink in the courtyard and started washing up. Inhaling, exhaling, kneading the dishcloth into a lather, running her fingertips over the rough glaze of the earthenware bowls, feeling the water spill over her skin. Slowly. Slowly. Her parents had been ambushed on the way to some sort of rendezvous. The police suspected a love triangle—a crime of passion. It wasn't true. As she'd learned in the years to come, it was the kind of slander the regime always used to cover up a political crime. Nonetheless, she still had no explanation for what her parents were doing that day or for the unsigned note the police had discovered in her father's pocket. Isabel rinsed each dish, watching the soapy water slither into the drain. Calming her, washing the fear, the pain away.

When she returned to the kitchen, Yasmin was not at the table. Soraida stood at the stove, cleaning and putting everything back in order, and Enrique, the empty litre bottle before him, was in his chair, swaying slightly as if to music.

CHAPTER 4

It was May Day, the first workers' celebration of the new peace. Soraida, Yasmin and Isabel had climbed to the footbridge between Guatemala City's town hall and the National Theatre to watch. It was already crammed with onlookers. Soraida scoured the crowd for pickpockets and troublemakers as Yasmin and Isabel squeezed their way to the bridge railing to get a better view.

"Yasmi, don't climb up like that," Soraida snapped. "You'll go right over."

Yasmin leaned farther out. "Auntie hates May Day," she confided to her mother, perched next to her. Isabel shot Soraida a look, more baffled than condemning, before she turned her eyes back to the long grey stripe of Sixth Avenue that ran underneath them, empty of traffic, empty yet of people.

Soraida was not in the habit of celebrating May Day, it was true. She didn't see the point. But she knew the day was important to Isabel. Almost sacred. She'd opened her shop despite the holiday—can't afford to close every time somebody gets it into their head to hold a parade—but she'd left Byron in charge so she could join her niece and grandniece and thousands of others who lined the streets waiting to cheer on the marching workers. She was here to show good will, to do her part.

On either side of them, young men sat astride the bridge railing and another group—students probably—stood on one of the cement blocks that broke the railing into sections. One wore the pointed capirote of one of the university faculties over his head and face, his eyes alone visible above his T-shirt and jeans. Another had a red bandana over his mouth and nose, like a bandit from an old Western. There was a girl, too, in a blue URNG T-shirt and a paper visor. Just beyond the bridge, a young woman in a capirote was spray-painting a wall. *Army = Murder*, she scrawled in large red letters. The words sent a shiver along Soraida's arms and neck, despite the heat. Such recklessness. Words like that read like a challenge. But what was a can of spray paint against bullets and firebombs?

"They're coming!" Yasmin yelled.

The first marchers appeared in the distance, a large red banner on bamboo poles stretched between them, one of the national labour federations trailed by the Coca-Cola union. A squat woman lugging a megaphone shouted slogans and the marchers answered: "A people with hunger ... is a people without peace." The same slogans they'd been chanting for as long as Soraida could remember. Other banners followed, held high by hundreds of men and women, factory workers, small farmers, Indigenous, ladino, who jabbed them at the sky every time they repeated the refrain. They formed two long queues as they marched. Many of the Mayan women balanced babies on their backs. A few carried umbrellas to protect them from the sun.

"I wonder how far they've come," Isabel said to no one in particular.

"They bus them in from all over," Soraida answered. "A free lunch and a trip to the capital—that's why they come." She called over a boy who was selling plastic bags of drinking water and paper visors and bought one of each. The sun was ferocious. "Do either of you want?" she asked, but Isabel and Yasmin were intent on the parade. Soraida bit off the corner of the bag and sucked back the icy water. Around them, the spectators—Yasmin, too—aped the marchers, echoing their slogans. Isabel hadn't joined in, but Soraida saw anticipation in her face, as if she were hoping for something but was not sure she would get it. Many of the older people in the crowd were silent too. Watching.

Isabel turned to her. "Are you surviving?" she asked.

Soraida flapped the visor at her face like a fan and was about to answer when the young men to her left unfurled a long narrow banner, letting it drop over the bridge railing, and then secured it at the four corners. Soraida had barely registered their presence and they were gone. Isabel bent to read it. *URNG is here.* "I guess the boys won't be long in coming," she said.

Soraida knew enough of rebel parlance to know she meant the guerrillas, or former guerrillas. That's why they were really here. But Soraida was no longer interested. Why did they bother, year after year? The chanting? The slogans? As if a slogan would change anything. She drew her handkerchief from her apron pocket and mopped her forehead.

Yasmin was the first to see them. "Look, Mami. Let's go down."

Isabel was surprised how much it buoyed her to see her old comrades marching under the noonday sun toward her, waving at the crowd like celebrities, chatting to each other, breaking formation, such as it was, to run and greet somebody on the sidelines. Catching up on all the gossip. It was the grand homecoming, the hero's welcome, so unlike the intimate reunion with Yasmin and Soraida, which, though tender and warm, had left her feeling more like a fugitive in need of shelter than any kind of champion.

She heard somebody roar and turned to see Claudia approaching.

"I told Danilo you'd come," Claudia shouted. "Where have you been?"

Claudia had energy that would outlast the Hundred Years War, let alone Guatemala's three and a half decades. She threw her arms out to embrace Isabel and then turned to the rest of the family. "This must be Yasmin!" Another warm hug before she called to two gangly teenagers, a girl and a boy, who joined the circle, their toothy smiles as big as Claudia's.

"Look, honey," she said to Yasmin. "Here are my babies. Giants both of them." She nudged them toward Isabel. "Kids, do you remember … what do they call you?"

Isabel gave her name and pulled Claudia's children to her. She didn't know whether it was joy or grief that had her rocking, struggling to stay afloat, a tide of emotions threatening to capsize her. These two were safe, returned to them. How many others were not? She gripped them tighter. Then she introduced Soraida, who continued to fan herself with her visor as she offered her cheek to be kissed. Erika, the girl, wrapped an arm around Yasmin—like sisters already—while Yasmin gazed with fierce admiration at Erika's elder brother, Jorge, who had Danilo's thin frame but had outdone him in height. His hair was short and tidy, quite unlike his father's mop or Claudia's wild curls.

Claudia's children had been toddlers when Isabel last saw them. She'd been assigned to bring them to a house tucked away in a Mexico City suburb where they were to live out the war with a dozen other rebel offspring. They'd barely said a word during the journey but had clasped each other's hands, even as they slept. She'd visited once or twice after that, but all too soon, she'd been reposted. She might not have recognized them if it weren't for the strong resemblance to their mother. And like Claudia, they were warm and open. Or perhaps Mexico had given them that gift.

"Just look at you two," Isabel murmured.

"We've been meeting so many of Mama and Papa's friends today," Erika said. "And old friends of ours, too."

Claudia nodded vigorously. She whisked a tear from her eye, laughing at herself. "People we thought we'd lost."

Jorge had moved off and was talking to Yasmin as the marchers swept them forward, through the crowd of onlookers, their backs pressed against walls of hot stone and broiling metal. The sun's rays bathed the street and everything in it in a sharp white light. Businesses had drawn their shutters. In front of the Bancafé and Pollo Campero, guards in grey and black uniforms and bullet-proof vests stood at the ready, cradling their shotguns. But there were no police or soldiers to be seen. Today, the marchers owned the streets.

Isabel thought she might cry, too. "And Danilo?" she asked.

"He's on security. You didn't see him, but he probably saw you."

Isabel scanned the sidewalks. "Who's he covering?"

"Who else?"

Isabel searched for the guerrillas' commander-in-chief and found Danilo three metres away watching the crowd.

"You should come for dinner at the Foundation!" Claudia said. "Everybody's going afterwards."

As they crossed Eighteenth Street, Isabel noticed Soraida look wistfully at her shop. Broom in hand, Byron waved from the entrance as they drifted by.

"Byron's a worker," Yasmin said loudly to her aunt. "He should be allowed to march with the rest of us. It's his right."

Byron started sweeping.

"Everybody's out here watching. It's not fair," Yasmin said.

"You mean everybody's hiding so those hooligans from the university don't spray-paint them blue or something."

Yasmin laughed. "It's not that bad." She turned again to her mother. "Last year they spray-painted a skull and crossbones across Auntie's American flags."

"Those flags don't mean anything. All the bale shops have them. It's not like I've got the CIA hiding in the back room. It's not like I'm helping them out!" Soraida slapped her hand over her mouth and cast around her, afraid perhaps she *would* get painted blue. But nobody in the crowd was paying her any mind: there was too much to see and too many people to greet.

Isabel heard her pseudonym and soon caught sight of another compa hailing her.

"Excuse me," she said. "Soraida? Are you okay for a moment?"

For Isabel's sake she'd said, yes. *Yes, yes, run along. I'll be fine.* But she wasn't fine. It wasn't just the heat and the noise and the smells and her sore feet. On this hot, hot day, she did not want to be here, surrounded by five thousand subversives, Indians and hoodlums. These people were dangerous. A few signatures under the word "peace" wasn't going to change that. And the whole reason for coming out—*her* reason—was to spend the afternoon with her niece and grandniece. But they'd both taken off and left her here, where she didn't belong.

Bodies jostled her along. A barrel of a man bumped her arm. Apologized. Moved on. Soraida had half a mind to push back, hard. But she didn't. Instead, she made sure she kept her eyes on Claudia who, with all her jumping and gesticulating, was easy to spot. They were happy. They were all so happy.

By the time Isabel returned they had reached Congress, an elegant stone building pinned between a mechanic shop and a walled parking lot. It was alive with demonstrators, who stood and sat along the windowsills and clogged the archway of the main entrance. The graffiti artists had arrived before them: *Out with the Yankee invaders! End neoliberalism now!* The walls were covered.

Isabel was beaming, and Soraida regretted her bad humour. "I think I'll get going," she said.

"I'm sorry I was so long. You must be getting tired." Isabel looked about her. "Where's Yasmin?"

"She went off with those friends of yours."

"With Erika and Jorge," Claudia broke in. "We're meeting at the Foundation afterwards. You can pick her up there or if you need to take your aunt home, Danilo can bring Yasmin back after dinner."

"But the park's just a little farther," Isabel said. "Auntie, you really don't think you can make it? It'll be quite a sight."

The throng squeezing through the narrow street was growing. It would be worse in the park unless they stuck to the edges. Though her feet could probably handle more, Soraida wasn't sure her heart could.

"I can find my way home from here," she said. "I'll take a bus down on Tenth."

It was clear from Isabel's face, from the way she was constantly glancing around, to the left, to the right, behind her, tottering on the tips of her toes to see past Soraida—it was clear that taking Soraida home was the last thing she wanted to do. But she would do it—Soraida could bet on it—because it was her duty. And Soraida would accept, because it was high time Isabel learned that home was where she belonged.

Isabel looked doubtfully at Claudia.

"Go," Claudia said. "You can meet us back at the Foundation, or we might still be in the park. The kids'll be fine. Jorge's got a good head on his shoulders." She gave Isabel a big hug. "You should come back after you've settled your aunt, though. There's so many people you'll miss."

Isabel sat on the end of Soraida's bed and massaged the older woman's feet. Her aunt reclined against a thin pillow, hands folded across her nightdress, just below her thick abdomen. The bulge of her stomach dropped off suddenly to reveal two gnarly legs, ramrod straight, emerging where the nightdress ended. Isabel worked the oil around bunions and callouses, over the discoloured toenails, sliding her thumb down each arch and cupping each heel with her palm. She'd given up on joining her old comrades at the Foundation. It was already past seven. Soon it would be dark. At least Yasmin would get to meet some of them.

"I appreciate your coming today," she said.

The room was small and damp, a wardrobe, its doors closed, on one side and Soraida's bed on the other. An unlit candle sat on a stand by the bed.

"I suppose I don't get out enough," Soraida said. "So much has changed. For Yasmin's sake, I should." She sighed deeply. "Sixth Avenue isn't what it once was. We used to stroll there every Sunday afternoon —everybody did—your father and I when we were kids, our parents. *Sexteando* it was called. Visiting the boutiques, maybe taking in a movie at the Lux. Now it's all dirty and crowded—street vendors all over the sidewalk. Can't see a thing for all the signs sticking out everywhere. It's beginning to look like Eighteenth Street. Back then it was really something."

Isabel gently rotated her aunt's feet, each toe. She wondered whether she'd ever gone sexteando with her parents. *Back then*, she suspected, the only Mayans who'd strolled Sixth Avenue in the downtown core had done so as street cleaners, custodians or maids. She said none of this to Soraida, who had closed her eyes, her chest rising and falling in a slow, easy rhythm.

"So those were the people you were with all these years?" Soraida asked, her eyes still shut.

Isabel started. She'd thought her aunt had fallen asleep. "Some of them. There are a lot of people who weren't there." She worked on her aunt's feet, mentally counting and recounting the toes to keep any tremor from entering her hands. "Some I'll never see again."

Soraida opened her eyes and raised her head. "Do you ever hear anything from Yasmin's father?"

Another jolt. Soraida knew perfectly well that Yasmin's father had left without a word before Yasmin was due. Why think about him now? Why think about him at all? "No," she said. "Never."

"You know, Yasmin asks about him sometimes. You should be prepared."

Isabel had stopped massaging. She started again, head down. She had no intention of meeting her aunt's eyes. Why was Soraida always so intent on ruining a good moment? More than a few of the short visits the rebels had allowed them over the years had ended this way.

"Thanks for the warning," she said.

Soraida propped herself on her elbows. "I've never understood it, Isabel, how those people let him get away with it. Why they didn't protect you. How are they supposed to sweep in a new age if they can't even keep their own people in line? I've heard about other things they did, too. There's been articles in the paper."

Isabel dried her hands with a towel and faced the old busybody. She was fuming. "What did you want them to do? Stop the war and chase him down? They ... *we* had more important things on our minds."

Her aunt waved her hand, dismissing her. "If your mind was where it was supposed to be, you wouldn't have got yourself in trouble."

An insult, flung casually. Typical petite bourgeoisie—fretting over what the neighbours might think while the country goes up in flames. Still, Isabel was determined to remain calm. She didn't want a repeat of last Sunday's dinner. "You're ignoring the big picture," she said.

Soraida sat upright, hands reaching. Not pleading. They were part of the argument. "I know about the big picture, but I'm not talking about that. I'm talking about you and Yasmin. About the so-called new man who dumped you and took off and has never spent five centavos on either one of you. Is that what your revolution would bring?"

"I slept with him of my own free will."

"That's exactly what I'm talking about. Too much freedom and not enough responsibility. I bet you've been with others, too. And who's with you now? Who's going to support you?"

Isabel felt ready to burst. There was no getting through to Soraida. There was no meeting her halfway. She stood up, but the room was too small to move around in, unless she were to walk right out the door. "Why are you doing this? Are you trying to drive me away? Do you think you'd get Yasmin if I left?"

As soon as she said it, Isabel knew she'd gone too far, again—Soraida was shaking her head violently. Still, Isabel let her words sink in before speaking again, more gently this time. "I look at you, and I see a woman who's made a good living, a good life, for herself and for her grandniece. I don't see any man around."

"Don't talk about what you don't know. I didn't choose this."

"And I did?" Isabel rubbed her face, her neck. If she could ease the tension, she could respond the way she should. With dignity. With truth. She rolled her shoulders forward and back, let them fall. "Look, the revolution isn't perfect. Revolutionaries aren't perfect. I'm not perfect. But of all the things I've done, the one I'm not sorry about is Yasmin." She was calmer now, but she was perspiring. After a moment, she reached for Soraida's feet and stroked them. "What would I have now if not for her?"

There was a knock at the front door so Isabel, grateful for the interruption, went to get it. Danilo stood in the doorway in the half-light with Yasmin just behind him. As Isabel opened the door wider, Yasmin stole past and disappeared down the corridor.

"What was that about?" Isabel said to Danilo. Dusk had fallen. The street was dark.

"Um … I think she doesn't want you getting a whiff of her breath."

Isabel looked behind her, but Yasmin was already gone. "She's been drinking? Danilo?"

"I had nothing to do with it, nor Jorge either. She hooked up with some friends of hers and they were all pissed to the gills."

The night seemed to shift; the black sky felt blacker. Somewhere over on the next street, people were arguing, lobbing words at each other like hand grenades. "Jorge was supposed to look out for her. She's only fifteen."

"He was. He did. He tried to get her away from them, but there's this boy she likes. Isabel, that girl's been up to things … You'd better ask Soraida about it." Danilo moved his arms as he spoke, as loose and relaxed as always, the glowing tip of his cigarette bobbing in the dark. Light from the doorway pooled at his feet.

Isabel's throat was tight. It hurt to speak. "You were supposed to take care of her."

"She's fine. She only had a little. Like I say, when Jorge couldn't persuade her, he came and got me and I had to lay down the law. He didn't even know these people. They're school friends or something."

"Or maybe Jorge was disappointed, wanted to have some fun with her. He wouldn't be the first—"

Danilo flapped his arms. "Okay, now you're talking crazy. Jorge's as straight as they come. Me and Claudia are bohemians by comparison. But even so, this bohemian never took advantage."

"Maybe no one ever gave you the chance." Her voice, clear and sharp, cut across the night.

Danilo stepped away from the door, hands raised, palms out, the smouldering cigarette wedged between his knuckles. "Yeah, well, you're welcome. Glad to be of service. But next time you want to give me a kick in the teeth, I think I'll pass."

The words came like slaps, echoing through the city, mixing and rebounding with the arguments of other houses, with the feathery talk of lovers, with the crimes that would be committed that night. The light from the house left him partly in shadow.

"Stop! Come here. I'm sorry."

Danilo made a half-step toward her.

She pressed her fingers to her temples. "Sometimes I think I'm losing it, that I'm really going to lose it. Thank you for bringing her home," she whispered. "Thank you for taking care of her."

Danilo came closer. He lifted his hand as if to touch her shoulder or her face and let it fall again. "You don't have to grovel. I understand the mother jaguar." He smiled. "Don't be a stranger, okay?"

When Isabel approached the room she shared with Yasmin, the light was already out; the air, still and close. She made her way to the barred window and opened it an inch. "Yasmi, baby?" She sat beside the blanketed lump and started stroking her hair. "Come on. Turn over."

"I heard what you said. The whole neighbourhood did."

She ran her fingers down the girl's cheek. No tears, but they were warm. From anger? Alcohol? "Forget about that." Isabel kissed her. The sweet aroma of rum was faint on her lips, masking who knew what mysteries of her complicated adolescence. Years of thoughts and feelings shored up inside looking for release. Questions unanswered. Longings unmet. "Are you okay?"

Yasmin hugged her pillow. "Why did you leave me here with Soraida? Why couldn't you have done like Claudia and Danilo? All those kids, they all know each other. I didn't know anybody."

Isabel waited before she answered. It frightened her to think of the mountain of things Yasmin could accuse her of. This was surely just the tip of the iceberg. "I thought you'd be better off with family."

"A family of one. The organization would have been my family—that's what Jorge called it—just like it was yours, like having a whole pile of cousins. Jorge and Erika know everybody, they know everything about their parents and what they were doing and why."

"Jorge and Erika . . . it was like an orphanage there. A few compas taking care of them. Their parents hardly ever got to see them. They didn't go to regular school. They kept getting moved around." She touched Yasmin's cheek again. Her daughter's eyes were on her. She saw herself as she was at Yasmin's age, her parents lost to her without explanation, her grandparents struggling to carry on, to stand up for themselves and their community. "I wanted you *safe*." She tried to say more—Yasmin needed reassurance—but old pains and sorrows stormed her senses and the words collected and knotted in her throat before they could reach her lips. She was afraid that if she plucked one or another from the tangle, the rest would come tumbling out in an incomprehensible stream until it all unravelled and she was left with nothing to hold herself together.

She took the pillow and placed it under Yasmin's head. Perhaps she could still communicate something, if only by the expression on her face or the touch of her fingertips. "You might be too old for it now, but do you want me to tell you a bedtime story? Tío Chevo?"

Yasmin giggled. "You tell Tío Chevo stories?"

"The best."

Her daughter snuggled down with the blankets yanked up to her chin. "Ready," she said.

CHAPTER 5

ISABEL STANDS ALONE *among the tangled vines and mossy trees of the Ixcán jungle, turning the canvas pack round and round in her hands, shaking it just to be sure. Empty. Impossibly empty. On all sides of her, an emerald silence. How did she wander off like that? Like a stray thought? Now she can't find her way back to camp. Her compass, its needle spinning madly, is useless, and on top of that, her pack is empty. She looks to the ground in search of her own footprints, but the leafy mass offers no signs. People lose their way all the time, but as far as she knows they always make it back, even after days of tracing circles through the tropical forest. She sits against the trunk of a fat grey ceiba. Perhaps something will nudge her in the right direction. Perhaps something in the relentless green will strike her as familiar. Before long she hears a rustle, and a small wild boar appears from between the vines, munching as it goes. Isabel smiles. She is lost but not alone. Where there is one boar, there will be others. She reaches for her gun and lifts it. The little boar catches her scent and sounds the alarm, its teeth clattering like castanets. Suddenly, it is not a boar but a man, a Kaibil whose painted face and camouflage—shredded green fabric sprouting from his helmet and pack—make him seem part man, part beast. And the little boar's snout has become the lean barrel of a Galil rifle.* Rattatat tat. Rattatat tat.

Yasmin was at school and Soraida at work, so Isabel spent the morning in the sunlit courtyard doing laundry, both their own clothes and the ones that would later hang in Soraida's shop. Luckily, her aunt had invested in an electric washer, something of a luxury in Guatemala but justifiable given her line of work. As Isabel sorted the remaining dirty laundry into lights, colours and darks, the machine chugged away beside her, sloshing soapy water back and forth, its motor droning in her ears. When the water had turned black, she shut it off, detached the nozzle strapped to the side of its cylindrical white basin and hooked it over the sink's edge. She flipped the switch for the pump and watched the water level sink to reveal a wet mound of jeans and dark trousers. When all the water had drained, she refilled the basin with buckets of water from the tap and turned the machine back on. One side of the cement sink and a rubber trash can were also full of water, as backup for when the taps inevitably ran dry. After the clothes were rinsed, she drained them again and started extracting pairs of jeans, wringing them and feeding them through the electric mangle perched over the washer's basin. As each item emerged stiff but still damp from the press of the rollers, she dumped it into a large round tub. It was time-consuming work, but—apart from the motor's deafening hum—not unpleasant.

Washing by hand had been one of her chores as a child living with her grandparents. They'd wash down at the river, kneading the garments with a ball of black lard soap and beating them against the large stones along the riverbank. Her grandmother would pile the clean damp clothing back into a basket, lift it high and rest it atop her head. Isabel did the same with a smaller, lighter basket. Then they'd walk the long trail back to the house, where, being nimble, she'd climb to the roof, pitched higher at the front of the house than at the back, to lay the laundry out and let it bake under the noonday sun. Bright *uq*, *po't*, *peraj* covered the red clay tiles like a quilt. It was clothing she no longer used. She no longer dressed as a Mayan woman. At eighteen she'd exchanged her multicoloured *po't* blouse and black *uq* skirt for green fatigues, and now, for the ladino fashions of her daughter and aunt—fashions that were "made in USA" or in Europe, though they were usually stitched together somewhere else. Often in Guatemala.

If she'd had a choice, she'd have returned to that life, but there was nothing to go back to. The army had seen to that. A surge of queasiness rippled through her like a spectre passing through a closed door, and she faltered, gripping the rim of the washtub until she had regained her composure. Then she breathed deep, hoisted the tub and mounted the stairs to the roof. Instead of laying the trousers out, she hung them from a nylon line stretched between a hook on the wall and a post at the other end of the flat cement deck, wedging a pinch of material from each garment between the line's twisted threads to fix it there. As she worked, a warm breeze lapped at the trouser legs, rousing them to a muted, aimless shuffle. The city spread out before her, grey rooftops dotted with clutter and debris, dust and exhaust pooled in the streets, the clamour of people and machines floating up from the market below. Apart from the ravines that sliced through the areas to the west and east, there was barely a patch of green to be seen. In the distance, the volcano Pacaya shimmered against a powder blue sky, its peak piercing a single white cloud. Seeing it, she suddenly yearned to be there, if only for a moment, wandering the mountain skirt, feeling at each step the power of its molten belly in the soles of her feet. She scuffed her shoe against the cement deck. Cinderblock had nothing to say to her. She was glad Soraida was sending her out to the countryside. And she was glad she'd be taking Yasmin with her.

By lunchtime two of Soraida's lightweight polyester dresses were dry, so Isabel took them down to her aunt's wardrobe. She opened the walnut-stained door and looked for an empty hanger. To one side was a small shelf with a bible and a dog-eared copy of the *Popul Vuh* on it. The bible was not really a surprise, but Isabel wondered vaguely why Soraida would keep a copy of the famous Mayan text. Then she noticed a photo lying face up at the back of the shelf. She withdrew it carefully.

It was a wedding portrait, an old black and white. A man in a suit and a woman in *po't* and *uq*, embroidery zigzagging across her chest like an electric heartbeat. Her parents, a paper chain of flowers strung around their shoulders symbolically uniting them for life.

Isabel studied the photograph: her mother's features were delicate, almond eyes, the trace of a dimple barely visible on either side of a generous smile; her father so tall, his forehead broad, his nose long, the moustache that used to tickle her when he kissed her good-night hiding his upper lip, eyes that drilled into you. Around them crowded her grandparents, aunts and uncles, cousins—all of them short and dark like her mother. She closed her eyes and tried to conjure them. Her mother's laugh, like running water, the way it made her grin. Her father lifting her high and then pretending to drop her, the delicious thrill of falling barely long enough to feel it. The warmth of her mother's touch, comfort in the grainy roughness of her skin. Her limbs folded around Isabel with an intimacy unmatched by any other, until Isabel gave birth to a daughter of her own.

She heard movement and opened her eyes. Soraida was at the open door.

"I was just putting your dresses away," Isabel said. "I didn't mean to snoop, but ..." She held out the photograph. "I didn't know you had this."

Soraida stared at Isabel's hand, her face drained of colour. Then she took the photo and sank onto the bed. "Your father sent it to me after ..." She wiped her eyes, looked another long moment at the image, and passed it back to Isabel. "Keep it."

"Auntie." Isabel sat, too, and put her arm around the older woman. "We can make copies."

Soraida nodded and rested her hand on Isabel's thigh. Although her father was what connected them and there were many questions Isabel would like to ask—about his past, what he was like as a child, as a young man, how he came to know and fall in love with her mother, a woman from a different class, a different culture, how ... *how* they met their deaths—Isabel didn't ask. It was clear from Soraida's own silence on the subject that her father's death had hurt her aunt deeply, and Isabel had no desire to reopen old wounds. There was something else, though. A family of one, Yasmin had said.

"If you have a moment," she said, "I'd like to talk to you about Yasmin. She's been having some difficulties, I understand. The other night, when she came home, she'd been drinking."

"I've done the best I could," Soraida said.

"I don't doubt it. I just need to know, to understand what's eating her so I can try to fix it." Blissful one moment, angry and bitter the next, Yasmin struck Isabel as more taciturn and erratic in her emotions than her adolescence warranted. But what did Isabel know about teenagers or mother-daughter relationships?

"What's wrong is easy," Soraida said. "You've been away."

Isabel felt her face flush, but she kept her voice steady. "She was telling me the other night that she's missed having family. That it's only been the two of you."

"And Cousin Quique every Sunday." Soraida chuckled. Then she said, "Enrique's been very good to us. We've been able to count on him."

"And your parents? Aunts? Uncles?"

Soraida said nothing.

"Why?"

"They were afraid."

"Of Yasmin?"

"And of you. Everybody knew you would come back one day, unless . . ."

Isabel waited for her to say it, but she didn't.

Soraida went on. "I don't know, really. It's not like they ever told me. They only told me don't do it."

"When I brought you Yasmin."

"And then they never talked to me again."

Isabel was stunned. How could they turn their backs on their own family? "I thought . . ." But she didn't know what she'd thought, what she'd imagined would happen.

Soraida stroked her thigh. "I knew before I agreed to take her."

"How?"

"Because . . ." Soraida looked to the ceiling and then to the barred window next to her bed before her gaze settled on the books on the wardrobe shelf. She sighed. "They never approved of your father's choice of bride." She turned again to Isabel. "You didn't know?"

Isabel examined the photo. In her mind, she was following her mother and several of her aunts along a trail, repeating the names of the plants they were harvesting for her grandmother's teas: *eya, tzoli'j, much'*. She'd always assumed they'd lost touch with her father's relatives after mounting death threats had forced them to take refuge in her mother's village. But that wasn't what had happened.

"*Much'*," she repeated.

"What?"

All the words from her relatives came to her in Kaqchikel. "It's a plant. You call it chipilín."

Soraida didn't respond. How could she? It was a world her family had refused to meet, refused to know.

"I was remembering," Isabel said. She ran her finger along the photo's edge, careful not to touch the image, an ancient grief welling in her. Her mother. Her beautiful, intelligent, courageous mother. They'd rejected her. "So it isn't just that they were afraid. It wasn't because I went to the mountains."

"No." Soraida's voice was a whisper. "Keep the picture, Isabel."

And Soraida? She'd got as far as Eighteenth Street and this little room—it couldn't have been where she'd started—and she'd stood by Yasmin and protected her.

Isabel rose to go. "I still want to talk to you about Yasmin's behaviour. Another time?" She turned at the door. "And thank you. For everything."

After Isabel left, Soraida sat a while longer. Through no fault of her own, her niece had awakened doubts she'd long tried to keep dormant. Even after so many years, her brother's memory filled her with longing, remorse and dread.

She got up and took down the tattered copy of the *Popul Vuh* from the wardrobe shelf, flipping through its brittle pages until she found the place she'd wedged the passport-sized photo Hugo had sent her of his baby daughter just after she was born. A dark little face peeking out between folds of swaddling and a white woolen cap. Piercing black eyes even then. Soraida slid the photo back between the book's leaves and turned to the first page. There was Hugo's signature, its flourish a reflection of his self-confidence and, perhaps, his pride. Above it, the inscription to his little sister: "The world is big but it's beautiful. Don't be afraid." She'd read his message a thousand times—the book, too—but it still hadn't got through. She *was* afraid—now more than ever.

She closed the book and replaced it on the shelf. Then she checked her watch. 12:15. This was not the time to be reading or wallowing in memories. Lunch was waiting and Yasmin would be home soon and then she must get back to the shop. She couldn't saddle Byron with all the work. Before she left, she shut the wardrobe door.

The next day, Isabel boarded the bus that would take her to the Toriello Foundation. Ever since the May Day parade, she'd been eager to see her old friends there—to talk to people who understood her.

The old bus, a repainted Bluebird sent down from the States decades earlier, raced down the city streets, stopping wherever somebody hailed it. It wasn't full, as they often were, packed in fact to overflowing, hapless passengers clinging to the bus's frame as they sped through the city. Isabel found a seat midway back next to a young woman dressed in a school uniform.

Three stops later, two young, tattooed men got on. On seeing them, Isabel felt for the gun at her belt, but there wasn't one. Her neighbour twisted toward the back, looking for a way to escape. It was too late. A very tall and muscular youth had boarded by the rear door and was standing in the aisle with his arms crossed, a large revolver in his hand. It was a holdup.

Isabel and the girl faced the front again, where the larger of the tattooed pair was waving a Glock and shouting instructions. Isabel knew that holdups had become commonplace, but she hadn't realized what it would be like to be confronted this way—victimized—with no means of defending herself. A chill crept through her.

As the third of the crew moved with a canvas sack from passenger to passenger, demanding they hand over money and possessions, she reminded herself that this was not the army—they would take the valuables and leave. Nobody, if they all cooperated, would get hurt. That was exactly what the young thug at the front of the bus was yelling at them—*do like I say and nobody gets hurt*—as his partner collected jewellery, watches, bags of groceries, cash, from the passengers in front of her. When he got to Isabel, she had her money, less what sat in the bottom of her shoe, ready. The youth snatched the bills from her hand and shoved them into the deep pocket of his baggy jeans. "Where's the rest," he demanded.

"That's it." She showed him her arms, both wrists, and turned her head so he could see she wasn't carrying anything, not even a knapsack. Mounting anger was steadily melting her fear—just like in the jungle. She was ready for whatever might happen. The youth leaned heavily across her now to grab the money from the hands of the young woman at Isabel's side, who held it there like a candle, trembling, her tear-filled eyes fixed on the floor. Their assailant put this money into the same pocket where Isabel's had gone.

"Earrings," he said and held out his hand. The young woman slid the small silver hoops from her earlobes and, without looking at him, placed them in his palm. Isabel could feel the girl's heart pounding. He dropped the jewellery into his sack and then leaned back, grinning at the young woman. Isabel saw the thought forming behind his eyes, so when he lunged forward to yank her neighbour from her seat, Isabel stood and caught his wrist. "No!" she said.

He brought his face close to hers and exhaled, his breath hot and moist on her skin, his temples pulsing. Glistening Roman numerals seethed over his face and skull—the elaborate thirteens of the Salvatrucha. A heifer branded by its owners.

Then his partner at the front of the bus called out. "Leave her, Chato. No time for that."

Isabel released the brute's hand and he slapped her hard before hurrying on. The blow knocked her off balance but she didn't fall. Nor did she raise her hand to the injured spot. She sat again in her seat, humiliated, furious, and stared straight ahead, the side of her face radiating heat. The girl beside her had not moved but her tears were flowing and she was shaking. When the gangsters finally stepped off the bus and it pulled away, resuming its route as if nothing were amiss, she leaned into Isabel and began to wail. Isabel said nothing. She was too angry to speak. She was watching the other passengers, the way they carried on, animated, repeating to each other moment by moment everything that had just occurred and then sharing the stories of the last time they were robbed and the time before that and declaring at intervals how terrible it all was. She also watched the driver, who throughout the whole ordeal had sat hunched over the steering wheel, silent, picking at his nails, and she wondered what part he had in all this.

"It's still red but it looks like it's not going to swell up." A Q'eqchi' compa named Lola was dabbing at Isabel's cheek with a damp cloth while they sat at one of the long tables in the Foundation's cafeteria.

Since the electricity was out, as it was throughout the city every day from noon till six, she gently raised Isabel's chin to better capture the sunlight that filtered through the glass tiles overhead. The Foundation was full of people trained in first aid, though Isabel's injury hardly required such fuss.

"You've got to be careful, Isabel," Danilo said, sitting across from her. Claudia was next to him, and a few other compas had gathered around to hear her account of the robbery. "Those guys would just as soon kill you as look at you," he said. A number of people nodded in agreement.

"I wasn't thinking. I just reacted." Her face hurt but she didn't like the attention she was getting. Nor did she like the mild scolding tone that went with it.

"You were lucky," Claudia said. "You have to treat it like going through an army checkpoint. Complete passivity, like you wouldn't hurt a fly. That's how people survive."

Isabel thanked Lola, who having finished her work got up to return the cloth to the kitchen. The other compas began to meander off as well.

"I've been through a few checkpoints myself, you know," Isabel said to Claudia. "But there's no greater cause here. Am I supposed to sacrifice other people just to save my own skin?" She was tiring of the conversation. "It turned out all right."

"We wouldn't want to lose you," Claudia said.

Danilo must have sensed Isabel's unease because he made a joke of it. "The organization has invested a great deal in you."

Claudia slapped his shoulder, her long curls jiggling. "Stop!" To Isabel, she said, "He never stops."

Isabel smiled, but Danilo went on, his brow furrowing behind his glasses. "Seriously, we've got to take the country back from the gangs, from organized crime—and the peace accords are the only way to do it."

Claudia nodded. "And by building the party." Claudia, Isabel had learned, was going to run for Congress in the next election.

Isabel, in contrast, hadn't even joined the party and hadn't decided whether or not she would. She shook her head. "I will do my part, I promise, but for now, as a citizen only." She added, by way of concession, "Yasmin would like it if I was more involved here."

Compañeros puttered in and out of the large room, greeting them in passing. The place had a tone of quiet industry, like an indoor guerrilla camp, everybody with something to do and plenty of time to do it.

"You should bring her round," Danilo said. "There's a whole group of young people now. A lot of them are the kids of militants but others are brand-new and eager to join in."

"They're so funny, too," Claudia said. "One of them said to me, 'I wish I'd been born ten years earlier so I could have fought the army.'"

"They have no goddamn idea," Danilo said.

"It's the guerrilla mystique they're after."

"And the fashion!" Danilo held his sides and rocked with laughter. He looked in pain.

"When I was in the demobilization camp," Claudia said, "people would actually come and have pictures taken of themselves dressed up as guerrillas—guns and everything."

"Guerrilla tourism," Danilo said, still laughing.

Isabel was laughing, too, trying to imagine it. It made her face hurt. She thought of the nightmares that ambushed her every night. Sometimes there was only a labyrinth of green and a pack that was too heavy to lift, yet she still woke up shaking and dripping with sweat. In daylight, she'd remember—it was her duty to remember—the people they'd lost: Lucía. The desolation as they laid her, still in her bloody, bullet-punctured fatigues, in a shallow grave in the jungle, a place her loved ones would never see. Rodrigo. Isabel's trying to stem the bleeding after he slipped in the mud and his assault rifle discharged, the bullets tearing into his throat. There were so many people she must hold on to.

Claudia was talking now. "That life made us who we are. It's going to be hard for the next generation to understand."

Danilo reached across the table and poked Isabel's arm. "C'mon. I bet even you miss something about it. Have you ever been as close to anybody as we all were in camp?"

It was true. The guerrilla life had stripped them to the core. You were who you were, and it showed in everything you did. Even the smallest act was open to the scrutiny of the entire camp. Body and soul completely exposed.

"Not even my own daughter," she said.

Isabel sat behind the counter of Soraida's shop, flipping through a newspaper, as two women stood speaking in Kaqchikel by the shelves of men's clothing. She knew by their dress they were from Comalapa: the red band across the shoulders of their woven *po't* was said to represent the fires of the Spanish conquistadores that had ravaged their ancestors' homes. They were trying to decide between two and three T-shirts.

Soraida had fixed her up working the slow shifts, easing her into what Isabel supposed would be her new role in life. It was not a bad role. Compared to the lot of many people it was downright comfortable. And yet ... The fact was the talk with Danilo and Claudia had left her unsettled. She missed them and the other compas, but more than that perhaps, she missed the conviction she'd had of having chosen a difficult but righteous path in life. She wished she was not so full of doubt now.

During the war the way had been clear. They—Isabel and her compañeros—couldn't give up. People's lives were at stake. She'd learned of the massacre of her own village from the rebel radio station and spent the next two nights awake, eyes wide open, straining to keep the news that had reached her ears from touching her mind, her soul. But she'd never doubted that she must go on. The survivors of the massacres had taken refuge in the jungle—they needed protection. And though a rebel victory was no longer possible, giving up would have been a death sentence. Everybody knew that in Guatemala there was no such thing as a political prisoner.

A man and a woman strolled by Soraida's shop, swinging a small girl by her arms. Each time the child landed, her shiny black shoes slapped the pavement and she squealed for more. "More, more, more, more!"

Isabel thought of her parents. What would they have done? They had launched headfirst into the movement for change in the country. Without any weapons to protect them, her father had defended the workers of a sugar plantation who'd been fired en masse for daring to organize. Her mother had joined the student-run literacy campaign, teaching adults from hers and other villages to read and write. It had cost them everything. All that remained were the few memories Isabel struggled to retain and the wedding portrait Soraida kept hidden in her wardrobe.

Things were different now. Working on projects to advance the peace accords and everything they contained wasn't quite as likely to get you killed. But it was still soul-consuming. When you lived that life, you had little time for anything else. Isabel suspected that for some of her compas, carrying on with the old life was just a way of avoiding the new one. She didn't want to make that mistake.

And that thought brought her back to Yasmin. She'd lived without a mother long enough. If Isabel was going to devote herself to Yasmin, she had to take on Soraida and her shop, too. They were part of the package.

She closed the newspaper she'd been perusing. On the front page was a colour photograph of a young man collapsed in the street, tattoos along both arms and spilling over his skull, a splash of red across his chest.

Outside the shop, an argument had erupted between a young man and an older one. What it was about, Isabel couldn't discern. *These* are the people I have to get to know, she thought.

CHAPTER 6

Yasmin's school was holding a Mother's Day event, and Soraida had closed the shop to attend. She fretted about it the whole way there. "I'll go broke if we keep this up," she said to Isabel.

In the school courtyard, a sterile expanse of grey cement and mint green stucco walls, they sat on long benches arranged in rows as they listened to the adolescent choir intone the virtues of their mothers: love, self-sacrifice, hard work, dependability. The choristers sang with their hands clasped over their hearts, their gazes hovering somewhere over the heads of their audience, from time to time drifting up, one then another, to the white clouds above. Isabel was entranced. It wasn't their words that moved her; it was *seeing* them, hearing their young voices, high and pure and clear. And Yasmin, right there among them. A wide range of ages as students always were in Guatemala, they were lucky, these boys and girls, to have made it so far. Years 1 to 3 of this middle school were the stepping stones to studying for a career, as an accountant, a farm technician, a teacher—the only three options when Isabel was their age—and nowadays as a computer technician, a bilingual secretary, a travel agent, a project manager. For a very few students, university awaited. Isabel's father had studied at the public university. Her mother had scaled barriers of race, gender and poverty to graduate from high school. But even that had been beyond Isabel's reach. Her grandparents had considered it too dangerous for her to leave the village, as her mother had, to attend a school like this one.

Up next was a short skit by the third-year class: a typical bus ride through the neighbourhood. Stock characters got on and joined the other passengers, seated in two columns of hard-backed chairs, who bumped up and down and swayed from side to side in simulation of the journey. There was the harassed mother trailed by her brood of whining brats, the silver-tongued hawker of miracle cures, the mournful beggar delivering his long entreaty to the passengers, now and then reaching out his upturned palm, the faux bourgeois princess complaining on her mobile phone that her private jet had been grounded for repairs, and last of all a tattooed youth who boarded the bus and stood before the seated passengers, legs apart, arms extended, a plastic water pistol between his palms: "Good morning, ladies and gentlemen, this is a holdup!"

The audience up and down the benches howled with laughter. But Isabel couldn't laugh. She could hardly breathe. Her heart was pounding, and she'd begun to sweat. Because all she could see, as if time had stopped or she had stepped outside time completely, was Yasmin, just minutes before, shuffling from the patio with the rest of the choristers, washed white by the glare of a merciless sun. Yasmin chatting and giggling with the girl ahead of her, and then, as though she'd just remembered, looking back for an instance to give her mother a small wave, one innocent among many in a country that did not tolerate innocence. Isabel struggled to keep her seat. To regain control. Her head was burning, her hands shaking. Every breath she took had become an act of will. But she did breathe. *One and two and three and* . . . She counted silently, commanding her mind to move through her body and speak the soothing words of order and sense. *Breathe.* Two days ago, another transvestite had been killed in Eighteenth Street. Another pickup raging past. Gunfire flashing. Another life extinguished. Today, she was surrounded by people laughing at a skit depicting their country's destruction. She felt wounded. She wanted to protect these children from the horrors they were bound to meet but knew she was unable. Not all of them. But one? Her Yasmin?

A boy had taken the stage and was reciting a poem he'd composed for his grandmother:

> *Mother of my mother*
> *I remember you this day . . .*

Still lightheaded, Isabel focused on the boy, his stubby fingers, the odd twist of his nose, the puckered stucco wall behind him. She was returning. She felt stable now. The boy left the stage, and a girl stepped forward to declaim Gabriela Mistral's "Madrecita Mía." For a final number, the boys, who outnumbered the girls by almost two to one, invited their mothers or aunts or grandmothers to dance.

Yasmin approached, one hand thrust toward her mother. In it, she held a folded piece of paper emblazoned with red pencil crayon flowers. "Mami. This is for you."

Isabel received the card and read it: "All my love, darling Mami, home at last." The dot over the *i* in *Mami* was heart-shaped.

She kissed Yasmin's cheek and held her tight, until Yasmin coughed and pulled away. She was almost full grown, this intriguing, frustrating, precious child Isabel hardly knew, a woman in body if not in mind or spirit. Yet this was the first Mother's Day they'd celebrated together. Isabel watched as all along the bench, students were delivering their gifts to their mothers. It was hard not to feel like an intruder.

She opened the card and reread it. *That i!* Surely Yasmin still needed her mother. And Isabel so wanted to be that person for whatever time were left them.

"Did you see?" she asked Soraida, showing her the card.

Soraida barely glanced at it. "It's lovely," she said as she dabbed at her forehead with her handkerchief.

Cranky even now, Isabel thought. Still, the patio was uncomfortably hot. "Why don't we find some shade?" To Yasmin she said, "I just want to meet your teacher and then we can go."

"Can't I stay with my friends?"

"You haven't eaten. Come and eat first, and then you can spend the afternoon out."

Yasmin frowned.

Soraida leaned back against the cool courtyard wall and closed her eyes. The day had started badly and it had just turned worse. She should not have closed the shop for this. She pressed her handkerchief to her eyes and sniffed. Yasmin had not given *her* a card. After years and years of standing in as the child's mother—honoured on Mother's Day for it—she'd been replaced by the real thing. It hurt. She didn't like to admit it—a silly thing like a card—but it did. And Isabel hadn't even noticed, hadn't thought twice about getting the credit, giving the orders. She'd fidgeted for most of the children's presentation. And now, despite that, she was off meeting Yasmin's teacher, somebody Soraida had known for years and didn't need to speak to again. She should have been prepared for this, but she was not. Why had she come? She should be working in her shop, where she made the decisions.

"Doña Soraida?"

Soraida opened her eyes. Byron stood before her, a young pregnant woman at his side. His sister Élida, no doubt. Her warm brown eyes and wide lips were almost identical to Byron's. And there was something gentle about her manner, the way her right hand rested lightly on her brother's shoulder, her fingers playing absent-mindedly with the loose curls at the back of his neck.

"I wanted to introduce you," Byron said.

Soraida kissed Byron's cheek and then Élida's. "And how is the little one?" she asked.

"Two more months to go," Élida said. She looked flushed but content, her smooth round belly pressing against the fabric of her T-shirt. Tiny pearls of sweat sat on her upper lip. Was there anything more beautiful than a woman with child?

Soraida asked after their mother, who couldn't make the trip. She asked about Élida's work and Byron's grades. It was clear from the responses that Élida was every bit the dutiful child Byron was—proof that money did not decide conduct. The pregnancy had been a mistake, obviously, but at least the girl was taking responsibility for it. No reason the child should suffer the faults of its parents.

And Byron looked happy, even though his mother—a cripple, poor thing—had not come. He never showed rancour toward the rags life dealt him. Of course, his interactions with Soraida were always somewhat formal. It was possible he behaved differently at home. But his face was open, nothing hidden there. Soraida was sure—she felt it in her heart—that she'd found in Byron one of those rare people who was exactly what he appeared to be.

After he'd gone to bring them some horchata, she asked Élida, "Is Byron ever a moody teenager? He's always so polite with me, always content."

Élida laughed. "Mother says he was born under moonlight. The moon gave him his character."

Soraida didn't give much credence to folk wisdom, but observing Byron as he returned with two plastic cups brimming with the chalky rice drink, taking care not to knock any of the many students and adults crowded under the blazing sun, she thought it might be true. Yasmin had been born in a war zone.

Isabel watched as Yasmin sought out a boy who hung at the edge of the crowd, one hand in the pocket of his blue jeans, the other caressing his chin, the ducked head and stooped shoulders of somebody who is trying not to stand out—or is simply a little abashed. He wore no school uniform and looked older than most of Yasmin's classmates. An ex-classmate perhaps? Their expressions as he and Yasmin met, his head inclined, hers raised, murmurs, tender smiles, suggested something else. This must be the one, Isabel thought. She decided to introduce herself but before she could reach them, the boy lifted his eyes from her daughter's face, his smile evaporating. Then he confided something to Yasmin's ear, grinned, and left.

"What? Is he afraid to meet me?" Isabel asked when Yasmin turned to see what had prompted her friend's departure.

"What are you talking about?" she said. "Why are you spying on me?"

"I just wanted to meet your friend."

"Spying." She turned away, her face eclipsed by a curtain of ebony hair.

Isabel touched her shoulder. "Call it what you like," she said, "but I'm part of your life. I want to know what's going on in it. That's what being a family is about. That's what you said you wanted."

"I wanted, like ten years ago."

All around them, the patio bubbled with the happy prattle of mothers and children, their bursts of laughter and exclamations of love and pride. "For Mother's Day," Isabel said. "Let me have this one."

Yasmin flicked her long hair from her face and crossed her arms, but she stopped protesting.

Lunch did not go well. Yasmin spent most of the meal fuming, headphones looped around her neck, ready to block her elders out at the first opportunity. Isabel, in Soraida's opinion, behaved no better. They'd barely finished eating when she announced she had business to attend to. As if she were trying to beat Yasmin at her own game. Soraida found it hard to watch—a mother should set a better example. But Soraida, unlike her niece, was used to Yasmin's ways. Maybe too used to them.

When Isabel had left, she decided to find out what was going on.

"It was very thoughtful of you to make your mother such a lovely card," she said.

Yasmin shrugged. She had not moved from the table.

"Is there anything wrong? Did you and your mother have a fight?" Soraida reached out her hand to stroke her niece's hair, but Yasmin shook her off and got up.

"Can I go out?" she said. "Mama said I could go out."

It was true, but nobody had consulted Soraida. "I need you in the shop. I'm going to open."

"You don't need me. Besides it's not my turn. Why doesn't my mother help you? She's the adult in the family."

"We've always worked together in the shop. You used to like it."

Yasmin raised her hands to her head and paced like a trapped animal. "Is that all you ever think about? Your shop? It's like nothing else exists." She gave Soraida a stony look. "Other things do exist, you know."

Soraida winced. "You've no right to mock a person's livelihood."

Yasmin lowered her arms. Her expression softened. She eyed the door. "Can I go now?"

It was like watching a circus performer—the pirouettes, the somersaults. Or like trying to follow the pea during a shell game. Soraida couldn't keep up. "Go, then. Go, go, go!" Dealing with a hundred customers would be easier than dealing with Yasmin all afternoon. "Go do whatever it is young people do."

The angry furrows vanished from Yasmin's brow. She kissed her great-aunt. "You see. You're the only one who understands me."

She was out the door before Soraida could correct her.

Isabel had gone to the registrar's office to start the weary process of replacing or getting for the first time her different pieces of identification —birth certificate, cédula, drivers licence. She hadn't planned on spending the afternoon this way—Mother's Day of all days—but after enduring her daughter's morose silence during their return from the school and their midday meal together, she'd decided she'd had enough fraught emotion for one day. At least here, in the heart of the city's government district, she'd be doing something useful.

She pushed open the glass doors of the dimly lit office tower and mounted the stairs to the third floor. She'd expected to find bureaucrats and plenty of red tape, which she did. But she also found Claudia.

"What are you doing here?"

"I work here." Claudia leaned across the counter and kissed her cheek. She lowered her voice and jerked her thumb to the left. "And I'm not the only one." Isabel peeked around the corner in the direction Claudia had indicated, and there she saw Max. Older now, greyer, his hair trim, spectacles unbroken, he looked fit and healthy if not exactly happy. He was smiling tightly at the man in front of him. Isabel hadn't thought about Max in she didn't know how long. Yet now that she saw him, she wondered how that was possible. How had it become possible to put people aside for years and still feel your heart tick faster when they reappeared in your life? How many times could they pick up where they'd left off? Could they this time? She approached.

An hour later they were sitting next to each other in a booth of a bar near the registrar's building. Claudia was there, too, and Danilo was on his way. Max was grinning at her, the same frank, reassuring smile she remembered. It both thrilled and calmed her.

Claudia was talking. "We're in the registrar's office, in the police force, even in that new department—strategic analysis. Strategic is right!"

"Like we're practically co-governing," Max said with a smirk. He sat hunched over his elbows, cupping his hand behind one ear to hear better. A grenade attack had left him deaf in the other.

Claudia balled up a paper napkin and threw it at him. "Oh, shut up. We're working, anyway. And these are key positions to have."

Max rolled his eyes, but then he chuckled.

"I still can't believe it," Isabel said to him. "I didn't even know you were in the country."

"Max likes to keep a low profile," Claudia said.

"Probably wise."

Max dipped his good ear toward her. "I just got back from Cuba. Alejo's studying there—computer engineering."

Isabel had last seen Max's son when she'd last seen Max, maybe four or five years ago. "He's all grown up then. Handsome?"

"Takes after his mother, so, yes."

"Is Eva here or there?" Isabel asked. And that's when Max put his arm around her.

"Neither. She's in Switzerland with an ex-compa." He squeezed Isabel's shoulder and looked at her. "How is your Yasmin?"

Of course she went home with him. Of course she did. Danilo came and gave them all a ride, dropping Isabel and Max off at the little apartment he rented in the back of a carpentry shop.

Danilo poked his head out of the window of his pickup. "I'll stop by and let Soraida know you won't be back tonight." Max had already stepped into a corner pharmacy to buy condoms. Danilo grinned. "Or I'll say you had to do some favours to get the bureaucrats to fix your papers."

Isabel pushed his head back into the cab. "Go away! See you, Claudia. Say hi to the kids."

Max's room was small and barren, as if he were only staying the night. A single bed with a metal frame and a lumpy mattress. An ironing board, the iron on top of it, stood in one corner and several pressed shirts hung in the open closet. Isabel waited as he put down his leather briefcase and removed his tie. Then they were kissing, undressing, clambering onto the bed. She pulled him to her, his familiar smell, his bulk, his heat. From somewhere inside her, a rage she was not even aware of turned to desire, burning through her, leaving nothing behind but the delicious void of sex.

When she awoke the next morning, Max was already shaved and showered, standing at the hotplate waiting for water to boil. She watched him until he glanced her way and smiled.

"Coffee?"

Before he left for work, he leaned down to kiss her. The smell of his cologne, as warm and sharp as sunlight, dispelled the last of her slumber.

"It's good to see you again," he said.

She knew then that they would continue to meet up, now and then, on and off. It was the way their relationship had always been. The sex was full, committed. Max was reticent by nature, but he was honest and dependable in the things that counted. And he made no demands—which was what she wanted. The only future that should concern her now was Yasmin's. The alarm clock by Max's hotplate read 6:30. An hour yet till Yasmin had to be at school. Isabel jumped up and searched the bed and then the floor for her scattered clothing. They'd had their chance, she and Max, and they'd used it to try to change history. Now it was up to the next generation. She'd barely reached middle age, but she couldn't help feeling that she'd done all the living she would ever do.

When she got home, Soraida was making breakfast.

"I'll just change and come help you," Isabel said.

Soraida didn't raise her eyes from the mixing bowl. She was kneading together Maseca and water to make tortillas.

"Is Yasmin up yet?" Isabel asked.

"Yasmin stayed at friends. She'll go to school from there."

"Really? Which friend?" Though she asked the question, she'd met very few of Yasmin's friends. She hadn't even managed to meet the boy Yasmin seemed to be dating.

"Maritza. They live right by the school." Soraida pounded at the corn masa.

Maritza. Isabel couldn't remember any mention of Maritza. "But on a school night?"

Soraida faced her. "What do you expect? As soon as Danilo came by and told us you were staying out, she grabbed her things and said, 'That makes two of us.'"

Isabel decided not to pursue it. "Maybe I'll pick her up from school."

But Soraida kept on. "What kind of example do you think you're setting for her, doing . . . doing what you're doing."

"This is none of your business."

"Yasmin is very much my business."

Isabel was too tired to fight. It seemed to be all she did, all she had ever done in one way or another. Let Yasmin have her sleepover—let them all forget about the rules and the wrongs to be righted, for once.

"When do you need me in the shop?" she asked.

Soraida slapped the dough against the side of the bowl and turned it again.

"I don't need you at all."

Isabel bowed her head. She'd failed again. She'd let Soraida down and, worse, she'd let down Yasmin. Again. She'd chosen escape, blissful escape instead of battle. Instead of disappointment. She rubbed her forehead. She felt exhausted. Weeks without a good night's sleep. Years without a real and prolonged sense of peace. Was it so wrong to want that? She entered the room she shared with her daughter, lowered her backpack to the floor and stripped down to her underwear. Mother's Day had come and gone like a tropical storm, and now, as she climbed into bed, she wandered mentally through the calm that followed, surveying the wreckage. There'd been a moment, maybe two, as Yasmin sang to her from the school's impromptu stage and again as she looked into her mother's eyes and delivered her card, isolated moments when Yasmin had let her in. Too soon, the door had slammed shut. As a child, Yasmin had always kept that door open. Her heart was there for the taking. At every rendezvous, she'd rushed to embrace her mother and cover her face with kisses. When they parted, she'd kept the faith, nodding obediently despite her tears as Isabel pressed her hand to her daughter's heart and told her, "I'm right here. No matter what, I am always with you, right here." No doubt, Yasmin had learned from her mistake, as least as far as her mother was concerned.

Isabel tried to recall her own mother. What would she think of the choices Isabel had made? Would she be proud? Ashamed? They were questions Isabel couldn't hope to answer. She knew nothing of her mother's mind or thoughts. No word of advice or warning had survived. What Isabel remembered about her mother was the shape of her face, the feel of her hand, the stories she would tell—not the stories themselves so much as the way they made her feel. Loved. Safe. By the time Isabel was old enough to make decisions for herself, her mother was long dead, and try as she might, Isabel could barely visualize her as the whole person she had been: student, pioneer, rebel, woman in love, young mother. How could she give to Yasmin what her mother had been unable to give to her? What would that thing be that Yasmin most needed? Patience? Wisdom? Love? Freedom?

Drowsy now, Isabel rolled over. One by one, like stones dropping into a well, she released all thought of her daughter, her mother, her aunt, and let the memory of Max's body engulf her. She slept.

Soraida collected the hot tortillas from the comal and sat down to a bowl of black beans she had prepared the night before. She was still angry with Isabel and hoped her niece would not appear for midday dinner but go on sleeping. Isabel's actions confirmed for her that the guerrillas, whatever their political aims, were a hotbed of immorality. Imagine a jungle camp full of men—atheists and communists, most of them—with just a few women between them, mere girls really. Too young to know any better. No parent to step in or guide them. No neighbours to shame them onto the right path. Who knew what orgies ensued? Was it any surprise so many of them came out of it pregnant? Yasmin's father had disappeared just about as soon as he knew Isabel had missed her period. So much for the cause. And Isabel? She'd dumped the poor infant with Soraida and gone right back for more.

Soraida stared at her food, still untouched. The tortilla in her hand had grown cold. She gripped it harder, determined to keep her anger alive, but already it was waning. She remembered Isabel's face the day she'd left Yasmin in her care. She'd looked straight into Soraida's eyes—decided, unembarrassed, resolutely alone. It was the face that a condemned man, having accepted his fate, might show to the world as he walked to his execution. There was resolve in it but no comfort or pity.

By the time Soraida had finished the last of her meal, her anger had passed and she saw clearly what she must do. Her job was to reunite mother and daughter. Yasmin needed that. Whatever kind of mother Isabel was, she was the only one Yasmin had. Soraida had done what she could—what family duty demanded of her and more—but the time had come for her to step aside. If she couldn't take that step out of love for Isabel and Yasmin, she would do it in memory of her dear brother. She owed him that much.

CHAPTER 7

ISABEL SAT TREMBLING, gasping for air, wrestling against a panic that had ambushed her in the depths of sleep and still had her in its grip. After a moment, she could just make out Yasmin's slumbering form in the next bed, the gentle rise and fall of her daughter's chest. In. Out. In ... Out ... Isabel tried to match the rhythm of her own breathing to Yasmin's until at last, her panic began to ebb. Soon, perhaps, she would sleep again. Lying back on her pillow, she listened to the night sounds of the city spill through the window above their beds and with them, as if floating on a wave, the lopsided singing of a drunk stumbling home.

She parked the pickup next to a stall on the fringes of the open-air Sunday market. They hadn't travelled far, but already it was a different world: the cobblestone plaza, the whitewashed adobe church, its bell tower silhouetted against the rising sun, women in traditional dress and a few men, too, their checkered woolen *xerka* wrapped like aprons about their hips. Barely a ladino to be seen. And beyond it all, the forested hills, scorched and brown at this time of year, rippling into the distance. Yasmin helped Isabel remove the blue plastic tarp they had secured over the clothing in the truck bed and spread it over the pebbled ground.

"What do you think? Are we going to make a killing?" Isabel asked.

Yasmin squinted at her mother, as if trying to place her against the unfamiliar backdrop. "Enough to cover gas if we're lucky."

Despite the surly reply, Yasmin didn't look unhappy. And by a stroke of luck—or an exertion of will?—she'd left her Walkman behind in the city. She was observing the people around her as she passed armloads of clothing to Isabel, who arranged the garments on the tarp, in groups by size and sex.

"Was it like this where you grew up?" Yasmin asked.

Isabel took in the town, its market stands and buildings shimmering in the burgeoning heat. It didn't strike her as strange. This, and places even smaller—humble clusters of cornstalk houses tucked into the pocket of a mountain skirt—this was her Guatemala. She felt at home here.

"Pretty much. This place is a bit bigger."

"Were you poor?"

Isabel smiled. "Not as poor as most. We had enough to eat." She was draping some of the better outfits over wire hangers hooked over the truck's panels. "In fact, early on, when we were still in the city, we were really quite well off. Better off than Soraida." She shaded her eyes from the sun's piercing rays. "Later it was different . . ."

Yasmin inspected the toe of her sneaker and tapped it against the pickup's back tire.

"After they killed Grandma and Grandpa," she said.

Something like a tremor moved through Isabel. "Yes," she said. This was good. Let Yasmin ask everything she needed to. "But even afterward, we were better off than many of our neighbours."

"What was it like?"

"What do you mean?"

"To be . . . Indian. What's it like?"

Another small shock. As if Mayans were something so other. As if she, herself, were so different from her daughter. But Yasmin was asking and Isabel wanted to answer. She thought before she did.

"I was a child, like any other child. Safe and happy in the love of my parents. I was barely aware of anything else. Then that ended."

Isabel shut her eyes and took a deep breath. Six years old again, she saw her neighbours lowering her parents' bodies from the back of the borrowed pickup. She watched again from where she squatted in the corner of her grandparents' front room as her aunts peeled back their clothing, black and stiff with clotted blood, bathed their grey, limp bodies and dressed them in their wedding outfits. She squeezed herself between the wooden tables where her aunts had laid them out and balanced on her tiptoes to take a closer look. She ran her fingertips along her mother's cheek and prodded the cotton batten stuffed into the places where bullets had torn away her father's skull. This was not her mother's skin. This was not the way she smelled. Her father's face was a distorted mask. His big hands lay there like slabs of clay. They were returned to her but unrecognizable, empty. The cotton batten had more life in it.

Isabel opened her eyes and forced a smile.

"Like all children I still learned to be happy, running around, playing with my cousins. I had the love and care of my grandparents."

The smell of roasting corn reached her from somewhere within the market. The smell of home.

"They taught me, my grandparents, to honour the Heart of the Earth, the Heart of the Sky. They told me the old stories: that long before the Conquest our ancestors had walked here from across the sea, that soon they became scattered and began to fight with each other. Eventually they all managed to meet up, somewhere in these mountains"—she pointed to the dry, distant hills—"and as they waited for dawn, they watched the morning star rise. Together. One people."

Isabel paused. She'd forgotten what it was Yasmin had asked her. But since her daughter wasn't objecting, she continued.

"The earthquake in '76 hit San Martín hard, especially in the main town. So many lives lost. A lot of people headed for the capital. Some of them started to organize, to make demands, to push for change, but we stayed in our village. We felt safest there. Then came the repression. People started to disappear—people we knew—kidnapped from a bus stop or on their way to school or the market."

She'd joined her neighbours as they made the rounds of hospital, city morgue, police station, army base, and returned, ghosts of their former selves, without news. They'd scour the highways, the ravines, the city dump.

"Sometimes we'd find their bodies and other bodies, too—tortured, mutilated." Isabel was feeling weak, breathless, but she was determined to finish what she was saying. "So I decided to leave. I decided to fight against what was happening around me. To the Kaqchikel people. To my family."

A woman had approached and was fingering a polka-dot blouse that hung from the tailgate. Remembering where she was, Isabel spun around. The woman consulted with a younger woman at her side, her daughter perhaps. They were speaking Kaqchikel.

"How much?" the younger woman asked in Spanish.

Isabel appraised the blouse and gave her answer in Kaqchikel. The older woman's face betrayed surprise. She began asking more questions, also in Kaqchikel, and soon she and Isabel were deep in a conversation about daughters and babies and the joys and trials of motherhood. As they talked, Isabel stole glances at Yasmin, who gazed at her mother as she might a stranger, her head high, back erect, a posture, so it seemed to Isabel, deliberately aloof, remote. It was a look she'd sometimes seen in Soraida. Isabel decided to ignore her. They had work to do. When she looked back, Yasmin had turned away.

When the transaction was complete, Isabel found Yasmin picking out articles of clothing for the Kaqchikel woman's daughter, who, it turned out, was fluent in Spanish.

"I'm going to be a secretary," the woman's daughter said. "I studied with the Bethlemitas."

Yasmin was refolding several pairs of jeans. If she was listening, she didn't let on.

Unperturbed, her companion continued. "I'll be moving to the capital soon, for work. I got placed with an institute. What's it like there?"

Yasmin appealed with her eyes to her mother, but when Isabel didn't answer, she said, "It's big. There's lots to see and do . . ." She smoothed the jeans she had just folded and, eyebrows arched, dimples absent, plucked a piece of fluff from the fabric. "But there's a lot of crime too. The other day, somebody got shot right outside our house."

The young woman's eyes widened. There was pain in them. "I've heard about things like that. But to have it so near." She looked from Yasmin to Isabel and then leaned in closer and whispered. "Isn't the violence supposed to be over?"

Yasmin shrugged and held up the pairs of jeans the woman had selected. "Do you want any of these or not?"

On the drive back to the capital, Isabel asked Yasmin what she'd thought about the people they'd met, people with whom Isabel had found such strong and immediate connection that as she drove, she couldn't help feeling she was leaving a piece of herself behind. She said as much to her daughter.

"They were okay, I guess," Yasmin said.

"For me, it was encouraging. I mean, that girl you were talking to, the one who's going to study in the capital. Just a few years ago, that would have been a rare, rare thing."

"Good for her."

"The sad thing is she has to leave home to do it. And work in languages that aren't her own."

"I don't see why you're so interested in her. We'll never even see them again."

The unpaved highway sliced through parched hills crowned with stunted oaks. Here and there deep caves ate into the sun-baked banks on either side where construction workers had mined for sand to mix cement. At other spots along the road, Isabel had to swerve to avoid fallen rubble and branches. The road seemed to bend under the sun's heat. She flipped the visor down to shield her from its glare.

"You're right. Let's talk about you. Soon you'll be deciding what you want to study, what career you'd like to pursue."

Yasmin shifted in her seat. "Maybe I don't know what I want."

"That's okay. You've still got time." It struck Isabel how changed Yasmin was from the little girl who'd scampered down the hallway to spring into her mother's arms on the night of Isabel's return. In just a month she'd become plumper, her breasts fuller ... Isabel remembered the boy she'd seen at the Mother's Day celebration and decided to ask. "Do you like him? How old is he?"

Yasmin scowled, but didn't answer.

Isabel made a second attempt. Too much had been put off for too long. "I know discussing this can be embarrassing. And maybe you think it's none of my business. But you're still very young. It's my job to look out for you, help you through things that can be difficult to navigate."

Yasmin was looking out her window as they talked. Hard to read the back of somebody's head. "He's just a guy at school," she said. "No big deal."

"Really? I guess I was a bit taken aback. He looks so much older than you."

They'd hit paved road and the hills were receding. Yasmin, too, seemed to be receding from her. Isabel had to find a way to call her back. "And, frankly, you seemed kind of smitten ..."

Nothing. Yasmin was glued to the window. Isabel chose another tack.

"I know about the drinking."

Silence.

"Remember? After May Day?"

"It was only one time."

"It's not just that. You're always out—I never know where you are. I never know who you're with."

Yasmin turned abruptly. "Welcome to *my* world."

Isabel let the words stand. She was trying to interpret her daughter's expression, see past the wall of defiance to whatever cowered in the shadows on the other side. She spoke gently.

"You're fifteen. You've got a long, long road ahead of you. You don't have to rush into anything. You don't have to do everything you see other people doing."

An intercity bus rounded the corner in front of them, raising a cloud of dust and surprising a pair of zopilotes that had been picking at some roadside carrion. Isabel watched them flap away, their giant black wings beating the hot air like a warning.

"Decide for yourself what is important to you, what you really want. But take time to do it."

"I do decide for myself," Yasmin mumbled. "You just don't like what I decide."

"Not when it's going to do you harm. That night, when you came home and you'd been drinking, I was so scared. All I could think of was all the things that might have happened. All the things I'd hoped to protect you from. The whole reason I asked Soraida—"

"Soraida!" Yasmin shouted. "Soraida doesn't know shit! Soraida is an uptight fossil who'd probably love to be rid of us both! She'd say anything to keep her precious little world from crumbling. Her stupid shop. Her stupid house." The expression on Yasmin's face, directed squarely at Isabel, was one Isabel had never seen before—a desperate anger shone from her eyes. "She'd turn her own brother in to save her skin."

Isabel pulled the truck over. She was shaking, breathing heavily, hunched over the steering wheel, trying to focus on its black plastic. There was a roaring in her ears. She couldn't look at Yasmin. Yasmin was not her daughter. Yasmin was not anybody at all. She did not exist. She was a roar in Isabel's ears. She was the buzzing in her eyes. A sea inside Isabel wanted to break forth. It was rushing from deep inside, pushing to the surface. Isabel held her breath and then released it slowly through pursed lips. She'd conquered fear before. She'd kept the boiling sea inside her in check. She was sweating. Yasmin had not said a word. Isabel still hadn't turned from the steering wheel.

They sat like that . . . two minutes? Five? Then Isabel straightened and started the engine, checked the mirror and pulled onto the highway. In the periphery of her vision, Yasmin curled against the door of the truck, cowering like a whipped puppy. Isabel knew that Yasmin would keep her eyes fixed on her, perhaps for the rest of the trip. Isabel kept her eyes on the road.

Soraida's heart was pounding, racing to decipher what it was her niece was telling her. She stood at the courtyard sink, in the dim shade cast by a translucent fibreglass awning, exactly where she'd been when Isabel barged in and confronted her. "I don't know what you're talking about," she stammered.

Yasmin lingered at the open door, neither inside nor out. Her eyes were wide, her face pale.

"Yasmin said you'd turn in your own brother," Isabel repeated. "What does she mean by that?"

"No, Mami, I—"

Isabel silenced her daughter with a raised hand.

Yasmin covered her mouth. She was choking back tears.

"She must have said it for a reason." Isabel was just inches from Soraida, sharp brown eyes drilling right into her. Surely she could read the fear there and would know that Soraida was hiding something. And then what?

"I don't know what it is you're asking me," Soraida said. On the street outside, the long whistle of a baked potato vendor pierced the eternal hum of sidewalk chatter and revving motors.

Isabel took a step backward, lowered her eyes to the hard cement floor and sighed. She spoke softly, as if she were speaking to herself rather than to Soraida. "I thought maybe you knew something. That maybe you could tell me something about what happened to them. You don't know what it's like not knowing." She was on the verge of tears, and Soraida thought she caught a glimpse of the little girl Isabel must once have been—eyes round with incomprehension and longing, as if she'd wandered off and become lost in an unfamiliar place.

Tell her. Soraida tried to make her tongue work, but her throat constricted; her mouth went dry. She wanted to confess, but what finally came out was more evasion. She eyed Yasmin, who was crying in earnest now. "I don't know why Yasmin says the things she does."

Isabel nodded—the fire Soraida had seen in her niece an instant ago was gone. Extinguished. She was still staring at the cement floor.

"I didn't mean to make you jump like that," Isabel said. "I overreacted—as usual." As she turned and moved toward her bedroom, Yasmin tried to approach, but her mother again raised her hand. "I can't," she said. "Not right now." Then she closed the bedroom door behind her.

Yasmin turned to Soraida.

"I don't want to hear it," Soraida said. "Don't you think you've caused enough trouble?" She was trying to recover her breath. She needed time and space to think, to decide what to do next. In a pretence of composure, she checked her watch. "Make yourself useful and go get the tortillas for supper."

Yasmin, still pale, her face damp, marched into the kitchen.

"Use the money from the Nido tin," Soraida called after her.

Once Yasmin had left, Soraida leaned heavily against the cement sink. She could not fathom what had led Yasmin to fabricate such a vile accusation nor how it was that buried beneath her monstrous, dirty lie there lay a tiny, hard diamond of truth. Her mind drifted to her brother: the times he'd cheered her up, the times he'd stood up for her, the times he'd shielded her from their father's wrath. She took her handkerchief from her apron pocket and pressed it to her eyes. She would tell Isabel everything when the moment was right—when things were better between them and Isabel was not so agitated. She had nothing to fear; she had done nothing wrong or, at least, she had intended no harm. But a sudden squeezing at her chest made her doubt her conviction. If she had nothing to fear, why hadn't she spoken up earlier? Why had she waited so many years? That fact alone would arouse Isabel's suspicion. Soraida brushed the tears from her eyes. Why couldn't things just stay the way they were? A bit better than the way they were? What difference would the truth make now?

She faced the closed door of Isabel's room and tried to imagine her niece on the other side of it, battling every night with nightmares that left her pale and shaken. Soraida didn't know—she didn't want to know—what horrors invaded Isabel's sleep. She'd learned long ago never to talk about the war or its victims. Never to ask questions. Never to question at all. Because people who tried to change things they couldn't were fools. They were wrongheaded. And Isabel was one of those people. Soraida's brother had been one of those people, too.

Soraida shook her head. The *truth* was, she still missed her brother. She'd spent most of her life missing him. He may have been wrong—about what he believed in and what he thought was possible—but that had never stopped her from loving him. Even that small truth would make a difference to Isabel. It would help her heal. Soraida steadied herself, approached the door, and tapped on it. After a moment she knocked a little harder. "Isabel?"

When she heard no answer, she opened it a crack. Isabel was just lifting a backpack to her shoulder. "I'm going out," she said as she slipped past Soraida. "I don't know when I'll be back."

Isabel was in Max's bed again, sprawled face down across the sheets, curling her toes as Max showered, wondering what had drawn her back here so soon. Max had wondered at it, too, when she'd appeared at his door fifteen minutes earlier. But he'd let her in. He'd said he'd take a quick shower and be right with her.

Now she was having second thoughts. She wanted Max—yes. Or perhaps more concretely, she wanted sex. She wanted it to transport her, if only for a few hours, even a few minutes, away from this place. Away from everything and everybody. From Soraida, of course. But also, she admitted, from Yasmin.

She hugged Max's thin foam pillow. Had she returned for her daughter only to give up so easily? Running away as if *she* were the adolescent? She should have phoned Danilo, or even Claudia. She should have tried to talk to somebody. After all, she'd endured far worse—the pressures of clandestine life, endless rules and codes of conduct, the terror of battle, the knowledge that one wrong move would cost lives. So why were the manias of an old woman and a young girl so hard to bear? She didn't know the answer, but she knew she must return home.

"Max?"

He had just turned off the water.

"I've got to go."

Naked and dripping, he poked his head out the bathroom door. "Did something happen?"

"No. No." She wanted to kiss him, to reassure him, but thought better of it. "I've just got to get home."

Max sighed his disappointment. But then he shrugged and continued to towel his head.

She let herself out.

Soraida sat at the kitchen table, worrying her handkerchief between her hands. Just when she thought they'd found their footing, the ground had given way beneath them. Things had been going well until that visit to the villages. It was as if they'd been bewitched, Isabel and Yasmin, by some evil spirit. Something reaching out from the past, trying to drag them all under. Or something luring them into a future where Soraida had no place.

Nonsense. She mustn't let her mind play tricks on her. The whole mess was just another adolescent outburst. Another adolescent prank. Because Yasmin knew, she *knew* that whatever she said or did, whatever her moods, whatever her missteps, Soraida would *never* turn her away. She would do anything to keep her grandniece safe. Safe at home, with Soraida.

The kitchen door opened and Isabel entered. Soraida jumped to her feet. "There you are. Is Yasmin with you?"

Isabel deposited her backpack on the table and started pulling groceries from it. "Why would she be with me?"

"She went for tortillas but she never came back." In fact, she'd never even made it to the tortillería. Soraida had checked.

Isabel stopped unpacking, a dark green squash in one hand and a small bag of tomatoes in the other. "How long ago was that?"

Soraida twisted the handkerchief around her fingers and tugged at it until her fingers hurt. Nobody in the street had been able to tell her anything.

"Hours. She left before you did."

"What about a friend? Maritza? Byron?" Isabel had started to root around the kitchen, as if for clues, lifting the alarm clock, turning over a newspaper. "Have you talked to anyone?"

Soraida got up to follow her niece as she paced. Moving felt better than not moving. And she had faith that Isabel would know what to do.

"I was waiting for you. I didn't want to miss you too."

"Where does she usually go when she goes out?"

"I don't know. She doesn't tell me." Soraida rubbed her arms. The room seemed very cold. All afternoon she'd dragged her brain and come up empty. How could she know so little about the girl she'd raised? "She was very upset."

Isabel stopped pacing and sank onto one of the wooden chairs. "What have I done?" She was not looking at Soraida but at her bedroom door.

"She's probably just out with friends," Soraida said. "It's not like it's the first time." But she wasn't convinced of her own words, even though it was the most likely explanation. Too many things could happen in this city.

Isabel leapt to her feet.

"I think Byron is our best bet. I'll go talk to him. Will he be at home? Where does he live?"

"You can't go there by yourself. It's dangerous at the best of times, and it'll be getting dark soon."

"I'll go and phone Danilo. If he's around, he'll help."

As Isabel charged down the corridor, Soraida called out to her. "You'll need money." She pulled down the old powdered-milk tin from an upper shelf, retrieved the roll of bills inside and started counting. She counted again.

With a trembling hand, she massaged the pain that was growing in her throat.

"She's taken two hundred quetzales," she shouted, her voice raw. "She's run away."

Down the corridor, something hit the wall. She heard Isabel's voice.

"Damn her! Damn her!"

Soraida covered her face with her handkerchief and began to cry.

CHAPTER 8

THEY'D AGREED TO meet at the eastern terminus of Eighteenth Street, that point where the road dipped a few metres into the ravine before vanishing completely. Isabel had reached Danilo on his pager, and he'd promised to join her down among the tin and cardboard shacks massed one atop another from street level to the bottom of the gulley. It was the neighbourhood known as La Limonada. Byron lived here and so, they had learned from Byron, did Yasmin's boyfriend. The footpath leading between the houses and into the ravine was steep and narrow.

"Can you imagine it in the rain?" Isabel asked Danilo as he headed down the hill before her. When he turned and grinned, she said, "Don't tell me. You used to work these parts." Guerrilla work was what she meant: organization, logistics, propaganda.

"All over." His gesture might have suggested the length and breadth of La Limonada or of Guatemala City. For that matter, it might have encompassed all Guatemala.

"Did you ever go to the States?" She wasn't sure why it had occurred to her, except as cover for the sea of emotions Yasmin's disappearance had unleashed in her. A surface of chatter bobbing her along the perilous current to her daughter.

"Just on business." He popped a cigarette into his mouth and lit it. "Organization business."

Running guns, no doubt. Isabel knew that had been Claudia's job for a while. Bringing all those weapons down from the United States, through Mexico, and into the Guatemalan jungle. Travel in the U.S. might mean fundraising or international diplomacy, but Isabel couldn't see Danilo in either role. He'd tell her when he felt like it, in a safer place than this, or maybe he wouldn't. Not everything must or should be told.

It was not yet noon, but the heat was fierce, the sun's rays, magnified. She batted flies away and coughed at a sudden whiff of sewage. Was this where Yasmin had come? To get away from her? To find what? Love? Still, love—or what passed for love when you were fifteen—was a powerful drug, strong enough to dull the senses to these surroundings, certainly.

The path was levelling off, still weaving through houses and shacks pressed together on every side. Now and then another path branched off between corrugated zinc walls. Danilo approached a young man reclined in a string hammock slung between two posts as Isabel scanned the neighbourhood that spread before them like a tin maze. Pinpoints of sunlight danced across the rooftops. She was baking.

"He says the boy lives down here to the right, just past the water tap and behind Doña Magda's grocery store."

"I wasn't sure he would tell you."

"I told him I was an uncle. Uncle Rogelio."

"What if he'd been family?" She hugged herself despite the heat.

"Those are questions not worth asking." He dropped his cigarette into a channel of greasy water that ran beside the path and put his arm around her. "No what-ifs about Yasmin either. We're going to find her and she's going to be fine."

Isabel leaned into him before she pulled away. She needed to stay strong—no giving in.

"You're right. God! When did I become so ... incapable?"

At the water tap, one lonely pipe rising from the baked earth, they looked around for Magda's store. Few people were about, and those who were studied them but left them alone. Danilo nodded at each in greeting and Isabel imitated him. This was all new to her. Most of her time with the guerrillas had been spent in the jungle, with occasional forays into Mexico on security details. But she wasn't afraid. They were just people, the very people she'd gone to war to defend. And look what had been won for them. The place was probably more crowded than it was thirty years ago and more dangerous, too, now that gangs had taken hold.

Danilo was buying cigarettes and talking to Doña Magda. He pointed the way to Isabel.

"Give Doña Irene my greetings!" Magda called.

They approached the crooked shack Doña Magda had indicated, a faded bedsheet hanging in its open doorway.

"Let me do the talking," Isabel said.

"I don't think so. They'll see this as a man's job."

With one foot, Isabel shunted aside several chickens that had wandered onto the path from between the huts.

"Really," Danilo said on seeing Isabel hesitate. "They won't take any guarantees from you because they'll think the dad could still come after them."

She joined him at the doorway. They couldn't afford mistakes, but she imagined Doña Irene would be as eager to protect her son as Isabel was to protect Yasmin. "Okay. I just want to see Yasmin."

"You can tell them that. But let me do the negotiating."

Doña Irene answered full minutes after Danilo rapped on the furrowed metal wall. She wore a dusty pink sleeveless blouse and a narrow jean skirt. A ladina. Though she was probably only in her thirties, her eyes and cheeks were sunken, her skin tight on her slender frame—as parched as the neighbourhood she lived in. She looked as if she knew exactly why they'd come. Danilo bowed slightly when he addressed her.

He did all the talking. Doña Irene listened, arms folded but expressing no urgency. They were in her territory now, with an army of neighbours who could make short work of just about any outsider. If a person disappeared down here, the world above might never know. Still, it was clear she was interested in what Danilo had to say, though she would neither admit to nor deny any of it. He kept his hands clasped before him, tapping his chest as he spoke. It was an attitude of prayer. "We don't want to break them up. We won't bring any harm to your boy."

Isabel thought Doña Irene nodded ever so slightly. Yasmin was a child, after all—it was statutory rape. Of course, Isabel had no intention of seeking help from the police or any other thugs, but Doña Irene didn't know that. They could, if they wanted, make her difficult life even more so. And even in these times of peace, it wouldn't take much to induce a police officer or a security guard to hurt or even dispose of her son.

When it was her turn to speak, Isabel had trouble keeping her voice even. She knew she mustn't rage or threaten, but she worried that if she didn't she'd just fall apart. She focused her mind on Yasmin and met Doña Irene's hollow brown eyes. The woman looked frightened. Isabel softened her expression. There was nothing wrong with pleading if it got results. "You're a mother, too. You know how I feel," she said. "I miss her. I worry about her. At least promise me you'll tell her I love her and I'm not angry and I just want to see her. Tell her I'll help her, I'll help both of them." Isabel wasn't sure what else she could offer. It was important to be honest. "I want to help them."

Doña Irene regarded Isabel for several agonizing moments. A patient woman. In the end, she said, "I'll see what I can do."

Isabel, remote in hand, sat at Soraida's kitchen table, flipping through the three channels available on the television propped between the stove and a rack of dishes. Soap opera, soap opera, public service message. The last channel had, until recently, belonged to the army but they'd relinquished it in compliance with the peace accords. Now it belonged to an evangelical church that seemed to alternate between terrorizing its audience with the coming apocalypse and enrapturing them with song. Isabel turned the thing off and went to make coffee. Soraida was working in the shop, and Isabel was beginning to wish she were, too. It had been two days and no word.

Coffee in hand, she returned to the table and picked up the newspaper Soraida had brought in earlier. She flipped through its pages. Violence, violence and more violence. On page 5 was a picture of the rebel leaders lined up beside their army counterparts on the National Day of the Army. "Traitors!" Isabel said and turned the page. There, a small story about a shooting at the Eighteenth Street market stopped her. Another transvestite killed. The third in less than a month—and Isabel hadn't even heard about it. She read the whole article and the next, which chronicled crime in another part of the city.

By the time Soraida arrived for eleven o'clock coffee, Isabel had read the entire paper cover to cover. Soraida steered straight for the stove, as she always did. "Do you want another coffee?" she asked.

"I don't know how you can keep on as if nothing's happened."

Soraida reheated the coffee Isabel had prepared and then poured herself a cup. "If I knew what else to do, I'd do it. Like you reading the paper. It's how I manage."

Such control. It was admirable, really, but at the moment it made Isabel want to smash every plate in Soraida's dish rack. Instead, she pointed to the newspaper, which lay open at the picture of the rebel commanders. "This is no place for her. It's no place for anybody."

"Isabel, it's—"

Isabel grabbed the paper and shook it at her. She wanted her to see what she saw. Thirty-six years of war. What had it won for Yasmin? What freedom? What future? Isabel had chosen this place to keep her daughter safe, but it hadn't worked. "Yasmin never had a chance," she said. She felt the tears and tried to brush them away. It was no good.

Soraida reached out to her but stopped partway. "I want to help, but what can we do? Danilo said to wait."

Isabel dropped the paper and got up. "I'm going to go get her myself." She retrieved her wallet and backpack from her room and headed down the front corridor, Soraida trailing.

"Isabel, you can't. It's dangerous there. A woman alone. Call the police if you have to. Get Danilo."

The sun caught Isabel full blast as she opened the black metal door and stepped alone into the street. She welcomed its fury.

Isabel followed the path she and Danilo had taken three days before. The sun beat even hotter, if that were possible, but Isabel was numb to it. It was as if her body did not exist, as if her mind alone, or perhaps it was her heart, drove her forward, nodding at the people she passed, confident finally that she belonged here as much as she did anywhere else. At Doña Irene's door, she banged twice and waited. She had decided it was still better to plead than to threaten, to find common ground.

But when the bedsheet curtain opened an inch and Doña Irene peeked out, the words Isabel had rehearsed left her. She stood there mute, eyes misted over, trying to make something, anything come out of her mouth.

It was Doña Irene, instead, who spoke. "She's here. I'll get her."

Before Isabel could reply, Doña Irene let the bedsheet fall back into place.

The next moment she poked her head out once more. "Though she won't say so, I think she was waiting for you." Again she left the doorway.

As Isabel waited, she heard movement inside the shack and the sound of lowered voices. Then Yasmin parted the bedsheet and stood before her, a bag in her hand, her head down. Isabel forgot about the woman and her son and took her daughter in her arms, kissing her head again and again as Yasmin pressed her face into Isabel's shoulder.

"It's okay. Everything's going to be okay," she said as she steered Yasmin toward the path away from the house.

As they climbed up the dirt path to Eighteenth Street, Isabel's arms wound tight around her daughter, Yasmin's face crushed against her neck, Isabel decided she wouldn't wait until they got home to speak. She thought a neutral space, one where Soraida wasn't either hovering anxiously or bullying her way in, might help Yasmin unload the things she'd been keeping back. When they reached street level, Isabel guided her to a small gardened square under a leafy oak and found a bench. Beside them, white flowers cascaded from the central stalk of a spiky yucca plant.

"Are you hungry?" she asked, but Yasmin wouldn't look at her. Isabel didn't insist. Three days, three days of waiting and worrying. Impotent. Helpless. Three days of anger building, till she thought she would burst. It was all gone. She had Yasmin back. She was whole again. More than whole. Overflowing. She embraced Yasmin gently and kissed her hair. "Don't ever do that again," she whispered.

Yasmin held fast to her mother. Isabel lifted her child's head and brushed the hair from her face. She cupped Yasmin's round, warm cheeks and tried to look her in the eyes, but Yasmin resisted. She clung tighter.

"What is it?" Isabel said. "Tell me."

Yasmin started to moan. Isabel could feel her shaking. The air was rich with the fragrance of warm earth and sun-kissed flowers. "I don't know what to do!" Yasmin said.

"Yasmi, Yasmi." Isabel spoke firmly now and held her daughter at arm's length. "Look at me."

Nothing.

Isabel could guess what was coming. It had been there at the margins all along: the absences, the mood swings, the disappearance, the chase, the boyfriend. But Isabel hadn't wanted to see it.

She remembered the morning she'd delivered the news of her own pregnancy to Yasmin's father. She'd been overjoyed when she realized that her missed periods were not a response to poor diet or heavy exertion or anxiety, that she was actually gaining weight. She loved Luís and he loved her. A baby was just more love for both of them. Their own little family. She supposed, now, at this distance, that she'd felt so lonely for so long, it hadn't occurred to her what bringing a baby into that world would mean—for them and for the child. She hadn't thought ahead at all.

She relaxed her grip on Yasmin's arm. "Listen to me, then." She stroked her daughter's face with her thumb. "Whatever it is, we'll handle it. You've got me. You've got Soraida. We've got the help we need."

Luís had said no. He didn't want the baby. Things were bad enough without adding a baby to the mix. He'd talked and talked that morning in their cramped, sweltering tent while Isabel sat there caressing her belly as if to soothe the unborn child within. She kept telling herself he would come around. It wasn't like they had any options. And he couldn't deny his child. The organization wouldn't stand for it. But she was wrong. Luís had options and he used them. The next time he was sent out on a mission, he didn't come back.

And now it was happening again. To her little girl. What had she been doing all this time if she'd failed to protect her own little girl? Blind and arrogant. That's what she'd been.

"Tell me," Isabel said again.

Yasmin blew heavily, as if she'd been holding her breath until now. "I'm pregnant."

Isabel studied her daughter, sitting there, head down, waiting to be told what would happen to her. She needed more than Isabel's self-recrimination.

"That's a big thing," Isabel said. "But we'll help you through this." She refused to let herself think of the boyfriend as she spoke. "You will get through this."

Yasmin had closed her eyes. She was shaking harder now. Then she collapsed against her mother, burying her face in her chest as if she was trying to escape through Isabel's body, trying to crawl back into it. "I don't want to be! I don't want to be!" she wailed. And it all came out. Sobs and more sobs. Isabel held her daughter as she cried. Held her, stroked her, whispered, "My poor little baby."

Soraida was just trying to be helpful. She knew that these things happened—far too often in her opinion—but even this situation could be salvaged. There were ways to smooth the waters, move forward with dignity. Appearances were important. Neighbourhood opinion was important. They were in the kitchen, all three of them at the table—Yasmin seated while Soraida and Isabel took turns walking around it—deciding on Yasmin's future. Soraida said to Isabel, "We can arrange a civic wedding. I've got money saved."

Isabel shook her head violently. "Are you insane? This is not the time for petit bourgeoisie pretensions."

Soraida folded her arms and stopped pacing. She was furious. "And what are you going to do?" she said to Isabel, the table between them. "Just make the problem go away? This is still a Christian household!"

"I would—if that's what Yasmin wants. I'm sure I could get her to Nicaragua."

Soraida nodded toward Yasmin—she was sitting right there. This was getting out of hand.

"If that's what Yasmin wants," Isabel repeated.

"I will not let that happen," Soraida said.

Isabel waved her off. "Frankly, I don't care what you do. My priority is Yasmin. She'll decide."

Yasmin shrank into her chair, hugging herself, looking anywhere but at her mother and great-aunt. Isabel was regarding her daughter. Apparently, she expected a response.

Yasmin put her hands over her face. The poor child. Soraida felt for her, but there was no undoing what had been done. They all needed to focus on repairing what could be repaired.

"I want to stay with Víctor," Yasmin said at last. It came out as a whimper. "I love him."

Isabel gently pulled Yasmin to her, rubbing her arms, leaning down to kiss her forehead. Touching her daughter seemed to calm her.

She said to Soraida, "Maybe instead of forcing them apart or forcing them together, we should invite Víctor here. That way we can make sure she's all right, that she finishes school ..."

Soraida shook her head. There'd been enough nonsense already. She was putting her foot down. "If they are going to live here, they can get married first. A child with one surname is marked."

"Like Yasmin, you're saying."

"This is a Christian home. This is no brothel."

Isabel released Yasmin. "What are you afraid of? What the neighbours will say? I think you've forgotten where you live. Or are you worried they'll find out that underneath it all, you're no different from them. No better than the market vendors."

"Insulting me in my own home, you should be ashamed." But Isabel wasn't listening. She'd made that clear.

"Yasmin is too young to climb into some straightjacket of a relationship just because she had sex," Isabel said. "Think what marriage would bring her. Before she's twenty, she'll have a heap of kids and he'll be working in the U.S., or off making another family, or at home getting drunk. Your rules do not apply here, Soraida. Independence. An education. A family that supports her. That's what she needs. And I don't care what anybody else in this country thinks. My daughter will be free."

Her voice rose as she spoke. Soon she'd be shouting, going on and on and on about rights, what she'd fought for, what Guatemala could be. Soraida was sure of it. Yasmin would be left far behind. But then, as if she were coming out of a trance, Isabel took a deep breath. "Soraida, I think I'd prefer to talk to my daughter about this alone."

Soraida gaped. Wasn't this her house? Her shop? Her money? Wasn't she the one who should be making the decisions? She glanced at Yasmin, who looked both frightened and miserable. Soraida watched as Isabel struggled to keep control of herself—control herself so she could take control of everything else. She was circling the room, calmer now, hands at her temples.

"Soraida," she said, "this is killing me . . ." She shook her head and tried again. She looked in pain. ". . . which shouldn't matter. But I can't be a good mother this way."

Soraida watched her breathing, collecting her resolve.

"I am Yasmin's mother and it is my duty to protect her. That includes protecting her from you."

Soraida could barely take it in, her shock was so great. She'd kept her temper, she'd been reasonable, she'd been generous. But there was no reasoning with people who refused to conform, people who were always looking to cause upheaval, people who wouldn't settle. After everything Soraida had done, Isabel was playing her trump card, right when Yasmin needed her great-aunt most. When she needed somebody who would steer her in the right direction, somebody who would teach her what had to be done to live in this society, this one, not some society that didn't exist yet. Isabel's ideas of motherhood were as doomed as the revolution she'd spent half her life chasing.

Soraida turned on her niece. "You'll make a slut out of her!" And then it just came out. "Like mother, like daughter."

Suddenly Isabel was the one with decorum. The one who thought before she spoke and spoke without raising her voice. She said to Soraida, "I think it's best that Yasmin and I find somewhere else to live. I think it's best if Yasmin doesn't see you anymore."

The world went black as Soraida reached out, searching the air for something to steady herself. She couldn't see. She couldn't breathe. Still, she strained to find the words. She had to fight back. "You can't. I won't let you." She could barely hear herself. She was sure this wasn't really happening. Isabel would calm down and see things differently, she would understand that family is family. They had to stick together. But somewhere inside her a tremor was building, a realization, borne from experience, that family breakup was possible, maybe even inevitable. She'd been through it before. And when she'd left, so long ago now, it had been final. If she could just reach out to Isabel, take her hand, let blood speak to blood.

But Isabel was on the other side of the room, facing the wall. She spoke quietly without turning. "You think that every choice I've made in my life was the wrong one. You believed the same thing about my parents. But you, you just stood by. They killed your own brother like a dog. Like he was less than a dog. And you did nothing."

All intention to resist or fight back died in Soraida. She'd been judged and found guilty. She wasn't listening any longer. She could feel her world growing cold and dark. Soon there would be no joy left in it. She closed her eyes, and, from somewhere, slender arms were around her, smooth warm skin against hers, flush with the sweet aroma of youth. Yasmin was embracing her, clinging, sobbing. Soraida cradled the child, bent her old head to her and held on for dear life.

PART II

ulew (earth)

CHAPTER 9

Soraida stood at the open door of her shop, heedless of the customers who foraged through the stacks of clothing behind her. She was watching the market vendors, her gaze moving from overstuffed stall to overstuffed stall, each festooned with fabrics and gadgetry, radios blaring, a kaleidoscope of colour and sound, her mind refusing or unable to rest on any one thing. She recognized many faces but couldn't say she knew them, not even to exchange greetings. They had always been, in her mind, the indistinguishable members of one group or another: the backpack sellers, for instance, defined by their merchandise. She'd never considered their losses or triumphs—it hadn't really occurred to her they might know any. And she certainly hadn't thought she had anything in common with them. She still didn't. But she did begin to wonder what made them tick. What kept them going.

She studied the vendors at one stand. Two, she decided, were brothers: muscular, their hair buzzed short in a slightly military style, a few years apart in age. And then there was a much younger version, a younger brother, perhaps, or nephew or son. The small boy perched on the shop counter, legs swinging, as the eldest of the trio lifted backpacks into place with a pole. The other boy leaned against a post at the entrance, gazing out, just as Soraida was, up and down Eighteenth Street, until his eyes met hers and she looked away.

"What do I owe you?" A middle-aged woman emerged from within Soraida's shop carrying several men's shirts. For a husband or a son? She showed them to Soraida.

"Fifteen," Soraida said.

"Ten and you'll get my business again." The woman proffered two newish five-quetzal notes.

Soraida accepted the money and left the front entrance.

"When will you be getting a new bale?" This came from a woman who was inspecting the dresses.

An invisible jet plane thundered overhead. Soraida thundered, too. "I have to move what I've got before I bring in anything new!" She wasn't in the mood for chatting with customers or encouraging them to buy. She hadn't been for months. What was the point? People bought what they bought. Let the business tend to itself. "Maybe this one here?" she said as she pulled from the rack a slim short dress—black with a white scalloped collar—that had made her think of Yasmin.

The woman, who looked to be in her early twenties, small and fine boned, smoothed the dress against her body. "To think I could have missed it," she said.

That transaction finished, Soraida returned to the open doorway. The boys at the backpack stand were serving customers now, pulling down two of the packs they'd just put up. At most of the stands, however, the vendors stood idle, playing with the contraptions they sold, listening to music, watching the passersby. Her side of the street was quieter still—just a few people at the shoe store and, as near as she could tell, no one at all at Estela's piñata shop. Farther along the sidewalk sat the homeless couple. They were sharing a piece of bread, their clothing, skin, and hair as grimy as ever. The woman no longer appeared pregnant. If there'd ever been a baby—if, in fact, it had reached full term—it was long gone. Soraida observed them as they ate, crumb by crumb, bent together, all four hands around the disappearing loaf.

Soon after she came to Eighteenth Street, almost twenty years ago, Soraida had developed daily and weekly routines she'd stuck to through all Yasmin's growing pains, through the appearance and intrusion of gangs in the neighbourhood, through war and now, through peace. On Sundays after closing time she'd stroll the park at the hippodrome, for many years with both Quique and Yasmin but now with Quique only; on Thursday evenings she'd stop by a church to pray for her parents, a private ritual she followed even though she almost never went to mass; on Wednesday afternoons she'd leave the shop in Byron's hands and visit with friends along Eighteenth Street. It had been difficult to keep the schedule up after Yasmin and Isabel's departure—much of it had been devised in the first place to accommodate Yasmin's presence in her life—but she tried. She got up at five, went to bed at ten. She bathed daily, and although at some point Quique had attached an electric heater to the shower head, she still preferred the water at the temperature it came from the tap. After showering, she sat alone at the kitchen table for a breakfast of coffee and biscuits. At noon, she ate her main meal, prepared the night before, alone. In the evening, she stood to eat, poking at the day's leftovers, her appetite defeated by solitude.

Today, being Wednesday, Soraida left the shop to visit Estela, who, she discovered, had been waiting for her anxiously.

"What is it?" she asked as Estela hurried her through the front door. The awning over the store front was stripped of piñatas—Estela, apparently, had not opened. When she had Soraida standing in the middle of her workroom, Estela said to her, "Raúl's been deported."

Soraida read her friend's face for clues about how to react. Estela's son Raúl had been in the United States for more than a decade, every month wiring a portion of his earnings to his mother. Was this bad news or good?

"Even if he tries to cross again, for now I'll have him here with me. Oh Soraida, it's been so long." Estela was practically dancing as she said it.

Soraida gave her a hug. "This is good news indeed!" She thought about the footage she'd seen on Notisiete of Guatemalans flown back from the United States in handcuffs, as if, in the air, they'd have anywhere to run. She tried to picture Estela's son among them.

"I've prayed and prayed for this day," Estela said. She crossed herself and kissed the crucifix that dangled from a thin chain around her neck.

They sat together for coffee and sweetbreads, discussing what might be done in preparation for Raúl's arrival. Around them, stacks of white, featureless elephants, ducks, giraffes, clowns, princesses, bathed the room in a creamy glow.

"I wonder if they'll let him bring anything back," Estela said.

"Well, you know where to come for clothes if he needs them." Soraida was happy for her friend. She really was. The aura of joy and anticipation warmed her. As they talked, they recalled each phase of Raúl's life—baby, toddler, child, adolescent—disregarding completely the painful parting it had all led to.

"He lights up the house when he's here," Estela said.

"It's your heart that lights it up because it's happy. Look how bright this room is right now."

Estela turned to see whether it was true. They didn't speak of Yasmin, just as, on so many occasions in the intervening years, they hadn't spoken of Raúl. Happy moments, however fleeting, were for savouring.

Twice that night, Soraida awoke from dreams that left only a chill in their wake. The third time, she sat upright and examined the watch that lay on the nightstand beside her bed. Two a.m. She felt restless, out of sorts. Every time she closed her eyes, she saw the spark in Estela's eyes, the flush on her cheeks, felt her breathless wonder as she spoke about her son. Soraida hated to admit it, but try as she might, she could not separate Estela's gain from her own loss, as if there were only so much happiness to go around, and God offered and withdrew it on a preordained schedule. Isabel would call that fatalism and then lecture Soraida about cause and effect. The future is in our hands, she'd say. Well, was it? Somewhere out there Isabel and Yasmin were looking forward to a whole new life together, with all the trials and tribulations but also all the joy that would bring. And Soraida would have no share in it. When Soraida imagined her future, all she saw was the slow unwinding of days, the endless, sleepless nights. Time marching mercilessly on. She curled into her pillow, no longer thinking about Estela or Raúl or even God. She was remembering Isabel and wondering, yet again, when and where the seed of this present they were all living had been planted.

Soraida had never seen Isabel with her parents. She had no way of knowing what their family life was like, how father, mother and daughter had behaved together. Soraida's parents had disowned Hugo the day he tried to introduce them to the Kaqchikel girl he hoped to marry. Soraida, sixteen at the time, had obeyed their wishes and severed all ties to her brother, even after he'd mailed her his wedding photo and invited her to celebrate his happiness with him, to wish them well, if only by return letter. Even after he sent her a photo of his newborn daughter. It had taken her eight years to muster the courage to defy her parents and seek Hugo out. It was a rash thing to do. It had ended in his death.

After that, although she'd wanted to contact Isabel, for the child's sake and—Heaven help her—because she'd hoped to find some inkling of Hugo in the daughter he left behind, she was afraid. Instead, it was Isabel, many years later, who'd contacted her.

It was arranged through messengers, a method Soraida would become familiar with in the succeeding years. A skinny man with a mop of brown hair and round glasses had approached Soraida one morning in her shop and said, "Are you Soraida Barrios? I believe I know your niece."

Soraida's heart had leapt in her chest. "Where is she? *How* is she?"

The young man scanned the shop, and just as it was dawning on Soraida that she'd seen him before, in the shop, perusing without purchasing, he said, "Maybe we could speak after you close. Somewhere public?"

She'd consented, although her heart was pounding: a brief meeting on the bench of a nearby park that would lead to another—this time with Isabel herself—at a Chinese restaurant on Sixth Avenue. Soraida got to the restaurant early, out of habit and because she wanted some sense of what she was walking into before she committed. It was a busy place, with double glass doors open to the street and two floors of tables alive with sprawling families and unruly students. A large blue-green fish tank occupied one wall. Soraida chose a small table near the entranceway and waited. A sweet floral bouquet tinged the pervasive aroma of hot grease. At the appointed time, Isabel entered like somebody risen from the dead. She was small and dark-skinned, dressed in jeans and a T-shirt, twenty years old, by Soraida's calculation. Soraida glimpsed something of her brother in those deep, penetrating eyes. She stood, tremulous, as her niece reached her and kissed her cheek with neither warmth nor hostility.

They sat without speaking. Soraida could do nothing but stare as she contemplated the stranger before her, this life that had taken shape and grown into a young woman without her help. And what was she doing now? Where was she living? Who was she living with? The questions tumbled through Soraida's mind, but she was afraid to ask.

Isabel surveyed the room, the bustling tables above them, behind the mezzanine's railing, the tables around them. Then she spoke: "How have you been?"

It was a question that expected no answer, but Soraida replied anyway. "Fine," she said. "Fine."

Then the waiter was there, and they distracted themselves with ordering.

As soon as the waiter left, Isabel leaned close. "Auntie, I've come to you for a reason. I'm pregnant and I need your help. It's big what I'm going to ask you. You can say no. And I can say no, too, if I change my mind, at any time."

She kept talking for the rest of the meal, never once mentioning where she was living or what she was doing, never invoking her father's name to soften Soraida up or curry her favour, just asking for help. She also promised money—not much, what she could manage when she could manage it—and asked Soraida a series of questions: about the shop, the neighbourhood, was it safe, did Soraida make enough to get by.

Other meetings followed that one, always at a different location, until, Soraida supposed, Isabel was satisfied and Soraida had said yes. Yes, she would take care of Isabel's child when the time came.

"As soon as I'm able to care for the baby myself, I will," Isabel said before they parted, Soraida going one way and Isabel, the other, melting like a phantom into the stream of window shoppers that coursed along Sixth Avenue.

Soraida woke to the sound of a fight on the street outside. In her sleep she'd heard the confused blows—bodies colliding, people shouting, somebody scrambling to escape—and as she stirred awake, a voice, still violent, receding.

She started her day, but the discomfort of that awakening, climbing gingerly, painfully out of her metal-framed bed as if she herself had been caught in the tussle outside, stayed with her. She fixed breakfast, she opened the shop, she tended to the dribble of customers who came to see what cast-off garments the USA had sent them this week, and she took their money. But she felt bruised and sore the whole day.

To her surprise, as Soraida was preparing to close, Byron and his sister came by.

"I want you to meet somebody," Byron said when Soraida went to greet them. Élida had her new daughter pressed to her breast. Soraida peeked into the folds of the blankets that swaddled the nursing child.

The crumpled face, the puckered lips, the tiny fingers made Soraida's heart swell. "She's an angel," she said.

She invited Élida to sit and offered her coffee while Byron kept an eye on the shop. The young mother was pleased, it was clear, and still in awe of the living being she had created.

"Are you managing?" Soraida asked. "Do you have enough milk?"

"And how." Élida lifted her engorged breast, the child still attached. "I'm getting used to it now, but I can't believe how much it hurts at first."

Soraida smiled. She'd heard the complaints of many new mothers, the discomfort and pain that tormented them after the delivery—what they'd thought of as the hard part—was over. They were experiences she would never have.

"How old is she now?"

"Just six weeks." Élida slid her finger into the child's mouth and unlatched her. She tucked her breast into her bra and shirt and then gently turned the babe onto her forearm, stroked the fragile spine and elicited two gurgled burps. Élida rolled her daughter onto her back again and raised her to Soraida like an offering. "Do you want to hold her?" she said. "We named her after you—Soraida."

Soraida gasped and turned to look for Byron, who was grinning. "What an honour!" she said. She could hardly speak. "To share the name of such a blessed creature."

"You've done so much for us," Élida said. "Who better to have as a model?"

"But I'm not even family!"

"Now you are," Byron called from the counter.

Soraida admired the infant. Such a gift. She was smaller even than Yasmin when Isabel—tears threatening—had bundled her daughter into Soraida's arms and turned quickly to go. Soraida tried not to let the memory undo her.

"You'll stay for dinner, of course," she said to Élida. "And you, too, Byron. Can you?"

"I've got the day off," Élida said.

She was so young, though she must have been over twenty. Yasmin was a child compared to her. "You're at the same place? You got your job back?" Soraida rocked the baby. "Poor thing. Do you leave her with your mother?"

Élida nodded in response to each question as Soraida tried to think of some way to show her gratitude.

"You can bring her here whenever you want," she said. "Byron can bring her to work. We can set up a crib." She added, "If you want."

"I can do that," Byron said.

Élida stifled a yawn, exhaustion in her face. "I have to nurse her. I get a break at the factory to do it." She massaged the breast she'd nursed from. "Maybe when she's older."

Soraida got up and handed the child to Byron, who accepted her like a proud father. "I'll warm up our dinner," she said. Seeing baby Soraida had overwhelmed her. Her entire body ached with remorse. Yasmin would be at six months now, her belly hard and round, the first kicks palpable. There was something horrifying about the image. Could anything have gone wrong? Surely, Isabel would have sent word if it had. Her heart was not made of stone. Soraida lit the gas stove and shifted a pot of pulique over the burner, the soothing, pungent aroma of epazote rising as the stew heated. Soraida breathed it in. Not soothing enough. She couldn't go on this way. Somebody had to make the first move.

Soraida studied the number embedded in the building's pale blue wall and checked it against the address she'd written down on the back of a hand bill. Yes, this should be the Toriello Foundation. She rang the buzzer, and when the lock clicked open, she entered and approached the front counter, where a small wiry woman with an untidy frizz of black hair sat grinning. The receptionist, she assumed.

"Good afternoon, compañera," the woman said.

There were a few people in the room, reading the newspaper or chatting, others seated, waiting patiently for something. A young man near the door scrutinized Soraida openly, but without apparent malice.

"I'm looking for Isabel Barrios," she said.

"Carolina!" the woman shrieked.

Soraida retreated an inch, though the woman continued to smile at her.

"Just have a seat. Carolina will be here in a moment to help you."

Soraida searched the small alcove and the hallway for an empty chair, but there weren't any. She'd decided to seek Isabel out, to make the first move, and this seemed to be a good place to start. She knew the former guerrillas came here for training and work. Maybe Isabel had found a job here, doing what, Soraida couldn't imagine. What did these people do now the war was over? Join the rest of the population trying to invent a living, she supposed. Make ice cream or kites or tamales, sell bubble gum or home-made detergent or used clothing, administer injections, set broken bones, cast spells—anything, anything at all to keep the belly full.

As she waited, she propped herself against the wall next to three Indigenous women in traditional dress squeezed together on a low sofa, speaking energetically in lengua. Round faced, ruddy with health, they were laughing, prodding each other's hands, lost in their own world as they chattered in their language of whispers. The young man still watched Soraida but she saw that his gaze also floated over the rest of the room, and every now and then he would peer out the window, up and down the street. He looked too relaxed to be working in security, but formality did not seem to be a habit of these people.

"Carolina!" the woman at the desk shrieked again. She flashed Soraida a smile. The sound made Soraida jump but failed to produce Carolina.

Several minutes later, Soraida again approached the receptionist, who seemed to do nothing at all as she sat there. Before she could speak, the woman turned to the young man at the door. "Tono, would you take this compañera to find Carolina."

Tono looked glad to be of service. "Right this way," he said as he led her down the hall, popping his head into every room he passed. "Carolina?" he asked the people he encountered, but no one supplied him with greater direction and they continued to wander through the building—aimlessly, Soraida thought—until halfway to the second floor, the young man stopped short and said, "I know." They returned down the stairs, down another hallway and into a large room at the end of it: the cafeteria. Sitting at one of several long rows of tables, they found Carolina. The young man presented Soraida, who repeated her quest.

"Isabel Barrios?" Carolina said. "Who's Isabel Barrios?'

It was the names, of course. Everybody here was known by a handful of names, none of which was the one they were christened with. Soraida began to reel off the ones she knew Isabel used and soon half a dozen ex-guerrillas had clustered at their table consulting with each other.

"She's at the housing project—that's where she's living. She doesn't work here," Carolina confirmed. "It looks like she's interpreting for the forensic anthropologists who are exhuming the clandestine cemeteries."

Soraida didn't know what she meant.

"The massacres," Carolina explained. "Isn't Isabel from Chimaltenango? They've found bodies there. They're digging them up."

Soraida felt ill. "How terrible," she said.

Several of the men and women around her grunted their agreement. They inched closer, drawing the small circle tighter still. Soraida suddenly did not want to be in this crush of people, people she knew nothing about.

Carolina took her hand and squeezed it. "Tono, take her back to Lidia and ask her to write down the phone number of the forensic team." She turned back to Soraida. "You read?"

Soraida blushed at the question but nodded.

"You can give her the address of the subdivision, too, the housing project." To Soraida, she said, "I don't know which house is your niece's, but you can ask when you get there."

Back at reception, Tono found the information and Lidia, the receptionist, wrote it down, her receptionist's grin still on her face. Soraida gripped the two scraps of paper as she left the Foundation, boarded the bus for Eighteenth Street, crossed the plaza and unlocked her front door. She placed them on the nightstand by her bed, under a squat candle that sat there, so they wouldn't blow away. But in the days that followed, she didn't telephone the forensic team and she didn't visit the guerrilla housing project. Every morning she picked up those scraps of paper and read them, only to return them to their place under the candle. *They've found bodies. They're digging them up.* The horror of those words hadn't left her. What they meant to Isabel she dared not fathom. And because of that, she felt more distant from her niece than ever. How, she asked herself, how could she reach out to Isabel while forensic anthropologists were pulling from the cold ground the people who'd loved her and cared for her and stood by her? An orphan at six. Her home and village destroyed before she turned twenty. Soraida had broken with her own parents and dedicated years to raising Yasmin—that was so. But where was she when those men, women, and children were agonizing? Was it possible she was haggling with a customer, trying to ratchet up the price on a used pair of jeans? Or was she in bed, asleep, door and mind locked against the world outside? Was she just another, who through fear and ignorance had allowed it all to happen? Well, Soraida wasn't sleeping soundly now. She didn't know when she'd sleep like that again.

CHAPTER 10

SUNLIGHT BROKE ACROSS the pit at Isabel's feet, a gaping, ragged hole, its mouth and walls scored by the teeth of the machinery used to dig it. To one side, jumbled together in a large mound of yellow and black soil, were hundreds of human bones and, here and there, the mud-soaked garments, leeched of their once vivid colours, that had clothed them. At Isabel's back, skinny, tightly packed trees crept up the mountainside, and to both sides of the pit, the forest slept, dark and impenetrable. Below her, the trees had been torn away right down to the highway. This clearing was the only place the sun reached.

"They've made a real mess of it," Aníbal, newly in charge here, said. He spat on the ground. *They* were the courts, which had ordered the exhumation but had no experience carrying one out. In their ignorance they'd scraped the remains out of the well with a backhoe. "We'll never be able to piece the evidence back together." Aníbal spat again and scratched at his thick dust-coloured hair. Small brown freckles peppered his forehead like flecks of dirt.

"What happens next?" Isabel asked. So far, her role had been limited to standing by the pit and watching the frustrated forensic anthropologists photograph and measure the scene of the disaster.

"We'll clean and bag the bones and try to sort them out back at the lab," Aníbal said.

"Will you be able to identify them?"

"Not unless we turn up something really unique—a ring, a good set of teeth from somebody with dental records." He shook his head. "No, I don't think we will."

The exhumation was Isabel's first but also one of the first for Aníbal's team. Forensic anthropology, she was learning, was something of a new science in Guatemala.

"We'll still need you when we interview the witnesses, possible family members and so on," Aníbal said. "Our job right now is to collect all the information we can and keep it safe." He lifted a skull from the mound. It was caved in on one side. "One day we may be able to use it."

Kaqchikel villagers had brought the case before the authorities. They said that in the early eighties the army had maintained a checkpoint on the highway below, stopping and searching each vehicle and hauling away anybody whose name appeared on their list of suspected subversives. Travellers without identification—and there were plenty of those—were seized as well. Once in army hands, the victims were tortured in the church in Xesuj and when their bodies finally gave out, they were thrown down this well. Isabel's gaze drifted over the yellow and black mound—an earthen tower of lives ripped to pieces. These had once been living, breathing, bleeding beings. If there were any justice in this world, she thought, their spirits would have escaped long before they drew their final painful breath.

Aníbal gently lay the skull where he'd found it.

"The team can get started here while we go into Xesuj and start interviewing."

"They cut me with a machete. On my head, my breast, and here." Her hands moved as she spoke: along the scar that wound from her temple to a sunken eye, to her chest, and finally, to the thick band of tissue across her palm. "And then they raped me. In my own home. One, two, three." She raised a finger for each of the men before folding her hands away, pressing them against her stomach. "They took turns while the other two held my husband and made him watch."

Her name was Paulina and she sat between Isabel and Fredy, a junior anthropologist, on a pine bench in Xesuj's small, dark church. She wore a black cardigan over a *po't* of purples, blues and greens and a thick *uq*, woven from the same colours and streaked here and there with white. A single long braid hung down her back. She was no older than Isabel.

"Then they dragged my husband away and brought him here." She scanned the church's dirty white walls, stopping when her eyes met the mournful figure of Jesus on the cross. She inhaled and continued. "They would play the radio all the time. Loud. So we wouldn't hear the screaming. But we did." Again she touched her chest.

As Paulina spoke, Isabel interpreted, and Fredy took notes. She spoke softly, raspy Kaqchikel consonants brushed against each other, vowels cut in two deep in the throat. Isabel tried to let the words flow through her without absorbing any of them, as if she were a smooth-sided vessel that would retain nothing of what it had carried after it was emptied. Fredy asked the questions, and Isabel interpreted those too.

"Do you remember what Mario was wearing when they took him?"

Paulina described her young husband, his red plaid shirt, his straw hat, the belt buckle his father had made for him, the ring finger that was crooked because he fell on it when he was a boy.

"Some of the women would wait here outside the door," she said, "for days, weeks, thinking maybe they would get their husbands back."

Isabel leaned closer to hear her better.

"My mother would go for me because I was too afraid." Paulina clapped her hands together and brought them to her forehead, shielding her eyes. "It hurts. It hurts."

Isabel spoke the Spanish words. Fredy wrote them down.

Since most of the exhumation sites were not far from their new home, Isabel would usually ride the bus there each day or catch a lift with one of the anthropologists driving from Guatemala City. But sometimes she'd have to stay over for several days at a time. When she did, she entrusted Yasmin to Danilo and Claudia. They made sure she got to school at the Toriello Foundation, her own school having expelled her as soon as her pregnancy began to show. Yasmin took classes with former guerillas and their family members of all ages and levels of education who had enrolled to make themselves more employable. Danilo and Claudia also fed her and let her sleep over if she was feeling lonely. Isabel didn't like spending so much time away from her daughter—especially given Yasmin's present condition—but the interpreter's job was a good one, and with few qualifications except a knowledge of guns and of jungle survival, she didn't have many options. They wouldn't go hungry, and when the baby was born there'd be enough for that, too. Yasmin, in spite of everything, seemed happy … most of the time. Happiest, perhaps, when Isabel wasn't around asking her questions.

It was the team's second day at a small exhumation near Chiuleu. Relatives of the victims had directed them to the site where, they said, soldiers had entered a house and killed everybody inside. The only survivors were out fetching water from the river at the time. On their return, they'd buried the victims in a single unmarked grave, grabbed a handful of belongings and fled. That was thirteen years ago.

Now Isabel stood beside them in her rubber boots as Aníbal worked the large square of dirt marked out with wooden stakes and divided into a grid by thin white strings suspended between the posts. He knelt beside one of the sections, scooping the earth from the ground with a trowel and passing it through a sieve. The morning mist was rising but moisture hung in the air, thick and close.

Isabel didn't speak unless spoken to, and the witnesses—a young man and his grandmother—said nothing as Aníbal worked. Another member of Aníbal's team labelled and bagged the objects captured by the sieve, and a third took photographs. Aníbal extracted a tooth from the ground and held it against the morning sunlight, turning it as he examined it, as if it were a precious stone. The old woman brought her hand to her lips. The young man bowed his head. Isabel said nothing and watched.

Within a few minutes, Aníbal had found the skull, its smooth frontal bone peeking through. Little by little he brushed the dirt away until the whole thing was visible, nestled in its earthen bed. He sat back and looked at the skull, judging its position before moving on.

By noon he had exposed the shoulders and rib cage of a skeleton on its back, clothed in a stiff and muddy *po't*, its embroidered collar of purple and red flowers frayed and black with dirt.

"A woman," Aníbal said.

A Kaqchikel *woman*, Isabel thought. The *po't* was identical in style to the one the woman at her side was wearing. Isabel turned to the witnesses to hear what they might say but the old woman only nodded. There were tears in her eyes.

Aníbal continued his work. There were more bones. Little ones. Isabel wondered whether they were broken. But no. Another skull appeared, in miniature, cradled by the woman's pelvis. Isabel's breath caught in her throat when she realized what she was seeing. The woman beside her began to moan.

"That's my mother," the young man said. "She was eight months pregnant when they came."

Isabel interpreted for Aníbal. Her ovaries ached.

Tono had called Isabel to the front desk. He said she had a visitor. "He can't go wandering round unless you can vouch for him," he said.

When she got there, she saw Víctor, Yasmin's boyfriend, stalled in the middle of the Toriello Foundation waiting room, looking around uncomfortably. When he spotted Isabel, his expression didn't change.

"Yasmin told me you'd be here," he said. "I haven't had time to go out to the house. And I work again tomorrow."

Isabel kissed his cheek and conducted him down the corridor. "She'll be very glad to see you. She's been staying with Danilo and Claudia. I just got back myself." She'd wanted to hate the boy when she'd first met him. She'd wanted to punish him, somehow, for what he'd done to her daughter. It still made her angry if she thought on it long. But what had been done couldn't be undone. He was neither bullying nor violent. And he'd shown himself to be devoted to Yasmin. He was working as a builder's helper and saving to set up an apartment. In the meantime, he sometimes stayed with them at the housing project, but more often at his mother's, which was closer to his work. Isabel didn't discourage him, though she had her doubts about the plan to ensconce her daughter in domestic bliss. Yasmin was still so young and as temperamental as ever. Víctor was practically a child himself. Lately, she'd even found herself feeling sorry for him.

"How's work?" she asked.

"Good, good. I'm saving every penny." But he looked tired.

"Don't overdo it. You've got to stay healthy, for the future." She smiled at him as encouragement.

"Yes, ma'am."

Isabel knew Víctor would never confide in her. And if he was anything like Yasmin, he might not feel able to confide in his own mother either. The pregnancy can't have been good news in that family any more than it was for Isabel and Soraida. Not good news, but not in any way out of the ordinary, Isabel suspected.

They came to the room where Yasmin took her high school make-up classes and where today she and her instructors were reviewing the materials she would need to complete the school year. Yasmin was at the back of the room talking to Jorge, who was a tutor for the program. When she finally looked up it was as if she'd forgotten who Víctor was. But then she waddled over, her belly jutting out before her, wrapped her arms around his waist and nuzzled his neck. Isabel thought Jorge looked a bit pained, but Yasmin and Víctor were oblivious.

"I'll just get my things and we can go," Isabel said as Víctor and her daughter engaged in a prolonged kiss.

Yasmin pulled away first. "There's a dance tonight," she said to Víctor. She raised her arms and moved her hips in a languid cumbia.

"At the housing project?"

"Sure. It's Friday night."

Víctor glanced around him and lowered his voice. "I've got work tomorrow. I thought maybe we could do something here, nearby. Maybe go to dinner."

Yasmin spoke bluntly. "What's the point of working so hard if it means we never get any time together?"

Víctor moved closer to her. "The point is . . ." He touched Yasmin's abdomen.

Yasmin let him rest his hand there, waiting for the little kick that eventually came. Víctor grinned and Yasmin grinned, too. "Okay," she said. "Let's go."

Despite Yasmin's acquiescence, there was a situation here that had been growing at about the same rate as Yasmin's belly. Her daughter still fantasized at times about her future as a "little mother" but increasingly, Isabel thought, she was beginning to resent it, and to resent Víctor, too. From the outset, Isabel had proffered the option of abortion—a safe, and legal, procedure in Nicaragua—but the Catholic in Yasmin had won out. Or was it her dream of being a better mother than Isabel that had replaced her daughter's initial panic and flight with a complete embrace of the nuclear family? At any rate, it was Yasmin's choice, and Isabel had respected that. She had, however, opposed her daughter's bid for marriage. They could marry, if they still wanted to, when Yasmin became an adult under the law. From the way things were going, that marriage would never happen. Yasmin spent most of her time now with Erika and Jorge—especially Jorge—and the other URNG youth. When she did see Víctor, frequently they'd quarrel. Víctor didn't understand, Yasmin would say. His ideas about the world were so small. Isabel didn't understand either, but she was pretty sure Yasmin would be at the dance tonight, with or without Víctor. It was painful to watch. But all Isabel felt she could do was support her daughter through her ups and downs and try to pick up the pieces afterward.

Isabel finished collecting her belongings and said goodbye to Jorge, who was poring over the homework of one of Yasmin's classmates, or pretended to be.

"Dinner's on me," she said to Víctor.

The doctor leaned over the smooth brown globe of Yasmin's belly, his white sleeve moving back and forth across it as the silver disc in his hand found what he was looking for. The lub lub lub of a tiny heart echoed through the doctor's machine. Isabel smiled at Yasmin, who lay on her back on the examining table, and then at Víctor, who hovered near her daughter's pillow, clasping her hand, his head inclined just like the doctor's, as if that would help him hear better. Perhaps he just wanted to be nearer his unborn child's heart.

"All good," the doctor said. "Now for the ultrasound." He reached from where he sat for a plastic tube from which he squeezed a clear jelly onto Yasmin's skin.

Yasmin gasped and wiggled her toes but managed to keep her belly still.

"Sorry. We don't have anything to warm it with," the doctor said. He selected another instrument, attached by a cable to another machine, and rolled its tip around in the jelly. Next he pointed to the TV screen by Víctor's head, where Isabel saw a grainy sea of grey waves coil and uncoil. After a moment, the form of a baby appeared. The grey sea churned again, and she could see the feet, a delicate arm. A mystery surfacing. Just peeking through. And then black again. Isabel looked closer. She felt queasy.

Another movement and the grains had turned into tiny bones. A skeletal fetus resting in the pelvis of his mother, grey bones in a cradle of black earth. Isabel went cold. She began to shake.

"Doña Isabel. Are you okay?" Víctor had abandoned Yasmin and taken her arm, but Isabel was searching for the door. She was suffocating. She needed fresh air. As she escaped the room, she saw the look of shock on Yasmin's face as her daughter's eyes swung from the monitor to her mother and back again. Then Isabel was racing down the dim hallway with Víctor right behind her.

"I'm all right," she sputtered, batting him away as she flew for the light of the street. "Go back to Yasmin. She needs you."

By the time she cracked open the glass door that led outside, Víctor had turned back. Isabel bent forward, hands on her knees, and sucked in air. *Breathe.* She started pacing, slowly, up and down the sidewalk, bending and straightening, swinging her arms back and forth, breathing deeply, deeply, looking, she was sure, like an idiot. But it helped. The pressure in her head and chest was easing. The nausea that swirled in her stomach, subsiding.

When she re-entered the building five minutes later, the doctor was just leaving his office, a clipboard in his hand. He looked annoyed. "Can you *please* get them out of there," he said as he passed her. "I need my office for the next patient."

Isabel opened the door to Yasmin, seated upright on the examining table, shouting at Víctor. Her face was puffy and red. Víctor's was stolid but ashen. When Yasmin saw her mother, she turned on her. "What is wrong with you! First *you* leave, then Víctor? I'm the one who's pregnant. I'm the one who needs help."

Isabel went to her and pulled her close, which stopped the shouting but started the tears. Yasmin leaned into her, sobbing. "Why did you let me do this? Why didn't you stop me? I don't want this baby. I don't want any of this."

Isabel hugged her and stroked her hair. Her own strength was returning, but she couldn't tell, even now, which of the two of them most needed somebody or something to hold onto. "We're here for you," she whispered. "We are. It'll be all right. Everything will be all right." And she kept saying it until Yasmin had calmed down and they could leave.

Isabel was in Las Escobas with Aníbal and his team. Another well. Who knew that wells—fountains of life in the countryside—could serve such a dark purpose? The anthropologists were boring a hole beside the filled-in well so they could reach the bodies without disturbing them.

Isabel's job was to interpret for the group of women who had guided them to the site in the hope of finding their missing loved ones buried there. She asked each for a physical description of the person they sought: sex, age, height, the condition and number of their teeth, illnesses and injuries they'd sustained in life, whether they were right- or left-handed. It was Isabel's fourth exhumation. By now she'd learned the routine, but she had yet to adjust to the anguish in the faces of the women and men she interviewed, the tremor in their voices, the hesitation in the touch of their hands when they greeted her.

Separate interviews would be conducted with anybody who had information about what had happened and when. According to the witnesses, the army had suspected the villagers of supplying food to the guerrillas. The survivors Isabel talked to would admit to no such collaboration. When it came to anything to do with the guerrillas, denial was still considered the best course. "We heard they were out there in the hills," they told her, "but we never saw them."

The anthropologists had already recovered twenty-two complete skeletons. "They were all thrown in from above," Aníbal said from where he knelt in the pit beside the well. He turned to the frieze of skeletons trapped in the mud wall, tracing with his index finger the twisted figure of one of the dead. "Some had their hands tied behind their backs and others in front. This one here"—his hand moved to a skull wrenched sideways, the jaw spread wide above her stained and decaying *po't*—"has a hypodermic needle in her neck. See?" He got up, absent-mindedly shaking the dirt from his pants. Mud trailed down his trouser legs. "We've found bullets, but it's not clear they were all dead when they went in."

Several ID cards had been retrieved along with the human remains, so they would be able to identify some of the people killed here.

Isabel listened numbly. She could not explain, even to herself, why she was doing this work or what she expected to come from it. Justice? Closure? She was never invited to touch, as Aníbal did, the objects or clothing or skeletal remains the forensic team exhumed, but she still felt them, under her feet, like a tremor at the earth's core, a thousand heartbeats lost in the underworld, muffled voices calling . . . to her?

She remembered as a child visiting their village cemetery every first of November. While her grandparents tended the graves, decking them in marigolds and pine branches and offering the departed banquets of steamed squashes and cane liquor, she and her cousins skipped among the wooden crosses. Death, she was taught, was always with them. It was not something to be hidden away, not from children, not from anybody. At this exhumation, too, children watched the anthropologists dig out the skeletons. They chased each other around the gravesite as Isabel interviewed their parents. Isabel had seen her own parents' bodies washed, reclothed and buried, but it hadn't brought her peace. Something was missing. Like the people here, she was searching for answers. Until she had them, all she could do was to try to hold on.

Isabel cast around to find her bearings. She was feeling lightheaded. Rows of cornstalks ran like stitches across the slopes below her, golden tassels shivering in the cool November breeze. Above her a grey-green ribbon of trees threaded the earth to the lemon-bordered sky.

Aníbal climbed out of the pit and approached. "We found this wooden statue," he said. "It must be their patron saint or some sort of Rilaj Mam." He showed her the muddy figure, edged with rot, and then wrapped it again in a stained piece of cotton. "Ask them. They may want it back."

Isabel took the bundle and watched Aníbal descend again into the black hole, back to his eternal conversation with the dead. Her hands tingled.

"Why do you do it?" she asked him later over dinner. "Don't they haunt you?" They were seated with the rest of the team on a knoll near the dig. The victims' families had provided the meal.

"They haunt me. Everything about this country haunts me." He lifted a spoonful of soup to his lips. His hand didn't shake, as hers did, but dirt was etched permanently into its creases despite his vigorous use of a scrubbing brush before and after every shift. It was ground into his shirt as well. He noticed her staring and looked at his hands, turning them over. "I love working in the earth," he said. "It's not all about death. It's the source of life too."

"So be a farmer."

"Why are *you* here?"

Isabel searched the jagged horizon. "It's a job," she said. Despite everything, this place still felt like home. "And I want to know what happened. I don't want to turn my eyes from it. I feel I owe them that."

"Couldn't have said it better myself." He slurped his soup.

"But when the only company you have is dead people, what does that do to you?" Isabel asked.

Aníbal reached for the tortillas, took one, and passed the hot cloth parcel to Isabel. "The survivors aren't dead," he said.

"They are. They're halfway there. You haven't seen their eyes?"

Aníbal was quiet. He nodded but said nothing more. A gust of wind rippled up the knoll from the fields below. It carried the fragrance of green corn.

Isabel hadn't meant to shut Aníbal down. "They're here though," she said. "Bringing these cases against the army. Not dead. Heroic."

She extracted a steaming tortilla from the cloth serviette and passed the bundle along.

"You know, in the old stories, the heroes descended to hell," Aníbal said. "To the land of the dead, before they could be reborn."

"To Xib'alb'a. That's where Mayan heroes go."

"Yes." He smiled. A weary smile. This wasn't work a person could take pleasure in.

Isabel blew on a spoonful of soup, returned it to her bowl. She wasn't hungry. "But for us, for our generation, I'm not sure there's any new beginning," she said. "Sometimes I think my only role now is to bury the dead. Leave the living to the next generation. It could have been me in that well. Why not?"

"How old are you?"

"Thirty-five."

"And you've got a daughter and a grandchild on the way?"

Isabel nodded.

The exhaustion she'd seen in Aníbal's face just a moment ago had receded. "Life will claim you yet," he said.

"So it doesn't kill you, this work?"

"No." He finished his soup. "I also have a garden. It's a very beautiful garden."

After dinner Isabel rode into town with one of the other anthropologists. She didn't like staying at the exhumation sites. She wanted to see Yasmin. She wanted to watch her sleeping. She wanted to watch her wake.

CHAPTER 11

SHE IS TRYING to call to her brother but the sound lodges in her throat. Hugo, she mouths, Hugo. She strains to open her mouth wider, but the sound stays trapped. She wants to warn him about the men in suits. She sees them, identical, robotic, briefcase in one hand, machete in the other, scrabbling over the twisted steel rods and broken walls of the shattered city. Her brother and his young wife stand near an open door, the rusted iron frame of which pokes up from the rubble without any wall around it. They hold a photograph to the light. She tries to run to them but one of the men, a red beret yanked down over his left eye, suddenly appears beside her, machete flailing. She runs in the opposite direction. She knows the other men have reached her brother, but she runs anyway, tripping as she goes, picking up speed despite her stumbles, until her feet leave the ground altogether and she is flying, above the ruins, circling them like a bird of prey. Below her she sees the dark backs of the men, more of them now, flocked over something or somebody on the ground. As the men's arms flap over their quarry, she wants to laugh at her mistake: they are vultures, not men. Then she realizes her own circling has marked the spot out to them. A shot rings out. The birds scatter.

Soraida opened her eyes. More shots ripped across the night. The sound, deceptively close, disappeared without echo.

When Soraida was sixteen years old, Hugo gave her a copy of the *Popul Vuh* as a gift. They'd been drinking lemonade and playing conquián rummy on the airy gallery that framed the four sides of their garden courtyard, seated on matching rattan chairs, a rattan table—also part of the set—between them, its white lace overlay stirring in a delicate breeze. Behind them, beneath an adobe archway, tall wrought iron doors led to the rest of the family home. Clay-shingled eaves and a sprawling cashew tree, its red and yellow apples swaying like plump golden bells, provided shade.

"If you want to understand the other half of this country, you should learn to see the world through their eyes," Hugo said as he presented his gift. "You'll be amazed." He took a sip of lemonade and wiped his incipient mustache. She could smell his cologne, the starch of his newly laundered and pressed guayabera. A light film of perspiration shone from his forehead and clean-shaven cheeks.

Soraida set her glass on the table and accepted the slim paperback. On its cover, the sightless profile of a Mayan warrior or god glared into nothingness, a line drawing derived, she supposed, from one of the ancient stone carvings that yet endured.

"Isn't this from another time entirely?" she said. "I don't see anybody today walking around like this." She turned the cover toward him.

The truth was Soraida had no interest in understanding the Indians who waited on her, made her meals, washed and ironed her clothes, and cluttered the streets and markets with their wares, their clothing and their dark faces. She loved and admired her older brother, however, and wanted to please him.

"Give it a try," Hugo said.

So she did. The book was vulgar and strange, a muddle of gods who dabbled at creating humans, first from mud, then from sticks, and finally from corn; kings who changed into clotted blood; an underworld of houses dedicated to specific torments: darkness, cold, jaguars, bats, knives. It was like a long, torturous dream, beginning and ending in darkness.

"What did you think?" Hugo asked when she laid the book down at the breakfast table a week later. A bouquet of fresh-cut daisies bloomed from a vase at the table's centre. The room, which gave onto the courtyard, was cool and bright, sunlight from the garden slicing across its polished tile floor.

He was visiting for the weekend. During the week he was at the university, studying law, helping out in a student-run legal clinic that represented people who couldn't afford counsel. Despite their father's objections, Hugo had decided to practice labour law. With everything he did, he was moving away from them. Even the book's inscription had suggested it: "The world is big but it's beautiful. Don't be afraid," he'd written. Was that what it meant to grow up?, Soraida wondered. Becoming part of the world out there?

"I don't think I understand anything better than I did before I read it," she said. "What strange people."

"Well, yes, the stories are unfamiliar. But no stranger surely than the things we read in the Bible."

"The Bible is the Bible," Soraida said. "It's God's word."

"And God speaks in mysterious ways?"

Hugo had always encouraged her. She was good at math, he'd say, she should keep studying, she could be anything she wanted to be, she shouldn't let her parents hold her back. But she was her parents' daughter. She did as she was told. His attention was all she craved. She didn't need to understand anything about it.

He picked the book up and turned it over. "The Mayans also have their gods. Or some sort of equivalent to gods." He smiled. "As you can see, I'm learning, too."

There was something different about Hugo, besides his political talk, which, though she saw he tried to moderate, grew more pronounced at every visit. Their father didn't even bother to show up for breakfast anymore when Hugo was home.

Their mother arrived then and sat at the table, followed by Carla, who brought their breakfast of eggs and beans, fried plantain, fresh cheese, tortillas, each serving arranged on a wide porcelain plate, and laid it in front of them before returning to the kitchen.

"What are you reading?" her mother asked.

Soraida showed her the book. "Hugo gave it to me."

"He would." She cast a wan smile in Hugo's direction. "But it's a fascinating story. The old Mayan civilization produced splendid things, you know. Shame it's all gone now, just disappeared, even before the Conquest. They couldn't sustain it. The Indians now"—she nodded toward the kitchen—"you wouldn't know they were from the same race. Nothing but shoeless peasants, scratching out a living with machetes and foot ploughs, worshipping wooden idols. Most of them couldn't even read that book you're holding. Their own sacred book."

She laughed then, remembering something. "That Carla. She didn't know a thing when she first came to us. She must have scorched three shirts before she started getting the ironing right. But now she's like family." She pointed her fork at Soraida. "Remember that, Soraida. That's what it means to be Christian. Putting the needs of others first."

Hugo said nothing during all this. His eyes were fixed on his plate but he wasn't eating. Soraida felt his anger, but she didn't understand *why* he was angry. Her mother hadn't lied. Carla *was* like family. When she'd contracted measles soon after her arrival, Soraida's mother had sent for the doctor and paid for it herself. She'd often told the story of bringing Carla chicken soup and staying by her bedside. And when Carla got pregnant, Soraida's parents paid for everything and even arranged an adoption to take care of it. Carla was sad for a while—Soraida remembered that—but then she was fine. She had to know the impossible burden a baby would be—yet another mouth to feed. And what would she do with it while she was working?

Before Soraida could express any of this, Hugo stood up. He always got to things before she did. "I have to be going," he said.

He kissed Soraida and his mother, who was swallowing a mouthful of eggs and couldn't say anything to stop him, and he left the room.

In those days, Soraida saw little of her brother. He was a young man now, busy with school, with the legal clinic, with a new life. He was aglow with it, fuelled by a hot energy she'd known only in its milder form when she was a child and he would speak to her of imagined worlds full of fabulous creatures and stalwart heroes. As she and Hugo grew, these fantasies gave way to stories that had the semblance of the world around her but in inverted fashion. The poor were noble, the rich were evil. One day peasants and workers—Indigenous farmers and poor ladinos together—would rule the country. It was inevitable, he said. "You can't keep a people down forever." He had always embraced change, worshipped the new, but now she realized that what he really wanted was to see the way their family lived crumble.

"How can you say the rich are evil?" she asked. "Is Papa evil? Is Mama?"

"Have you seen where the people who work in Papa's factory live? Or the people who work in this house?"

"What business is it of ours where they live? They're lucky to have jobs at all. Who gave them that?" Even as she said it, she recognized the frailty of her argument. She didn't know where or how the people who worked for her parents lived. She knew only what she saw around her, and some of that, too, she tried hard not to see. Hugo didn't challenge her further. He just looked at her sadly, talking again about the world out there, instead of the one Soraida lived in. Soraida still considered his stories fairy tales, but because she was not sure—she knew so little of life outside her father's house—they also made her afraid. She listened because she loved the sound of his voice, steady and assured, telling her everything would turn out all right.

One day on the street corner by their house, Soraida saw him kiss an Indigenous girl and she began to doubt. She was returning from school, laden with books, looking forward to a visit from Hugo after a long hard week of exams. She'd just learned that she'd won a first in calculus, and as she marched along the grand avenue, she imagined herself in a lab coat, instructing the managers of her father's factory in a ground-breaking mathematical formula that would double production without doubling the workload. She was hurrying to tell Hugo about it—not about the lab coat and the formula but about the first. As she turned the corner, she saw them. At first she thought he was kissing one of the maids. But like Soraida, the Indigenous girl hugged several books to her chest. And the kiss Hugo gave her was tender, drawn out but not desperate with passion. It was a kiss, she realized in the years to come as she turned the scene over and over in her mind, that said they—Hugo and the girl—had already travelled some distance together and still had all the time in the world. This visit home was but a tiny hiccough in their relationship. Soraida felt robbed.

She was in her room when Hugo asked to speak privately with their father and only became aware of the conversation when their voices began to rise. But even with her ear pressed to the door, she couldn't make out what was said. Something thudded against a wall, something fell and smashed—she thought immediately of the porcelain clock on her father's mantel—a door slammed. Soraida rushed from her room in time to see Hugo pause in the middle of the front hall, pale and perspiring, a red mark like a slap across his forehead. He opened the front door and fled. A moment later she heard the gate at the end of the drive rattle violently and snap shut. She remembered it, thirty-seven years later, as the moment the colour went out of her life.

Her parents never spoke of their son after that and Soraida understood, without being told, that she must not speak of him either. She was angry at first, hurt that he had chosen something or somebody over her. But anger never lasted in her. And so she began to imagine a happy life for her brother. It looked very much like the life Soraida led, though she would try to include the face of the dark-skinned girl in whatever scene she concocted, and a home that was not so large or clean or impermeable as the one Hugo had deserted. She imagined him at work, speaking to labourers, arguing with bosses, winning the day with his intelligence. She'd even started reading the newspapers in the hope of catching a glimpse of him or somebody like him or somebody he knew. All she found were tirades against the communists who were threatening the patria. Communists everywhere. Government forces everywhere too, rooting them out. And from time to time, the pale lifeless face of some young man would surface on the front page. She examined these photos carefully. Teacher, doctor, economist, poet, lawyer. The only good communist was a dead one, the papers said.

In the meantime, she went to dances, met the sons of her parents' friends, toured the chewing gum factory that would one day belong to her, or to her husband. But she took no step in any direction. Her life was on hold; she felt unable to move on. She needed to see Hugo.

Soraida was carrying an earthen vase of pink and orange daises from her shop to the kitchen when she heard Quique's knock at the door. "I thought I'd try and brighten the place," she said as she opened. She thrust the flowers at him. "Where should I put them? On the kitchen table or in the shop?"

Quique kissed her cheek. Good man, not a whiff of alcohol on him.

"And good afternoon to you, too," he said as he followed her down the corridor. "Wherever you will see them most, I say."

"That would be the shop." She'd bought the flowers to mark her resolve to start her life anew, to face the wrongs of the past and correct them if she could. But she'd lost her nerve and now she didn't want to put them down at all. "They might get damaged in the shop. Better on the table." She wandered toward the kitchen only to pause again.

"Leave them," Quique said. "You can decide when we get back."

Soraida nodded. She'd asked Quique to come and here he was—and sober, too. She couldn't keep him waiting. She nodded again and set the bouquet down in the courtyard sink.

"I'll just wash my hands and be right with you."

The Catholic Church was conducting an inquiry, a kind of Truth Commission, into the atrocities committed during the war. Guatemalans were invited to meet with the REMHI workers and tell them what they knew. It was a way, the church preached, to honour and remember the dead, to speak the truth, and to build a solid foundation for reconciliation. Soraida had learned about it from a pamphlet she'd picked up when she went to the cathedral the previous Thursday to light a candle for her parents' souls. At Sunday dinner, she'd told Quique about it and he'd agreed to escort her.

When they arrived downtown, they walked past the cathedral's enormous façade, pigeons scattering before them, past the beggars and the birdseed vendors, and stopped before a small oak door in the low building to one side. Soraida entered first, and after removing his baseball cap, Quique followed, his hands folded behind his back. Just inside the door, a young man at a simple wooden desk was bent over something he was writing. He had the look, with his fine white hands, of somebody who wrote all the time. As they approached, he raised his head and smiled.

"Can I help you?"

Soraida felt guilty already before this clean and Christian young man. She turned to Quique, who nodded his encouragement. She leaned forward and whispered. "I want to speak with somebody from REMHI."

To her surprise, the young man glanced around him—the room was quite empty but for the three of them—and whispered too. "Do you wish to give testimony?"

Soraida nodded. A secret pact had just been sealed.

The young man led them through another, larger wooden door into an open courtyard and then down the corridor that hugged the yard and into a large office with several desks and many stacks of papers and books. After turning them over to a young Indigenous woman in a red huipil who sat at one of the desks, he left.

The woman, Katia, explained to them the procedures for giving testimony, assuring them that their identities would be protected and that many other brave people were doing just as they were to bring Guatemala the lasting peace its valiant and long-suffering people so longed for and deserved.

"Without truth, there can be no peace," she said.

The little speech was clearly intended to reassure, but the young woman's words made Soraida doubt her decision instead. How could she count herself among these valiant people who deserved peace? How would truth serve the guilty?

"What will happen to us?" she asked.

Katia didn't understand the question.

". . . if we're guilty. If we've done something wrong." Soraida took out her handkerchief so she would have something to twist. Katia's warm expression had cooled somewhat.

But she said to Soraida, "It is even harder for those who have been part of the wrongs committed and have carried that burden for so long to come here and set it down. REMHI is here to speak for the victims, but to do that we need to hear from everybody who has information. The identity of every witness will be protected, no matter"—she was searching for the right word—"what *side* of the conflict you were on."

After assigning Soraida to a researcher and arranging a time and date for an interview, Katia delivered them back to the courtyard.

"Will it be worth it, I wonder?" Soraida said quietly to Quique as they found their way to the front entrance. "Is it the right thing to do?"

Quique took her arm. "How can speaking the truth be wrong?" And he led her out of the building.

CHAPTER 12

DANILO AND ISABEL were sitting in the moonlight on a cinderblock wall in the lot next to Isabel's new house. Across and along the street stood identical two-room houses in various stages of construction, all of them owned by former guerrillas. Beyond the housing project, stubbled fields and a single unpaved road stretched into the night. Danilo and his family lived just one street over. They'd been sitting on the wall, enjoying the cool night air, talking and not talking, leaning against each other, tapping their toes together. They were both a little drunk.

Danilo lit a cigarette, its tip flaring crimson as he inhaled. His bangs hung like a damp towel over the rim of his glasses, bathing his face in shadow. "How have you been sleeping?" he asked. "Are the dreams still bothering you?"

"You mean has the bag with the baby become a bag full of bones?" Isabel rubbed her forehead. She *had* dreamed something like that: hundreds of bones, she'd been trying to stuff them into her pack. But had she really dreamed it? When? Last night? It hadn't shaken her awake. In fact she wasn't aware of it at all until now. "The nightmares I see these days while I'm at work—they're worse than anything I dream at night."

Claudia was still at work and the kids had gone over to the basketball court to hang out with other URNG youth. Isabel, whose work was full of stops and starts, had spent the last two days at the project. The next day she'd head out again with the forensic anthropologists. Danilo was unemployed.

"I had another idea about what might be bothering you," he said between puffs. "You said your backpack's always really heavy?"

Isabel felt queasy. It wasn't just the beer. Any talk of her dreams made her feel this way.

"You never really talk," he said. "About the war. About your parents and grandparents." He listed toward her as he spoke, like a boat that had taken on too much water. "You only talk about Yasmin."

She prodded his shoulder until he was upright again. "So?"

"So maybe it's not Yasmin you're carrying around in those nightmares. Maybe it's everything else."

Everything else. The missions she'd undertaken. The claymores she'd planted below a bridge or along a trail. The firefights with soldiers—she had no idea who she might have injured or killed. Their names. Where they were from. How old they were. The compañeros she'd seen bleed to death. The death of her grandparents. The death of her parents.

"Maybe," Isabel said. The beer tasted sour upon her tongue.

A chorus of crickets chirped from the black fields that encircled the houses. Somewhere in the distance an engine coughed to life. Danilo dropped his spent cigarette and lit another.

"I think I want to carry those things," she said. "To hold onto them. What are we except the things we've done?"

"Those dreams might plague you your whole life."

Isabel shrugged. "Call it penance." She turned to face him. The alcohol had loosened her heartstrings as well as her tongue, and Danilo had long occupied a special place there, in her heart. She massaged his shoulder. "It's getting better. There's lots to keep me busy day to day."

"Busy hands."

"Sure, but it works well enough. Like you and the party. Aren't we all just trying to find a way forward?"

"It's important work you're doing."

Sometimes everything Danilo said sounded like it came out of a party pamphlet. Yet nobody was so completely sincere as he was, in his convictions, in everything he did. He was the quintessential true believer, a rare breed—rarer still because he didn't demand the same blind faith in return.

She took a sip from the glass in her hand. "I'm glad to be doing it," she said.

There were no streetlamps here—just the lights from her own and neighbouring houses and the moon above. She moved her glass to catch its reflection on the beer's golden surface.

"This is better than the city," she said.

Danilo exhaled a long stream of smoke. "You're with family here."

Isabel thought of Soraida, alone in her kitchen, checking her watch to see if the hour to open had finally arrived. She wondered whether Danilo, too, had exchanged the family he was born into for this one.

He was staring at his rapidly shrinking cigarette.

"How are *you* doing?" she asked.

He swept his bangs to one side and grimaced, his eyes glossy behind the glasses. "I'm learning to make granola. To sell door-to-door."

Isabel bumped against him in sympathy. Privately, she was glad the police force had sacked him. From what she'd heard, the new force was quickly becoming like the old one. She wouldn't want to lose Danilo to that. "Granola," she said. "*Shit.*"

"We're lucky Claudia's got a good job." He crushed his cigarette against the wall. "I love Claudia."

"I know you do."

"I love you too."

Isabel didn't respond. This was hazardous territory. She hopped down from the wall and then helped Danilo down, keeping hold of his hand even after he had both feet on the ground. He was drunker than she was, though not drunk enough to absolve him of whatever happened next. He was bending toward her, head inclined, hair falling forward. He had no intention of ambushing her with a kiss. He knew better than that.

They'd been lovers, a long time ago when they were travelling together on guerrilla business, a brief affair that she remembered fondly. It had ended as naturally as it began, no harm done—as far as she knew. Claudia, too, had taken lovers from time to time. They all had. Who didn't need love or sex or both when they and everything they cared about hung in the balance between life and death? She knew compañeros who would say it was the correct thing to do. Give love, freely, when you can. While you can. She was so tired of keeping herself in check, and he was right there, smelling of beer and tobacco and begging with those glossy eyes for her kiss—this man who for fifteen or twenty years had endured hardship and hunger, put his life on the line, only to discover that all his country wanted from him was homemade granola, and maybe not even that. An invitation to float away expanded inside her like a balloon.

Danilo rocked forward and back, heel to toe, pulling her hand closer to steady himself, trying, she thought, to draw her gaze. She looked at her sneakers, rooted to the spot, the only thing keeping them both standing. She didn't want to float away. She wanted her feet on the ground. She squeezed his hand, warm like hers. Peacetime didn't offer the kinds of excuses war did. They'd have to break with what most mattered to them—and for what? In the end, they'd still come up against the reality of each of their own lives, their commitments, and maybe just who they were.

"You love Claudia," she said. She pressed his hand again, gently but firmly—like a mother would, or an old woman whose sexual desire had withered, or a good friend.

"Sorry," he said. "Not sure what got into me." He stepped away from her, slapping his chest and stretching his arms. Exaggerating. Making a joke of it. He laughed, embarrassed. "Where's Max when you need him?"

It wasn't funny, but Isabel patted his cheek anyway—he was the best friend she had. She steered him toward the street and went inside.

Yasmin arrived about half an hour later. Jorge and Erika dropped her off after seeing another couple of friends home. She looked happy as she came through the door, waving goodbye to them. Was it the pregnancy that had her shimmering like that?

"I was just about to turn in," Isabel said.

"Me, too. I've got classes tomorrow."

She went to her daughter, who had not left the front door and remained, in fact, turned toward it as if at any moment somebody might knock. Lately, Yasmin had gone from rejecting her pregnancy to ignoring it. But she'd stopped drinking and, thanks in large part to Jorge's tutoring, she was progressing well in her courses, attending classes daily even though for most students her age the school year was over and vacations had begun. Isabel wanted to encourage her. "I saw Eduardo today. He says you should be able to graduate by spring." She gathered Yasmin's long black hair behind her neck and kissed her cheek.

Yasmin was still smiling at the door.

"Settling in here. All the changes. It can't have been easy," Isabel said.

Startled from her reverie, Yasmin turned. "I love it here," she said. "I wished I'd lived here my whole life."

Isabel reached for her daughter's arm. "Come. Have something to eat."

But Yasmin moved past her, stroking her swollen belly. "We had something at the snack bar. I just want to sleep." Without looking back, she entered the bedroom and closed the door behind her.

Isabel turned off the gas stove and slipped a lid onto the pot of black beans that had been simmering there. Then she cleared away the dishes and cutlery she'd laid out and sat at the table. Her mind turned again to Soraida. In her heart, she'd long since forgiven her aunt for the things she'd said. At this distance it was easy to see only Soraida's sacrifices, her good intentions. Yet Yasmin really did seem better off here. Nobody was going to judge or shun her. She could study and learn about the ideal the revolutionaries had fought for. And it would be a good, safe place to raise Yasmin's child. Isabel was loathe to disrupt their new-found stability by reaching out to her old aunt—even though she knew it was the right thing to do. It was a haven, this little house, barely furnished, the only adornment the newly framed photo of her parents' wedding that hung on the white stucco wall next to the table.

She got up to look at it, and as she examined each face, she noticed for the first time how like Soraida her father was. Long nose, broad forehead, square frame. He'd been very fond of his little sister. He'd harboured great hopes for her. That's what Isabel's grandparents had told her. He'd said Soraida was somebody you could trust. Isabel had been thinking a lot about her parents lately. The peace, the reunion with Soraida, with Yasmin—these things had unearthed questions and longings she thought she'd buried long ago. Why had her parents gone back to the city? Why had they left her behind? Who wrote the note the police found in her father's pocket? Was there, in fact, a note or was that another of the regime's lies? She'd heard her grandparents ask them, too, these questions. But nobody had answers.

Isabel stared at the photograph a long time, until with the chill of the night, she went to the bedroom she shared with Yasmin, found her bed and crawled under the covers.

She awoke well before dawn. The neighbourhood roosters had started up a ruckus, cockledoodling back and forth in long startled screeches. For a moment, in the room's deep shadows, she saw her mother, bending to the patio chickens, her long *uq* wrapped tight round her waist and thighs. *Chi, chi, chi*, her mother called, as she showered the birds with pale dried kernels of corn and they scrabbled and scratched to snap it from the hard ground. Then the image was gone. The roosters were quiet. Yasmin, in the next bed, slept soundly.

Isabel got up. In a few hours, she'd have to walk the dusty road to the highway and hail a bus to Öch äj. The forensic team was meeting with members of the town council to schedule a series of exhumations in the area. Isabel felt she'd seen so many bones she was losing track. Bones, clothing, a few belongings here and there. Once in a while a photograph. Each item they uncovered pulled at her heart, but in the end they—the people who had suffered and died—remained strangers to her. That might change in Öch äj. Eventually they were bound to come across a grave that held people she knew, people she loved.

She went to put water on the stove for a sponge bath. As she pressed the warm, damp cloth to her eyes, her throat, under her arms, her breasts, between her legs, she tried to remember what she'd been dreaming, but it had melted away at first light.

When Isabel returned home the next day, she surprised Yasmin and Jorge in the middle of an impassioned embrace on Yasmin's bed. Jorge scrambled to get up as Yasmin raised herself slowly and swung her feet to the floor. Isabel noted with some relief that both were fully clothed.

Jorge smoothed the creases from his shirt. "Doña Isabel. It's not ... I wouldn't ..."

Usually a thoughtful, articulate boy, he couldn't put two sentences together.

"Because the baby. The baby's what's important," he finally sputtered, a blush warming his brown cheeks.

"You should go," Isabel said. He obeyed, ducking past her and out of the house. Yasmin looked longingly after him.

Despite the sliver of shock that had pierced her on opening the bedroom door, the scene before her confirmed suspicions that had dogged Isabel for weeks. "I gather Víctor is out of the picture," she said.

Yasmin dropped her head. Was she really chagrined or just play-acting for her mother?

"Let's talk," Isabel said. She was about to sit on the rumpled covers of Yasmin's bed, but changed her mind. "At the table."

Yasmin hesitated, but then she followed and sat. Having a solid object under her seemed to lend her courage.

"I'm seeing Jorge, now," she said. She held her chin high and look squarely at her mother, though her hands, fingertips digging into her thighs, betrayed her. "But we've agreed. Nothing too serious till after the baby is born." Her blush was brighter than Jorge's.

"I'm glad you're thinking about the baby—I'm glad you're thinking, in fact, but ..." Isabel was trying to match Yasmin's attempt at calm, but her hold was slipping. "Don't you think you've got enough to deal with? First Víctor? Now Jorge?"

Yasmin gripped her belly. "Aren't I doing enough just *having* this baby? Am I supposed to lock myself up now? Is that it?"

"Stop ... stop with the dramatics. Let's start again." Isabel breathed deep and rested her hands palm down on the tabletop, feeling the cool, lifeless plastic. "I like Jorge. I also like Víctor, believe it or not. I don't expect you to stick with the first guy you fall for, or to worry too much about my likes and dislikes."

"But?" Yasmin said. "There must be a *but*."

"Two things. One is, whoever you decide you want to be with, you make sure you look out for yourself, and your baby, first. That means finishing high school, going on to university or into training. In this country education goes a long way. You can't depend on a boy for your future."

"I *am* studying. Jorge's helping me—"

"The other thing—have you told Víctor?"

"I will."

"When? You can't just pretend he doesn't exist."

"I don't want to see him."

"Why not? Did he do something? Did he hurt you?" Isabel would hunt him down if he had.

Yasmin lifted both hands and let them fall. Some sort of shrug. She puffed out her cheeks and pursed her lips. Isabel waited.

"It's nothing like that," she said at last, sniffing to hold back a tear. "I know he doesn't deserve it but I don't even know what I saw in him. We're not even interested in the same things."

Isabel was not sure herself what things interested Yasmin, but she wasn't about to say so. "So tell him that."

"I will."

"When?"

Yasmin slapped her hands on the table—just like a six-year-old. "I said I will and I will. And then it'll be over and I won't have to deal with him anymore."

"Of course you'll have to deal with him. He's your baby's father."

"The baby doesn't need a father. Fathers are useless."

They certainly could be. Yasmin's father had been. "He's been working hard to be a good father," Isabel said. "I think he's tried to do right by you."

"I can't believe you're siding with him."

"I'm not siding with him … I'm not." But she was. Why? Perhaps she'd grown tired of seeing families torn apart, whatever the reason. Víctor was bound to lose any struggle over custody—Isabel and Yasmin weren't rich by any means, but they had more resources and more support than he did. He'd give up the baby. It was inevitable. Perhaps he'd find that a relief. Or now that he was working, he could just start up a new family. It happened all the time. "If you don't love him, fine," she said. "But he does have some rights. At the very least, he deserves to know where he stands. Learning to be clear in your relationships is important."

Yasmin snorted. "You're one to talk. Where's *my* father then? You never even think about him. You haven't involved him at all."

It was as if she'd been reading Isabel's thoughts. Hands still on the table, Isabel willed her fingertips to absorb its indifference. "Your father left," she said. "He left both of us."

"And that was it. You never saw or talked to him again. You never gave him a chance to reconsider."

"What was I supposed to do? Go chasing after him? Track him down? There was a war on, and he just took off."

"But he was, he *is* my father!"

This was classic Yasmin. Turning one problem into another. Into one she hadn't created.

"If he wanted to be part of your life, he could have found you," Isabel said. "It wasn't that hard."

"How do you know? There was a war on. You said so yourself."

The war. When had it become the excuse for everything? Even Yasmin had learned that. Yet Isabel couldn't help thinking that her own decisions were what had led them here, to Yasmin's pregnancy, to this very quarrel. And everything Isabel had ever done was because of the war. The war had left them all off-balance.

"And now the war is over, and I want to meet him," Yasmin said.

"You're just trying to avoid responsibility for your own actions, bringing this up now."

"You're wrong." She was beginning to cry.

"You're serious?"

"Of course I am. People change. You said so yourself. You said that none of the choices you had back then were good ones. But you've never even talked to him. You don't know why he did what he did."

There was some truth to what Yasmin was saying. Isabel had put Luís so entirely out of her mind after she gave birth to Yasmin, it was as if he'd never existed. But for Yasmin he had always existed, if only as a spectre, a fantasy, a possibility. "How would we find him?" Isabel asked. "As far as I know he's in the States."

"Try."

"And what would you do?"

"I could write him." Yasmin brushed away her tears. She looked calm, determined, no longer angry.

"I'll try," Isabel said. "Somebody in the organization will know. They always do."

"Thank you."

"And you will speak to Víctor?"

"I will."

"If you don't, I will."

"I will."

Isabel smiled at her daughter. "I believe you."

CHAPTER 13

FROM HIS HAND a chicken dangles by its twine-bound legs, its wings opening at his side like a fan, contracting suddenly and, relaxing, falling open again. His back is turned, his young head bent forward, dark curls grazing the nape of his neck, as he thrusts his other hand into his pocket to retrieve something. He lifts his head and pivots as at a noise. Two young men, not so different in height or hair or dress, rush toward him, the arm of one raised in an odd sideways twist that reminds her of something she's seen on TV. The shot cracks the air. His head jerks back, his body follows, the chicken is airborne, beating its wings uselessly. His body hits the ground, a cloud of dust rises, the chicken lands heavily on his chest, its wings still flapping—against his chest, against his face, against the blood, the dust. Its feathers grow red as it struggles, painting his chest in his own blood, dusting his curls in his blood. He hasn't moved. His torn face is turned to the sun. She stands there, immobile, though she knows him. She can do nothing for him now.

Soraida swept the broom across the floor of her shop, from back to front, shaking the dust onto the sidewalk. Back to front and two sharp taps against the front step to release the dirt. Back to front, two sharp taps. When she'd finished, she took a bucket from the laundry sink in the courtyard and filled it halfway. After adding some powdered detergent and a trickle of bleach, she walked up and down the length of the shop, dribbling soapy water onto the polished cement floor. Next she grabbed a towel from the sink, wrapped it around the end of the broom and started mopping, pushing the dirty, sudsy water onto the street, delaying at the open door to see it drain away. She returned the towel and bucket to the courtyard and propped the broom against one of the shelves. Then she went to the entrance, checked her watch for the third time that morning, straightened her apron, folded her hands and waited. She was expecting Byron any minute.

A muscular young man with a thin mustache and short hair was crossing from the market.

"Doña Soraida?"

She recognized him. One of the backpack sellers?

"My mother sent me," he said.

Soraida nodded without replying. She didn't have time right now for market gossip. Byron was late. He was never late. She checked her watch again.

"Byron Velásquez works for you."

"He's not here," Soraida said. "He must have been detained. He's never late. Not without reason."

The young man looked away, back to the market, prompting Soraida to follow suit. But all she saw was the usual commotion of people: a round young woman in tight jeans and a ruby tank top slapping the hand of the little boy at her side as he reached to pluck the strings of a wooden ukulele; another woman, a vendor, folding up a green and white woven blanket for an elderly man whose hands trembled violently as he delivered her his money. Even at this distance she could see those hands dance. Every stand seemed to have somebody at it, selling or buying. But no Byron. Her gaze returned to the young man, who was sliding his index finger along his thin little moustache. He glanced once more toward the market, adjusted his belt, corrected his posture and addressed her. "I'm sorry, Doña Soraida. I have bad news."

His mouth was moving, shaping words. *Byron*, he was saying, *Byron*. A great cold weight grew in her, from her stomach to her chest, to her legs, arms, hands, feet. Her skin was ice under the beating sun. Ice on stone. Cold dead stone.

She didn't go to the vigil, which must have started as soon as Byron's sister and mother were able to transport his body home, as soon as they had washed and reclothed him, the coffin had been ordered and fitted and Byron shut within it. She wanted to go. She knew she should go. But she couldn't bring herself to step even an inch beyond her door. The sunlight hurt her eyes. Raging traffic, angry voices hurt her ears. The smell of rot was overpowering. She felt her heart was failing.

The young man from the market had helped her close, jumping up to grab the bottom of the overhead door and lower it, shutting out the wounding sunlight and locking the door in place, settling Soraida into the white plastic chair where, with Byron seated beside her, she used to enjoy her eleven o'clock coffee, asking her if there was anything she needed, a glass of water, peppermint tea, anything at all? Soraida, distantly aware of the young stranger and his enquiries, blinked her eyes in the half-light. "I'll manage," she said, her voice barely scratching the air. She thanked him and then she sent him home to his mother.

Seated there, in the middle of the shop, she kept her own private vigil, Byron's empty chair beside her, the empty counter behind the two chairs. She sat and she watched: the way light from the street slipped through the gap between wall and roof, the way it cast vague shadows that grew and deepened as the day progressed. She watched a fly touch down on the mopped cement floor and pick a blind path across it until it took flight again. She absorbed the slight tremor in the floor and walls each time a bus or truck rattled past, the quake each time an airplane broke the sky above. She sat there, at a loss, thinking of nothing at all, listening instead, listening hard—to the muffled shouts, the clatter, the groaning engines that reached her as if from another time, trying to comprehend that world out there, the message it had sent her. A message of chaos, of havoc. A message that made no sense.

Time slithered by without her marking it. She didn't notice the hour strike eleven. Or noon or one. She didn't check her watch. But at some point in the afternoon, somebody knocked on her side door. The visitor had been hammering she didn't know how long before she finally heard and understood what she was meant to do. She rose, slowly, and made her way down the long hallway, tapping the wall with her fingers as she went, for guidance, to whatever awaited at the end of the passage.

"Quique."

"You're not open," he said. "Are you ill? I've been knocking. I came to the market to get some fabric. Somebody's made me an order for a wedding dress, can you believe it? I thought I'd stop by. Are you ill?"

He stopped talking and looked at her. She'd begun to weep, the first tears she'd shed. But she couldn't speak. Her throat was tight and sore. Her lungs burned. So she turned and padded back down the hallway. Quique followed.

The next day, after mass at the church his mother occasionally attended, six classmates shouldered Byron's coffin through the streets, the knot of mourners behind them. On adjacent streets, the early morning traffic growled, horns tweeted, drivers cursed. Soraida and Quique walked just behind the family. They were not many, the mourners; the family, like Soraida's, a remnant of what had or what might have been. Byron's mother, in a black dress and supported by two canes, swung her bent legs forward one at a time to advance along the street. Élida, also in black, walked beside her, holding Soraida's namesake to her chest.

Upon reaching the graveyard, the group trickled through its gates, along the tree-lined avenues where the palatial mausoleums of the country's wealthiest families towered over the more modest structures that followed, on to the far end, filing into a maze of narrows alleys that bound the walls of the dead, block after block of sepulchral apartments stuffed top to bottom with the earthly remains of the city's poorer citizens. A rectangular cavity halfway up one wall marked the spot. The pall bearers set the coffin down before the tomb and then they all waited for the priest.

Soraida squeezed Quique's arm. She had yet to convince herself that the scene before her was anything but a bad dream. She could not connect, though she tried, Byron's ease and contentment—his grace—with anything she saw around her. He'd been shot, she had learned, near his home in La Limonada while he was running an errand for his mother. A case of mistaken identity, they'd said. The bullet was meant for some other seventeen-year-old boy.

When the priest began to speak, she wished she could block her ears. His words conveyed nothing. It could be anybody in that coffin. Her chest heaved, and she leaned heavily against Quique. The priest ended with a blessing and the pall bearers lifted the box, scaled a pair of narrow ladders they'd propped against the wall of tombs, and slid it into the awaiting niche. One of the mourners clambered up and laid a red, long-stemmed carnation at the foot of the coffin before the cemetery workers sealed it with a slab of plaster and fresh mortar. Byron's mother stood to one side, bent over her two canes, twisting her head painfully to track her son's ascent to his final resting place. Did she, perhaps, wish she could climb up into one of those stone holds and join him? Perhaps it was a comfort Byron was heading to. Perhaps, but Soraida refused to accept it. She wanted *her* comfort back. Her consolation. He had breathed life into everybody who knew him. They were all a little deadened by his passing.

"Can we stay a bit longer?" she asked Quique. The cemetery workers were fastening one of the small bouquets left at the foot of the wall to the plaster marker. The mourners were departing.

Quique led her to a cement bench still within view of the grave, and they sat in the mottled sunlight that reached them through the boughs of a nearby oak. He didn't hurry her. He gave her time. And eventually, after the cold from the bench had entered her body and her bones ached from the hard cement, she got up to go.

Awake in her rigid, metal bed, a thin blanket pulled up to her neck, Soraida folded her hands over the hurt in her chest. She stared at the ceiling, a dirty white that had yellowed in places. The room was dank; it smelled of old age. As she lay there, pressing on her at every instant was his face, his smile, his loose and easy movements when he swept or tidied or brought them conchas and hojaldras from the bakery for eleven o'clock coffee. Byron, born under moonlight, who had never been a threat to anybody, whose passage through this world had been as brief and gentle as a spring breeze. Though blood didn't bind them, he'd understood her pain when Isabel and Yasmin had left her, and he'd made her a member of his family. His sister had christened her first child Soraida. Because he believed in family, in reconciliation, in the good inside each of them. He'd told her so the day Isabel came back from the war. And look how the world had repaid him. The world's loss. When would such a light shine again?

Soraida tried to chase the images away, replace them with the map of yellow stains on the ceiling above her, but it was no use. Tomorrow, remembrances of his smile, his words, his attentiveness, would dog her as she plodded through her day, teasing her with fleeting moments of joy. And there was nothing she could do to put them to rest because there was nothing for her to do except carry on, alone, performing the same meaningless tasks she had always performed. She wanted to believe that Byron had gone to a better place but if that was so, why could she still feel him here? She pressed her hands against her chest, pushing back at the grief that welled inside her. Was she to live out the rest of her life in the company only of ghosts? She felt them now, circling her bed, drawing closer, whispering in her ear, tempting her with memories. She gripped her blanket. "Don't be afraid," her brother had written. She'd reread those words a thousand times, but to what end? Hugo's passage through life had been almost as brief as Byron's. Unlike Byron, he'd been energetic, purposeful, blazing like a torch that lights the path to the future. But this evil world would not tolerate him either. When they gunned him down, she'd run away. She hadn't even checked to see whether he was breathing. She didn't think once about his young wife, Rosario, cut down by the assassins' bullets right beside him.

And why had they been there in the first place? *Because of her. Because of her.*

It had taken all her courage just to write and send the note that had asked Hugo to meet her. When she received the reply, she'd shivered with fear—fear of her father's wrath should he ever find out. She'd read it over, aloud, following the cadence of Hugo's words, to persuade herself to follow through. They'd fixed a place and a time: the hippodrome at five o'clock.

She got there first and waited, watching the long paved boulevard for his approach. Soft gusts stirred the violet blossoms of the jacarandas that lined the median at the street's centre. The sky was bright and blue. She saw him, slim, smart, in a clean suit, a confident stride, and the woman at his side, chatting to him until she shifted her gaze and spotted, as Hugo already had, Soraida waiting. Hugo's wife smiled—the same dimpled smile Soraida would meet again in Isabel and then in Yasmin. Hugo was beaming. She'd never seen him so happy.

And then the van, a dark blue Chevy tearing up the street behind them. Hugo heard it and spun round, pulling his wife behind him. He knew that sound. Soraida moved, too, ducking behind the trunk of a jacaranda, its flowering branches dappling her in shadow. From her hiding place, she heard the van screech to a halt, its side door slide open, shouts, blasts. She shrank to her knees, shielding her ears, and peeked from behind the tree. Her brother was falling. But she saw. She saw the face of the man who stepped from the vehicle's side door to deliver the tiro de gracia. She saw his uniform, his beard, the tilt of his beret, his blue blue eyes. She hid behind the trunk and did not look out again. All she could think about was escape. She listened and prayed until she heard the van's motor change gear and the van drive off. She crouched there a few seconds longer, scarcely breathing, summoning the will to break through the paralysis that had gripped her. Then she ran, to the other side of the avenue—away from Hugo, away from his wife, down a side street, running and panting, listening all the way for the sound of the van's motor, veering again into another street when she encountered people or a moving vehicle. Soon she tired and began to walk. She moved onto larger, busier streets, seeking now the protection of strangers, of shoppers, vendors, pedestrians. She walked for nearly an hour. And then she had walked home.

In the company of ghosts, Soraida lay there, awake, waiting for shadows to engulf her and deliver her to the next pointless day.

Byron's mother invited her in. The hot metal shack was dimly lit, with a packed dirt floor, recently swept, and a low roof that inclined toward the back. A string hammock and a sheet that served as a partition marked off the sleeping quarters. Three wooden chairs placed near the door formed the common area. Élida, who was nursing baby Soraida, rose from one to greet her.

"It isn't much," Doña Fátima said. "My home is very humble."

Leaning on her canes, she moved to the chairs, offering one to Soraida before she lowered herself into another. Élida sat as well.

"But it is mine," she said. "And when I die it will belong to my daughter. I pay nothing to keep it and nobody will take it from me."

This was the first time Soraida had ever visited the neighbourhood, picking her way down the steep trail to the ramshackle colony below, sure that she'd get her throat slit before she ever made it to her goal. After asking the way, she was able to distinguish the corrugated zinc hut from the others by the black bow, fashioned from a plastic bag, posted above its door. Byron had worked for her for four years, yet she had never seen his home. It had taken his death to make her unafraid to venture into this metal hell, indifferent to what happened to her now or on the way back.

"My deepest sympathies to you and your family," she said.

Mother and daughter nodded in reply, before Élida blinked back a tear and looked away and Fátima bowed her head.

Soraida gave rein to the silence. What other response was there?

After a minute had passed, she broached the other purpose of her visit. "Would Élida come work for me?" She directed her inquiry to the girl's mother.

Doña Fátima moved her jaw as if she needed first to chew and then to digest the question. Élida had turned her attention to her baby, who suckled noisily.

"The maquila pays better," Fátima said finally.

"I thought it closed down," Soraida said. It was something Bryon had told her.

"One closes down, another one opens. They'll always need a girl who can sew."

Soraida was trying to imagine the baby and her crippled grandmother locked in this dark shack while Élida was at work. Of course they would manage. Didn't half the country? She wondered what else she could offer. "It's dangerous here," she said. "The gangs are out of control."

Hurt appeared in Doña Fátima's face; Soraida had gone too far. Her host struggled to her feet. "My daughter belongs here with me," she said. "You can't have her."

Soraida stood, too, trying to placate her. "That's not what I'm asking. I'm sorry. I've offended you. I just wanted to help." She turned to Élida, who remained seated, baby Soraida still latched to her breast.

"Of course your mother needs you here. Now more than ever." Soraida paused to measure her words before addressing Fátima again. "Byron was such a service to me. Such a good sweet boy. I miss him terribly. I guess I wanted to be closer to the people he cared about, the people he came from." She was embarrassed by the confession, by losing her composure. And now she was tearing up. Fátima urged her into her seat again. "Let me get you a coffee," she said.

Soraida bent to remove the padlocks from the corners of the overhead door, pulled at it and then pulled again. Finally it moved, and she lifted it past her head and thrust it into the dark cavity above, where it shuddered to a halt somewhere short of its final destination. She surveyed the shop's stands. Everything was tidy, every piece of clothing in its place. Stacks of clothing waiting in vain for bodies to fill them. She hadn't opened since Byron's death three days earlier.

She got the broom and started sweeping, slowly, more slowly, the strokes of the broom like sorrow itself. She straightened, breathed deep, and tried again. So much quiet. No, that wasn't it. People and things were making the usual racket all around her, but somehow nothing penetrated.

Then she saw the bent figures of that beggar and his girl amble past along the street outside, both heads tucked down, his arm around her waist, her nose against his cheek. Such misery. Such affection.

Soraida ran to the front step. "Hold up!" she called to them. "I've got something for you."

She invited them to sit on the plastic chairs while she reheated some soup and tortillas she had left over from the night before, nodding at them as they took their seats. They stank. They really stank. She resisted the temptation to hold her nose. When the soup was hot, she brought the steaming earthenware bowls, one at a time, and placed them in their filthy hands as the man grunted his thanks. A moment later she returned with the tortillas, wrapped in a blue cloth serviette, and set them on the counter. The couple dug in, ravenous, as Soraida stood by and watched them. She watched every spoonful, every gesture. She wanted to watch them forever.

CHAPTER 14

Through Claudia, Isabel asked Max to meet her again at a pub in downtown Guatemala City. Claudia had recommended the place, a locale Che Guevara was said to have favoured during his sojourn in Guatemala, long before the triumphant revolution that would propel him to world fame. Like most of the city, it was new to Isabel. Taking advantage of the remaining sunlight, she walked the ten blocks from Eighteenth Street, where the interurban had dropped her, first down Seventh Avenue and then over to Sixth. She felt a little silly choosing this route, contrived as it was to dodge Soraida's shop and, of course, Soraida herself. But she preferred the feeling to a chance encounter with her aunt. That's why she avoided the shop and its surroundings whenever her work or errands or Yasmin's prenatal appointments brought her to the city. Yes, a little silly. And ineffectual, since the turn down Sixth immediately brought to mind Soraida's stories about window shopping—*sexteando*—with her parents, the ladino grandparents Isabel had never met, and her brother, Isabel's father. There was the Cine Lux, with its soaring cream walls, multistory windows and curved marquee. There were the obtrusive neon signs, mobile stalls, food carts, shoeshine boys, glue-sniffing street kids, curled into each other in the shelter of a stairwell—all the people and things Soraida had said polluted the avenue now. Well, they should clutter Sixth Avenue. They should intrude and make people like Soraida uncomfortable. This space was theirs as much as anybody's. Actually, Isabel would have liked to see them intrude on people with more power than Soraida, to see them choke the avenues of Zone 11, demolish its walls topped with barbed wire and broken glass. Wasn't that what she'd always wanted? For herself and for the dispossessed and despised majority. To survive. To resist. But not just to resist. To push back.

When she reached the covered arcade that led to the Portalito, she noticed a bronze plaque embedded in its checkerboard floor. Late afternoon light glowed from windows high in the building's lemon walls, casting its warmth on a blind man who sold lottery tickets beside a kiosk of cigarettes, Chicklets, and candies. She crouched to read, brushing her fingers over the worn raised letters. The plaque marked the assassination in 1978 of Oliverio Castañeda de León, the charismatic secretary general of the university student association. It was a story Isabel knew well: how Oliverio had helped win a subsidy for the city's transit users; how, despite the growing number of death threats against him, he'd joined in the annual march commemorating the Democratic Revolution of 1944. In a speech in front of the National Palace he'd told the crowd, "As long as there are people, there will be revolution." As he left the rally, a death squad gunned him down at this very spot. That's what pushing back got you—something Soraida would say.

Still crouching, Isabel glanced over her shoulder to Sixth Avenue, seething with pedestrians, countless pairs of feet treading this ground year after year, treading these corridors of death, and feeling what? What would the streets of Guatemala look like, she wondered, what would all those people feel underfoot if the names of every man, woman and child murdered by government forces were etched into a plaque embedded in the ground? On some street out there, her parents had died, gunned down like Oliverio. And people were dying still. In a single month in Eighteenth Street, "social cleansing" operators had killed three transvestites. Too many deaths to record. Too many names to memorialize. Isabel traced the raised letters with her finger, reciting silently the pseudonyms of compas they'd lost, in ambushes, in firefights, in accidents, the ones who might not have anybody else to remember them.

Max was nursing a mojito when she arrived, spine pressed against the chair back, legs extended under the small circular table, drink half-empty. Here and there other couples and small groups huddled around polished wooden tables crowded with large goblets of blonde beer. It was an ordinary bar, dingy and dark, and perhaps like any bar, it seemed to invite its patrons to leave outside its doors whatever they had not brought with them: people, places, time, responsibility. She kissed Max's cheek in greeting and sat, and when the waiter passed their table, caught his eye and ordered a Gallo.

"Supporting the Castillos?" Max said as the waiter delivered her beer. He plucked the sprig of mint from his drink and popped it in his mouth.

"And you, the Botráns?" She nodded at his drink. "The mix may be Cuban but the ingredients are one hundred percent reactionary Chapín."

Max chewed and swallowed. "Except for the mint. Mint belongs to the popular classes."

Isabel raised her glass. "I'm in need of something more than mint today," she said. "Here's to the oligarchy and their ability to keep us well drugged."

"Salud." He clinked his tumbler against her goblet. They both drank and returned their glasses to the table.

Max inched his chair closer and dropped his voice. "The Castillos are higher up the ladder though. You know we kidnapped one of them, a Castillo, one of the grown sons."

Isabel wiped the froth from her lip. Funny how talk turned so quickly to the war. When she was with anybody else—anybody who hadn't actively supported the revolutionaries—they didn't talk about the war at all. "Higher up the ladder," she said. "Worthy of kidnapping." She held up her palm to quiet him as the waiter approached.

When the waiter had left with their food order, Max said, "He told us we should have taken his father—he wasn't sure they'd pay up for *him*."

Isabel thought about that. Were those families really so heartless? It's what you expected of them. "Did they?" she asked.

Max nodded. "As far as I know they always paid—except when something went wrong, of course."

Isabel sipped her beer. She wanted to change the subject. Kidnapping was one of the worst tools in the guerrilla handbook, worse even than assassination. If she could have put a bullet into one of those generals, she wouldn't have hesitated. But executing a hostage? Because somebody refused to pay the ransom? Yet she knew they couldn't have financed the war without it. She knew, too, that the generals were just hired guns doing the oligarchy's bidding. Kidnappings—and the war taxes they'd exacted from landowners—were the guerrillas' way of making war on the real kings of the country, the true enemy. Too bad it hadn't been more effective. They'd drained them of millions, but they hadn't toppled one of them.

"How's Alejo doing?" she asked. "Have you heard from him?"

The waiter arrived with a plate of tostadas, each of them slathered with guacamole, tomato sauce or pureed black beans and sprinkled with dried cheese. He placed it on the table between them.

"Studying hard, enjoying those golden beaches," Max said. "I'm taking holidays in December to go see him." He reached for Isabel's hand. "I'm glad I'm getting to see you before I go."

Isabel was glad too. She felt unsettled—a night with Max always helped reel her back.

He asked about Yasmin.

"Large—but good. She's doing well at her schoolwork, and she seems to be really fitting in at the Foundation."

"It's not a bad place for a young person to be."

Isabel agreed. "Why don't you ever go there?" she asked.

Max shrugged. He was eating a tostada, trying to keep the broken bits from falling into his lap or onto the table. "I guess I'm more of a loner."

"I don't really like it there either, but I don't know why. Yasmin—she just fits right in and, really, she doesn't know the first thing about the organization, what it stands for, what it's done—any of it."

"Neither did we when we joined up. It was a leap of faith."

"A leap into the abyss."

He laughed. "That too."

"We had good reason. I know I did. We knew what we wanted."

"Maybe. But we didn't know where it would lead, what would be asked of us, what it would become. We certainly didn't know how long it would last."

Isabel frowned. "We thought victory was right around the corner."

"And now, looking back, can you say you're happy with what we accomplished?"

"No. I can't."

"But going back fifteen, twenty years, you'd make the same choices again?"

Isabel didn't answer.

"You would, Isabel. I know that much about you."

"There's no point even thinking about it, is there? Past is past."

"Then why are you out there with the forensic examiners, digging it up?"

Isabel hated to admit it, but she was drawn to those graves as though somebody or something were pulling her there by a wire planted deep in her sternum. "You're right. It's all I think about. Maybe that's why I feel so distant from Yasmin. Obviously, a baby at her age is not ideal. But like my grandmother used to say, only death has no solution. And a baby is *life*. So why am I still back with the dead, stuck in that—not *past* because it's not past. At least not to me. It's very, very present." She stopped to catch her breath, trying to remember how the conversation had started. "But Yasmin doesn't even want to know about it, and maybe she's right." Isabel's face was hot. She hadn't come to Max for this.

He squeezed her hand. "What I'm trying to say is that you know where you're going. You think you don't but you do. You don't waver. You'll never be like some of them, our own compas—dining with the generals one day, eating right from their hands. They will." He raised his glass. "They'll be singing the praises of Castillo and Botrán. They'll be running their sons and daughters as candidates. You'll see."

"You're just bitter because they won't pick you."

Max lowered his glass and looked away, his deaf ear turned toward her.

Isabel took his hand and kissed it. "I'm sorry. I'm the one who's bitter. Yasmin seems to be finding a kind of home and I'm begrudging her it."

"I'm glad you came to me. You can make your home right here tonight." He tapped his chest with both palms.

Isabel wanted to be there now. They finished their drinks and took a taxi to Max's. They found the bed without turning on the lights. Its creaking metal frame made her laugh; its mattress, despite the lumps, offered bliss and relief. They were as far away from the rest of the world as if they'd been in a jungle in the Ixcán.

In her dream, her father was chasing her round and round their patio in a game of tag. She ran on her little girl legs, pumping her arms twice as fast and squealing with a mixture of terror and delight whenever he got close. It was impossible, with his long legs, that her father hadn't nabbed her. Yet just when she thought he'd overtake her, he would trip, his outstretched hand missing her shoulder, and she'd tear away again shrieking with laughter.

Then her mother was calling them to supper. Her father reached her easily now, scooping her up in one smooth motion, though her legs were still kicking, her head thrown back, laughing, *no, no, no.*

"I'm going to eat you for dinner!" He buried his face in her stomach, pretending to chew, spinning her round, which only made her laugh harder, an endless carousel of laughter.

Isabel awoke, laughter still rumbling in her chest. Max was snoring beside her, the greying hairs of his abdomen shivering in the morning light. She pressed her nose to them, kissing his navel, and then got up. The bed shifted and groaned but Max slept on. Before she left, she bent to kiss him again but he looked so peaceful, haloed by the sunshine that leaked from the shuttered window, she decided not to disturb him. She watched a moment longer to see if he would stir. Then she let herself out.

A yellow pickup sat in the drive outside her home, where no car had parked before. Isabel saw it as soon as she turned off the road from the highway onto the one that led to her front door. Pickups were ubiquitous. It could have been anybody's. But after running her hand over the dusty tailgate and peering into the cab, its black upholstery unremarkable yet familiar, she guessed it was Quique's. Yasmin would be thrilled. Quique had no reason to drive the hour to their house unless it was to bring Soraida. With Yasmin's caesarean just a month away, the timing could not have been better. A sudden warmth filled Isabel, evaporating the resentments she'd harboured against her aunt. Yes, Soraida was a bit of a fossil. Isabel had known that from the start. But maybe *because* she was unchanging, her aunt had been their anchor. All those years of caring for Yasmin, no questions asked. Unspoken, and sometimes spoken, recrimination. But no questions. That was important. It's what they'd needed. Isabel slapped the truck's dented roof and smiled. She could bear the aggrieved looks, the mumbled complaints, the barely veiled disapproval, as long as she, Isabel, remained in charge. And she intended to remain in charge.

She sprinted for the front door—open, as it always was during daylight hours when somebody was home—but as she neared, something else occurred to her. She slowed before entering.

"Soraida?"

Quique stood in the middle of the room, his baseball cap in his hands, Yasmin at his side. Yasmin looked like she'd been crying. Isabel scanned the room.

"What is it?" she asked Quique. "Where's my aunt?"

Quique lowered his eyes, turning his cap.

"It's not Auntie," Yasmin said. "It's Byron."

CHAPTER 15

SORAIDA'S BACK WAS turned when the young man slipped into her shop like a late afternoon shadow, but whether from a tremor along the cement floor or some rearrangement of the air, she felt it and spun about. He'd ducked between the stands of clothing and was visible—visible if you were looking right at him—yet he didn't stir or make a sound, as if he hoped by doing so Soraida would forget he was squatting there behind her best-selling blue jeans. Like a very small child in a game of hide-and-seek.

"What do you think you're doing?" she said. "Come out from there."

The young man stayed where he was but shook his head violently and raised a finger to his lips, which Soraida now saw, were red with blood.

She heard a noise at the shop entrance. Several men were stumbling up the front step, panting and sweating. They were joined by others, men and women, some of them brandishing long, thick sticks, as the first arrivals poked their heads into the shop or craned to see farther up the street or in other directions.

"Did he come this way?" the first man to appear asked.

"Who are you talking about?" Soraida said.

"He's here. I saw him run in," a woman said, trying to squeeze to the front of the swelling crowd.

Soraida addressed them with all the command she could muster. "I don't know what you're talking about but if you come barging into my shop making a row, I'll get the police."

"He's a thief. He robbed Doña Estela."

"Burn him!" somebody cried from the back of the crowd.

The thought of her friend victimized chilled Soraida, but not as much as those two words did. "Then you'd better get after him and catch him," she said. "You probably saw him go round the corner here—up Sixth Avenue."

A few in the mob strained to see past Soraida into the shop.

"Well, hurry up if you're going to find him," she said as she shooed them down the step.

That was enough to convince the youngest and the most eager, and the rest soon followed. Soraida stood at the door, her heart pounding, waving her encouragement to any who happened to turn back. She dared not leave the doorway but feared the whole time the young man behind her would abandon his hiding place and plunge a knife in her back.

When the street had emptied and the other shopkeepers had returned indoors, Soraida, too, quit her post. She went to the stand where the young man squatted, his head fallen forward on his knees. She shook his shoulder, and he snapped awake, his eyes wide with fright, his face bloodied and swollen.

As Soraida was about to speak, he scrambled to his feet and pushed past her, lingering at the open door long enough to scour the street before he disappeared into its white light.

No explanation. No thank you. All he left behind were two bloody handprints where he'd gripped the wooden stand.

"It was so quick. I didn't even realize what'd happened," Estela said. She was fine, as Soraida had discovered after she'd closed her shop to race over and check. She was humming along as if nothing had happened. "I had the mobile phone out to make a call and he snatched it right out of my hand."

Estela added more water to the glue pot. She was putting the final touches to a series of pint-sized Mario piñatas. "Raúl's the one that went after him. They caught him before he could get lost in the market stalls, but he got away again."

"They would've killed him," Soraida said. "They were going to set him on fire."

"It wasn't that bad. They were teaching him a lesson."

"What can a dead man do with lessons?"

Estela set the glue bottle down and studied Soraida. "If that scum hasn't killed somebody already, you can be sure he will one day. We've got to protect ourselves. The police are useless, when they're not in on it themselves. I'm lucky I've got Raúl here. Who knows what would have happened if I was here alone." She broke off and spoke again, more softly this time. "Forgive me, Soraida. I forgot about your boy. We were very sorry to hear it." She shook her head. "But that's exactly why we've got to stick together."

There was no point in arguing. Perhaps Estela had not seen the thief's disfigured face, his broken hand. Perhaps if he hadn't come to Soraida and placed his life at her feet, she wouldn't have granted it any value either. Questions bred questions. It was better to let the thing lie. "I'm very glad you weren't hurt," she said. "It must have been quite a scare."

Estela brushed the glue along the edge of a piece of royal blue tissue paper. "I'll need a new mobile phone. They aren't cheap." She looked at Soraida. "And you need a new hire."

Soraida returned to her shop and resumed her day—as if nothing had happened. But something had happened. In an unguarded moment, she'd stepped over a line, and now, to her surprise, she found herself unwilling to step back. Her neighbours were not yet aware of it, but sooner or later they would be. She knew that about them.

The next day, responding to a knock at her metal door, Soraida uncovered its little window and looked out. Isabel and Yasmin stood there: matching faces, one younger, one older, leaning together, concern in their eyes. Soraida fumbled with the bolt and opened to her grandniece's enormous belly. Yasmin rushed to embrace her, burying her face in Soraida's chest. Isabel embraced them both.

"We came as soon as we heard," Isabel said. "Soraida, I'm so, so sorry."

Yasmin was crying, which got Soraida started as well. It was all too much. She struggled to control herself, straightened and beckoned them inside. Yasmin continued to clutch her as they walked down the corridor, Isabel following. "I've missed you so much, Auntie," she sobbed. Her darling girl.

When they were all seated at the kitchen table, Isabel spoke. "I'm sorry we didn't get here earlier. We only heard yesterday. We would have come to the funeral. We would have been with you, Soraida. He was a dear, dear boy."

Isabel fixed coffee and brought them each a cup. Yasmin sipped her drink without once releasing Soraida's hand. It was like that first night after Isabel's arrival, though so much had changed in the meantime. Soraida could hardly breathe for fear of shattering the moment, of blowing away the warmth their small group generated.

"What of the baby? How are you feeling?" She stroked Yasmin's cheek.

Isabel answered for her daughter. "She's been seeing the doctor regularly. He says everything's fine. They're planning a caesarean because she's so narrow."

Soraida winced at the thought of her grandniece's perfect brown skin pierced by a scalpel.

"The baby's fine. Everything's fine," Isabel repeated.

They planned to stay for a few days, they said, and Yasmin promised to help in the shop while she could. She'd graduated from third-year básico and was already investigating where she might continue her studies. It was admirable how hard she was working, but it would be even better, Isabel said, with her great-aunt back in her life. "Between the three of us, we can work it out. Are you willing, Soraida?"

Of course she was willing. They'd alighted like angels to lift her out of darkness, to comfort her and care for her. She wouldn't speak a word or make a gesture that would drive them away again. No she wouldn't.

Despite Yasmin's offer, on Wednesday it was Isabel who stayed behind to mind the shop while Soraida and Yasmin went for groceries. Though she never liked to be away from her shop for long, Soraida was grateful. She wanted to spend time with her grandniece, to hear everything she had to say. There was new colour in Yasmin's face, and the pregnancy had sucked the remaining baby fat from her features, giving her cheekbones and nose an edge they didn't have before. Her legs and arms, too, were lean and toned. But to Soraida, Yasmin still looked in every way a child. Though she fought to keep any note of shock or surprise from her face whenever she turned to her, she was flummoxed by what she saw. The girl's belly looked like a poorly made prosthetic. It didn't match the rest of the slim, tender body. And what about Yasmin on the inside? This new Yasmin who no longer kept a pair of earphones either strapped to her temples or circling her neck. That was what Soraida hoped to learn about on this errand. To learn whether she still knew this beautiful girl and then to wonder to what extent she had ever known her.

They took their time, Yasmin slowing to keep pace with Soraida, pausing every few steps to look around her. Taking in the sights like a tourist. They passed Estela's piñatas, bright-coloured figures bulging from beneath the shop awning. Half a block farther, Soraida stopped to greet the homeless couple—their names, she had learned, were

Samuel and Paty—and handed them each a roll filled with fresh cheese and wrapped in a paper serviette. Yasmin watched but said nothing as her great-aunt delivered the sandwiches.

"I'm a bit late today," Soraida said as the man and woman dug in, bobbing their heads in thanks as they chewed. "I've got my grandniece with me." In response to this, the man and woman pivoted their jaws and bobbed and chewed in Yasmin's direction. Delivering them a bit of food each morning before she opened had become part of Soraida's routine, a routine that in the last year had suffered so many disruptions and modifications—imposed or elected—she wondered whether the word *routine* any longer applied. Samuel and Paty seemed very happy to accept the food she brought them, but they clearly didn't depend on her. Sometimes they weren't even there when she dropped by. Their lives were governed by rhythms and mechanisms that were completely opaque to her as, no doubt, her life was to them. *To each his own* was what she would once have said. But now, instead of holding fast to old habits, she found she wanted to *respond* to the world around her, to somehow be in sync. But how to balance so many competing demands on her time? Should she, for instance, close the shop as she usually did on Wednesday afternoon and visit the shopkeepers along Eighteenth Street? Or should that time be dedicated to Yasmin and Isabel? Or to the shop? Soraida rebuked herself silently. Change was good. This change was good.

"That's different," Yasmin said as they left the couple behind and made their way toward the far end of the block.

"The sandwiches? Yes, I've been trying some new things," Soraida said. "Byron's death . . ." She couldn't say more, even now, more than two weeks since. Just the mention of his name stole the air from her lungs.

Yasmin put her arms around her and kissed her. "I'm sorry, Auntie."

Across the street, two transvestite streetwalkers chatted, turning their heads in tandem to follow a car that cruised by. Their sequined dresses, one green, one blue, sparkled under the late morning sun.

Yasmin had noticed them, too. "They're still there," she said, a small, sad smile on her lips.

"Do you know them?" Soraida asked. "Or did you?"

Yasmin looked at her toes and shook her head slightly. "Not really. Sort of. They'd say things to me when I went by. Friendly things. 'Hey, baby doll,' they'd say. Or 'That's the way. Stay in school.' I learned some of their names."

"Like Menche." The name, mentioned to her but once, had stuck with Soraida. She repeated it in her prayers.

"They killed her," Yasmin said.

"Who killed her?"

"Nobody knows, do they? Nobody cares."

"Some people do. There were marches."

"I thought you didn't believe in marches."

Soraida was quiet. She resisted the urge to check her watch.

"Auntie, to tell you the truth—and please don't tell Mami—I think that day, when they shot Menche, I think that's when I decided I didn't want to live in this place anymore."

Soraida was stunned. "In Eighteenth Street?"

"In Eighteenth Street, or Guatemala City, or Guatemala, I don't know. The whole world can't be like this."

Soraida didn't know what to say. She'd thought things were better now, that—despite the pregnancy—Yasmin had adjusted to her new home. Despite the pregnancy, she had accomplished so many things. That's what Isabel had said. That's what Yasmin herself had said.

"I don't understand. Where would you go? What about the baby? And the new boyfriend. Your mother says he's a very good lad. What about us?" She started walking. Better, perhaps, to put the transvestites behind them.

Yasmin took a final long look across the street—one of the transvestites had doubled over to rummage through a large black bag, silver bangles flashing at her wrists, tight-skirted bottom jutting out provocatively, as the other watched the road. Yasmin caught up to her great-aunt. "You're right. There's nowhere to go. This is it."

"Oh, sweetheart. You'll feel better once the baby comes. You'll have somewhere to direct all that love I know you've got stored up inside you. Believe me, once you start loving and caring for another human being, you'll stop dwelling on what you might be missing."

Yasmin didn't seem to be listening. She was scanning the stalls of the market, scrutinizing the sky. But she said, "Okay." And then she smiled. "I know I love my auntie and I'm glad to be back with you."

This time it was Soraida who circled her arms around her grandniece and hugged her. "The way it's supposed to be," she said.

Soraida and Isabel had just finished their midday dinner together, when Yasmin, who'd been watching the shop, showed Estela into the kitchen. Soraida rose from her seat and kissed Estela's cheek.

"I was about to start my rounds," she said, offering her friend a chair. "I hadn't forgotten you." She had forgotten, but no matter. She was distracted. It was understandable. And Estela had not forgotten.

"Relax," Estela said as she kissed Isabel, who had got to her feet as well when Estela entered. "I see you've got a good reason to stay home."

"Have you eaten?" Isabel asked. "Can I bring you a plate?"

Estela declined the invitation by raising her hand. "I can only stay a moment."

As Isabel gathered the used plates and cutlery to take to the courtyard to wash, Estela patted Soraida's hand. "Just what you needed, Soraida. Some extra help around here." She glanced toward the open door that led to the courtyard. "And Yasmin looks very well, too."

"As well as can be expected, I suppose," Soraida said. She tried when she spoke to others about Yasmin's condition not to show any shame or remorse, but it was difficult. Her predicament was as common as contraband, as common as corruption, as common as crime. But none of those were things you actually wished for.

"You mustn't worry," Estela said.

Soraida pulled her handkerchief from her apron pocket and wiped her hands and mouth. "I tell myself that every morning. I know it does no good to worry. But I can't help myself."

"Pray then."

Soraida stirred more sugar into her coffee.

"And how is your Raúl?"

"Very well. Very well indeed." Estela's eyes sparkled. "You know he's heading north again, so we can expand the business. And he wants to build me a house out in Alotenango."

"I'm so sorry—"

"No, Soraida. He's quite right to. I realize that now. It's the only way."

"But you'll miss him, I know."

"Of course, I will." Estela frowned slightly but puffed up her chest bravely. "But it really is the only way. He wants something better for us and I want what's best for him. The shop is his inheritance—it's his, really."

Soraida sipped her coffee. Alotenango was a long way from Eighteenth Street—not any better, although perhaps it could be. There were certainly many reasons to leave their neighbourhood. She herself had only stayed all these years because she had nowhere else to go.

Estela spoke again. "But that's not why I stopped by." She began to examine her hands, turning them over before folding them in her lap. She met Soraida's eyes. "There's been talk," she said.

Soraida's mind went first to Isabel and then to Yasmin, her unease growing as she waited for Estela to tell her what she'd heard. She was prepared to deny all of it, if necessary, and to defend whatever she could not deny.

"It's those people you're feeding," Estela said. "Our neighbours are concerned. You shouldn't be encouraging them."

Soraida was relieved. She chuckled. "What on earth am I encouraging?"

"You're giving them a reason to stay."

"But they've been here forever already."

"It'll attract more of them. Nobody wants people like that here."

Now Soraida was getting angry. "And what's it to you? You're leaving."

"I have my business to think about. Think what this place could be if we cleaned it up? If we could attract tourists. That's where the money is. Raúl thinks we can do it. He thinks the city would help. Everybody wants Guatemala to succeed right now. The U.N., the Gringos. There's money to be had if you know where to look for it."

Soraida stared. This was not the Estela she knew, the Estela who ignored politics and avoided newspapers, the Estela whose entire world, her aspirations, her dreams—as far as Soraida was aware—fit within the three or four blocks between Otto's tire repair shop and the contraband market. She lived for gossip, but for gossip that was as small and petty and fleeting as any single life in Eighteenth Street. Soraida didn't know what to say.

"Perhaps you think you're acting from your heart," Estela went on. "But you need to use your head. You've always had a good head"—she tapped her own head as she said it—"and a good nose, too, for business. You know I'm right."

Soraida cheeks were burning. She hoped Estela didn't see. And suddenly she felt very tired. She didn't feel like explaining why it was that Samuel and Paty had suddenly become for her the most important people in the neighbourhood. Why she would go on bringing them food, whatever her neighbours said or thought. Why she felt no compunction about telling her neighbours whatever they wanted to hear. She had learned it was actually very easy to say one thing and do another.

"I'll think about it," she said.

Estela rose from her chair, and so did Soraida. They kissed each other's cheeks before parting. At the open door, Estela looked back.

"We're counting on you," she said.

CHAPTER 16

TWO WEEKS BEFORE the scheduled caesarean, Isabel and Yasmin moved back into the room they'd shared in Soraida's house.

"For three weeks, maybe a month," Isabel told her aunt. "It shouldn't be more than that."

Isabel wanted Yasmin to be close to the hospital in case the baby came early. She'd also taken time off work so that, in an emergency, she'd be available.

"If she wasn't so young, I'd have got a midwife," she said to Soraida as they sorted through the mound of outfits for newborns her aunt had been setting aside from her stock for months. "But the doctors seem to think this is best."

Soraida grunted, nodded and then shook her head before gathering up the outfits Isabel had rejected and returning them to one of the wooden stands. An appropriate response, Isabel thought. Motherhood was risky, especially at Yasmin's age.

"What about a nightie or a housecoat?" she asked. "Do you have any?"

Soraida showed her where to look and helped her find slippers, too. They still had to buy cloth diapers and baby wipes and sanitary pads for the hospital stay, and then it was simply a matter of waiting. "I hope Yasmin brought her toothbrush," Isabel said.

Yasmin sat out most of these preparations. Isabel was glad to do them for her daughter—they were just the distraction she needed, and they were a simple way of showing Yasmin how much she cared. But she was concerned. Yasmin had become very quiet lately, moving from room to room with barely a sound. Isabel didn't know how to reach and reassure her.

"Anybody home?" Danilo appeared at the shop entrance, stopping to finish his cigarette before crossing the shop floor to kiss Soraida's cheek and then Isabel's. It was odd to see him. He'd never dropped by before.

"I was running errands and thought I'd see how you were doing," he said. "Thought maybe I could lend a hand . . . or at least say hi."

Isabel looked around the shop. "There's really not much to do. We're all just waiting."

Danilo smiled. "How is Yasmin?"

"She's napping, I think. I can call her."

"No, let her rest. I'm sure she needs it."

"Can I offer you a coffee?" Soraida asked.

"Again no, but thank you." He turned to Isabel. "I was wondering if I could speak with you a moment."

"I can leave," Soraida offered without masking her disapproval.

"I didn't come to put you out, Doña Soraida," Danilo said. "Isabel, come for a walk with me. I need to buy cigarettes."

She went with him. Something was up. Something important enough to bring Danilo to a part of town he had no reason to visit. He got his cigarettes, and they walked along Eighteenth Street as he lit up and smoked and scanned the street, the sidewalk, the passing stalls and shops. When they reached the final block, they stopped to look out over the broken tin shacks and steaming open sewers of La Limonada. The last time they'd come here was to fetch Yasmin home.

"I found an address for Luís," Danilo said. "In the United States."

With everything that had been happening, Isabel had forgotten she'd asked Danilo to help track down Yasmin's father. His news made her wish she hadn't. There would never be a perfect time, but this time, this tender time before Yasmin's baby was due, this time when Yasmin needed her mother before anybody else—Isabel didn't want to share it with a ghost from her past, a ghost she feared might spirit Yasmin away to a future that didn't include her. She turned away from him. "God, Danilo, why are you telling me this now?"

A trip of goats was crossing Eighteenth Street, a boy of eleven or twelve following them, flicking their heels with a string that dangled from a long stick he held in one hand. A bell at the neck of the lead goat jangled. Heavy udders swayed between the animals' hind legs. Isabel watched as they reached the other side and a woman brought the boy an empty glass. He took it and kneeled by one animal, grabbed a tit and squirted warm frothy milk into it. The woman paid him and he continued on his way, urging the animals along with a high-pitched wordless call.

Isabel faced Danilo. "I suppose I've got to tell her," she said.

Danilo shot his cigarette into the ravine and lay one hand on Isabel's shoulder. "The sooner, the better. You want it to come from you, don't you?"

On her return to Soraida's, she and Danilo having parted before they reached the shop, Isabel found Élida and Yasmin sitting together on Yasmin's bed. Élida's daughter, baby Soraida, lay on her back between them, kicking her chubby legs in the air. Despite the heat, the baby was warmly dressed, knitted tights and sweater, a knitted cap on her head. A single strand of red yarn circled her tiny wrist. "To guard against the evil eye," Élida explained when Yasmin asked. Isabel watched from the doorway as Élida showed Yasmin how to change her. After setting out her supplies, she removed the baby's tights and the soiled diaper and tucked them away in her bag. Then she gripped little Soraida's heels and lifted, so that the baby's bottom lifted too, and arranged the clean diaper, a thin yellow cloth, beneath her.

"I'm sure Doña Soraida has you eating well," Élida said, one hand firmly on the child's chest as she folded the diaper down, slipped it between the gyrating legs and arranged it over the round belly. "No hot foods. You have to cool your stomach. Fish is good. Green mangoes, too. Everything that's cold, but not too cold of course."

Isabel smiled. A pregnant woman's body was hot and powerful, but like anything in life, it needed balance. So the recommendation was to eat cold foods—not cold on the tongue: they were foods that would chill you inside if you ate too many.

Élida reached for the faja—what in Kaqchikel they called a *pas*—a narrow cloth belt she wound twice around the diaper at her daughter's middle before she tied it off. "The faja is better than pins because there's no danger of pricking the baby," Élida said. So many things to remember as a mother-to-be. Through it all, Yasmin watched intently. And Isabel watched Yasmin.

Élida held up her wide green rebozo—*peraj* in Kaqchikel—wrapped it around her waist and shoulder and then around baby Soraida, who gasped and gurgled as Élida adjusted the cloth so that Soraida sat snugly against her mother's chest. "See. No hands." Élida lifted both arms above her head. Her daughter followed the movement with her eyes, reached out her dimpled hands, and squealed with laughter.

Yasmin tugged gently at the child's stocking-covered toes, which made her squeal even harder. Despite herself, Yasmin laughed too. "Wouldn't a stroller be easier?" she asked.

Élida shook her head. "The rebozo is safer and your baby will be happier next to your body." She leaned forward and back, turned one way, then the other. Baby Soraida was certainly secure. "Strollers are no good, on the street, on the bus, climbing up and down. And if somebody decides to steal your baby, you've just made it much easier for them."

Yasmin's eyes turned to her mother.

"The less you have to carry the better," Isabel said, taking Yasmin's hand. "Élida, your daughter is lovely."

Élida looked pleased. Perhaps it was the first time she'd had the chance to share her new mother wisdom. Though Yasmin looked a little taken aback by so many instructions, it was good for her to see another first-time mother managing so well. When Yasmin was born, Isabel had relied on the women around her, too. Unlike other combatants who became pregnant, she'd decided not to leave their mountain refuge when the time came. After the massacre of her village, there was nowhere, outside the guerrilla camp, she felt so safe or at home. They brought in a compa, a midwife before she'd joined up, who massaged and bathed Isabel and stayed with her through the long labour. When Yasmin was born healthy and without complication, the whole camp celebrated as Isabel and baby Yasmin slept.

That night in Soraida's house, mother and daughter lay next to each other again, in their twin beds in the room they shared. Isabel had thought Yasmin was already asleep, but then she spoke. "What if I can't do it?" she said. "What if . . . I don't know if I can do it."

Isabel turned toward her. "You can do it. You can." She propped herself on one elbow.

Yasmin was staring at the ceiling, her hands pressed against the mound, covered in bedsheets, that was her belly.

"Think of all the women, since the beginning of time, all those women who've given birth," Isabel said. "Lots of them young like you. Lots of them not as well off. They all had a first time, and they were probably scared." She lay back against her pillow. "I was, when I had you. But I thought about the women around me, the women who came before me, and I thought, if all those millions and millions of women across the world can do this, I can do this."

Yasmin turned to her now. "Okay," she said. "That helps a little."

Isabel and Soraida sat outside San Juan de Dios hospital waiting for news. The nurse had told them they must not even ask before two hours had passed. Relatives of patients were not allowed in without authorization from the faceless administrators inside the hospital's cold grey walls.

"It's inhuman," Isabel said. They weren't the only ones crowded outside the hospital doors. Anxious women and men hung about; a few had camped out for the duration. There were a couple of carts selling chuchitos and enchiladas, another offering runt-sized hotdogs. Soraida was very quiet.

"She'll be fine," Isabel said, hoping that saying the words would make it so. "She's very healthy. The baby, too."

"She's just a little girl," Soraida said.

Isabel didn't want to think about how little Yasmin was or to think of her alone in that old and threatening place. She had to believe it would come out right. She put her arm around her aunt. "I'll see if there's any news."

The woman at reception frowned at her. "You must wait until the doctors send for you."

"Can't you check?"

"There's nobody to check with. They'll call you when there's news."

"I don't know why I can't go in. I'm her mother."

"Do you think you're the only mother here? The doctors have their job to do. You would only get in the way."

Isabel returned to where Soraida sat on the curb. "Do you think Yasmin told Víctor not to come?"

"It doesn't matter to me what Víctor does," Soraida muttered.

Isabel smiled. "So you're not still fixed on getting them married?"

"I'd like to wring his neck. And I have half a mind to send Yasmin to a convent."

Isabel laughed. It was good to be on the same side as her aunt for once. "She'll be all right," she said again.

Four hours after they'd arrived and handed Yasmin off to the nurses with her nightie, her sanitary pads and her toothbrush, the receptionist called Isabel's surname.

"Congratulations," she said. "It's a boy." She handed Isabel a slip of paper. "Second floor at the end of the hall."

Yasmin was asleep in a bed in the middle of a row in the middle of a large ward. Isabel observed her daughter, her round face relaxed in a deep, drugged sleep.

"The babies are this way," Soraida said, leading her to the glass window at the end of the ward. At one end of the back row was "Barrios boy."

"Oh, my little treasure," Soraida said.

The tiny face was a ruddy pink, his eyes closed, his pinch of a chin trembling every few seconds, a white cap on his head. He was swaddled in a blue receiving blanket.

Isabel whispered, "I would never have thought it possible."

"A miracle, indeed," Soraida said, wiping away a tear. "I'd forgotten how tiny they are."

Isabel watched her grandson's delicate lips open and close, his nose wrinkle. So fragile, though he must have drawn on formidable forces to have made it this far. He was creation's gift to them—to Yasmin, to Soraida and to Isabel herself. Another chance to get it right. Yet he didn't belong to them. It was their duty to protect him and care for him and love him, but his life was his own. She knew they had no right to burden him with their desires, with their hopes and dreams.

They returned to sit with Yasmin until she awoke, which she did an hour later, groggy and sore.

"Is it over?" she asked when she finally understood where she was.

"Oh, I think it's just beginning," Soraida said.

Isabel couldn't have said it better herself.

When it was time for Isabel and Soraida to leave, Isabel asked her aunt to give her a moment with Yasmin alone. After Soraida had walked the length of the ward and pushed her way through the heavy, swinging doors marked *Exit*, Isabel slipped her daughter a scrap of folded paper. "Your father's address. Danilo tracked it down. He's in Los Angeles, he's got a wife, and you've got some half-brothers and -sisters." Isabel tried to smile as she delivered the news. Grief—for what, she didn't know—was flooding her body. "Danilo says your father would love to hear from you, and to send a picture." She forced another smile.

Yasmin held the square of paper, her eyes fixed on it, neither a smile nor a frown on her lips.

"You okay?" Isabel asked.

Yasmin nodded. "I'm going to write. I'm going to send him a picture of Leo."

"Leo? That's what you've decided on?"

Yasmin nodded again.

It wasn't a family name. It wasn't even a name Isabel had heard Yasmin mention. She realized once again there was a world of things she didn't know about her daughter and probably never would. But then, Yasmin didn't belong to Isabel any more than Leo did. Her path was her own. It was time Isabel accepted that.

The plaza was already dark, lit only by hundreds of candles held by the hundreds of people collected there. They faced the National Palace—the seat of government—waiting to see what would happen. Despite their numbers, the place felt quiet. Somebody to Isabel's left was saying the president was there among the crowd milling through the square. Isabel wondered where the URNG commanders were. She'd left Yasmin sleeping with her newborn son, Soraida watching over her, to come here. The date was December 29, 1997, the first anniversary of the peace.

Nearby flickered the eternal flame lit at the signing of the armistice the year before, and all around her spectators were passing out slender white candles, one to another, and lighting them. This was a celebration, so why did it look more like a vigil? Isabel took a candle from the man next to her, lit it from his own, and held it out before her. Its light illuminated her hand and the heads of the people right in front of her, but beyond that she couldn't see. Danilo and Claudia and the rest of them were probably here somewhere, and she might run into them yet. The person she really wanted to share this moment with, however—more than with Soraida or Yasmin or even her brand-new grandson—was Max. But Max was still in Cuba. Maybe he wouldn't have wanted to come. Or maybe he would have. As Max sometimes said, the company made all the difference.

A fireworks display started: red, green, white and blue starbursts lighting the sky above their heads. Following each, a delayed boom shook the plaza. The first started Isabel's heart pounding, but with the second and the third, the colours, the rapt faces turned skyward, she relaxed. They were at peace. For twelve months, they'd kept the peace. And peace was better than war. Nobody disputed that. What Isabel could not figure, however, was the cost of getting them this far. So much sacrifice, so little gain. And the people responsible for it all—for the massacres, the tortures, the disappearances—were there in the palace, celebrating this peace, while they were all outside in the dark.

As the display ended, the air thick with the smell of gunpowder, Isabel closed her eyes and listened to the cathedral bells, which had not ceased their tolling. She didn't know what they were counting.

PART III

ya' (water)

CHAPTER 17

SORAIDA WENT TO the presentation alone. She didn't even invite Quique. Despite the public forum, she approached it as an intimate act. Like communion. Or confession. Like coming face to face with your maker. At any rate, she didn't want anybody to distract her or get in the way of whatever it was she was going to see or hear or feel once she passed through those large oaken doors. Almost a year had passed since she'd given her testimony and she was nervous, but hopeful too. Hopeful that something good would come of this. She crossed the cathedral's threshold, worried now she might see one or another of Isabel's friends in the audience (Isabel herself was away working), but the people crowded under the high vaulted ceiling were so many, it wouldn't have mattered. There were men in suits, women in their church-going finery, reporters, Indigenous men and women in traditional dress, their children scattered around them like loose beads. Noticeably absent was anybody in uniform. The country's yellow-haired president had also declined to put in an appearance. This was not, after, all, the official Truth Commission. Soraida, being older than many of those in attendance, was soon offered space in a pew near the back. The light was dim, the glow of candles bringing slight warmth to the cold stone walls.

Bishop Juan Gerardi opened the ceremony. Dressed in a slate-blue suit, a clerical collar circling his neck, he rested his large hands on the wooden lectern and spoke of the atrocities committed: kidnappings, torture, rape, tens of thousands of disappearances, hundreds of massacres, hundreds of Mayan villages burned to the ground. He spoke of the old people and children and pregnant women who had died. The perpetrators of these crimes, as identified by witnesses, had been named in the report he was presenting, something the official Truth Commission would not do. He spoke slowly, clearly, words chosen and given with care. His deep voice filled the sanctuary. Forgiveness could not be granted, he said, unless it was asked for and asking for forgiveness required an admission of guilt. So far, nobody had admitted any such thing. But the victims had spoken. They had broken their silence, given a name to what they'd seen, what they'd suffered, what that suffering had cost them, what it cost them still. The bishop's voice didn't waver. His hands lay motionless upon the lectern.

Everything he said had been said before. Soraida had heard similar things from REMHI workers, and she'd heard people speak this way in interviews on the news. She'd read the same sentiments in the paper in the opinions of the more daring columnists. The difference today was that *he* was saying it, and he was saying it here, in this cathedral, backed by months of research and investigation and surrounded by people who, like herself, had lost loved ones or had witnessed war crimes and had decided, loosening the decades-long stranglehold of fear, to speak out. The faces around her shone with sorrow and anger and pride and triumph. Nowhere did she see fear, not even in the frailest of old women who sat in their pews, sheltering the flames of their votive candles with bony hands. Whether from their own conviction or because they believed in the bishop, they'd all gathered here, publicly, and they were strong. Their numbers, their truth, made them strong. Soraida, too, had spoken out. She'd taken that first step and now she would take the second. She would show Isabel the church's report. She would show her where her parents' names appeared in the list of victims. Not forgotten. Not unmourned. That was the other reason Soraida had come tonight—to collect her copy of REMHI's four thick volumes.

Gerardi turned the proceedings over to another, younger man in a dark suit and a red tie. The old bishop stood now in shadow, a tower of a man, as solid as a church pillar. Soraida had never met him and knew only a little of his reputation. He had spearheaded this project against the advice of many within and without the church hierarchy. She had followed it in the newspapers, columnists from the political left and right battling it out in words. Some of what they wrote frightened her, but she felt comforted now—by the bishop's calm, his quiet authority, by this old cathedral, its size, its grandeur. It had been on this spot for more than one hundred years. Sanctioned by the church. Sanctioned by God. For the first time in months, Soraida felt she'd done something that was absolutely right, something she was completely sure of.

But when she stepped from the cathedral's soft candlelight into the night, barely fallen, the black street loomed again as a threat, its shadows hiding unknown dangers. Head bowed, she broke from the stream of people draining from the sanctuary to scurry past the decrepit men who loitered by the cars parked along the street—paid by motorists to guard their property, paid by the army, so it was said, to pass along any inkling of subversion. She found Don Julio's cab exactly where he'd said it would be, not ten metres from the cathedral door, and without looking back, she yanked the car door open and scrambled inside. Shut it. Locked it. Rolled the open window up as high as it would go. As Don Julio pulled away, she rubbed her stomach, her arms, which felt suddenly tight and sore and cold. The wind from the gap in the window whipped her cheeks as they sped through the dark city.

The forensic team had invited Isabel to Cuarto Pueblo, in the Ixcán, to attend the reburial of villagers unearthed the year before from a mass grave. The timing of the ceremony, organized in part by the Catholic Church, was to coincide with the presentation in the capital of the church's much-anticipated report on war crimes. It was the first such ceremony the team had been involved in, and although Isabel would not be working—most of the victims were Ixil, Q'eqchi' or Mam—they wanted her to be there with them.

They flew in a small plane to the flat heart of the jungle, a spot first cut open by settlers and then enlarged by the army. The one road that led there from a town north of the capital was washed out most of the year. There'd never been telephones or electricity. And after the army offensive fifteen years ago, there'd been nothing left at all. No houses, no animals, no crops. Even the birds had all but disappeared. Survivors had taken shelter in the jungle or escaped to Mexico. Some had, like Isabel, only returned home recently.

As the plane crossed the last of the highlands' volcanic ranges, a green sea of treetops stretched before them. Isabel, who'd spent many years and still spent her dreams wandering among the Ixcán's magnificent strangler figs and ceibas, had never seen it from this angle. She'd arrived eighteen years ago on foot and left the same way, days of walking without meeting a soul who wasn't part of her guerrilla unit. After landing on the packed-earth airstrip, they disembarked one by one into the thick, humid air and proceeded under a hazy sun to the pickup that would take them to the exhumation site.

At what had once been Cuarto Pueblo's market square, Isabel and the forensic team unloaded again. It was a large barren patch between cornfields. Nothing marked this place that had hidden the charred remains of so many people, except that it was empty. Journalists, church representatives, victims groups from other parts of the country and U.N. observers waited on its periphery for the ceremony to begin. Behind them, at a distance that suggested either idle curiosity or contempt, stood a row of men, dressed—like most of the campesinos of the region—in straw hats, plaid shirts and rubber boots. "Patrollers," one of the anthropologists said to Isabel, though she had guessed as much. They were locals who had participated, by force or willingly, in army-sponsored militias, and they opposed the exhumation and the ceremony that was about to take place. Today, however, they were outnumbered.

A man in the traditional red woolen jacket of his village walked to the square's centre and gave a greeting in Ixil and then in Spanish, thanking the Heart of the Sky and the Heart of the Earth for this opportunity to lay to rest the people killed there and to bring some peace to the survivors. The oldest, he said, had been eighty-two when he died; the youngest, an infant of two months. Then the man read the names of the victims, all three hundred and twenty-five of them. As he spoke, a spiritual guide lay out a circle of pine needles and yellow petals over the hard earth and prepared a fire at its centre. At each of the cardinal directions, he planted a candle: red, black, yellow, white. The four colours of corn. Copal incense wafted over the crowd.

Isabel tried her best to focus on each name as the Ixil man pronounced it, to imagine who she or he was, who they might have become had they been allowed to live. But soon, her mind foggy with incense, the names glided one into the next, an endless chain of vowels and consonants that wound through her like a magic spell. She could almost feel the surrounding jungle inhaling and exhaling, the heat and moisture of its breath a caress on her skin. From somewhere, she heard the reedy whine of a chirimía, the thudding of drums and tinny jingle of leg bells. She saw again the festivals of her childhood, magnificent dancers who spun and stamped in bright costumes adorned with silver piping and silken ribbons, their faces hidden by painted wooden masks. Pink-faced Pedro de Alvarado, the Spanish conquistador, battling against the doomed leader Tecún in a slow dance that lasted three days. Kaqchikels re-enacting their own defeat by the bearded strangers, year after year after year for five hundred years. Isabel blinked. The Ixil man was still reciting. The smell of resin was sharp in her nostrils. Would the cruel history they were commemorating today—the razing of Cuarto Pueblo, of Tzalbal, of Sacalá, of her own village—be recorded this way? In the steps of their dances? In the stitches of their clothing?

After the last of the names was read, a group of men and boys lifted the mahogany boxes that held the victims' broken bones. One balanced a coffin on his shoulder, another used a tumpline against his forehead to place the box across his back. Isabel counted. There were twelve caskets in all and forty-four plastic bags of human ash. Behind the pallbearers, relatives cradled large wooden crosses, each marked with a name, one for each of their dead. The pallbearers led the way, trudging along a trail between two rows of green corn that soon opened into a field where the cemetery was located. Nobody spoke as they walked along. Isabel kept her eyes on the uneven path, her mind a grey blank. Inside the cemetery fence, they stopped at a high wall of empty niches, freshly painted light blue. The bereaved families lay their crosses one by one before the tomb. One woman set down five.

Isabel thought of Yasmin and Leo, safe at home, sheltered from these painful events, as they should be. Yet part of her wished they were here with her. Among the mourners, many a woman carried a baby on her back, a child on her hip. At one woman's feet, three small boys drove little metal cars around in the dust. For these Mayan families, for her Mayan family, too—from the tiniest babe to the most ancient among them—there'd been no shelter, nowhere to turn, nowhere to hide. And now they grieved together, openly, for the first time.

Two days later, when Soraida raised the overhead door of her shop in preparation for another workday, she felt the change. Everybody was moving about, as busy as they always were, but they seemed to lean together, to huddle, to hunch, as if they had turned back upon themselves, the candor that usually characterized the street gone. The racket at half-volume.

Estela stepped from her piñata shop and Soraida waved to her, turning her palm up in a question. *What's up?* Estela glanced at her doorway as if she wished she had never ventured through it, but then she closed her door and walked briskly to where Soraida waited on her shop step.

"What is it? What's going on?" Soraida asked.

Estela pushed her back indoors, whispering fiercely. "They killed him. They killed Monsignor."

Soraida went cold.

"Last night," Estela sputtered, lifting the crucifix at her throat and kissing it. "God help us, they're already making up stories about what happened—they have no shame—but you *know* why they did this."

Soraida recoiled. "Why would I know?"

"A bishop? God rest his soul. They've *never* touched a bishop. This is what happens when you put your nose where it doesn't belong. If they can do that to a bishop, just imagine. Soraida, they smashed his face in with a piece of cement." Estela wiped her face with her apron and prattled on, repeating herself, crossing herself, issuing warnings and prohibitions she and Soraida and everybody must heed until she was finally out of breath.

Soraida barely heard her. She couldn't move. She couldn't say a word. She wanted to close the shop, reverse the day, crawl back into bed and start over. Crawl back in and never come out. What was the world coming to? Was no one safe? She thought of the four volumes of the REMHI report that sat under her bed. What had she done? Should she burn them? Would they come after her, too? Her face grew hot with shame. If she'd been Yasmin's age maybe she would just run away. But what did running away solve when you took all your cares with you?

"I had no idea," she said at last to Estela. She thought for a moment. "We should pray for his soul and for the people he was defending. We could go to the cathedral."

Estela looked at her in horror.

"No, of course not," Soraida said. "What was I thinking?"

Sympathy returned to Estela's face. "It's the shock," she said. "Of course I'll pray for him, but at home. And that's where you should be, too. This has nothing to do with us."

The same words Soraida had uttered more than once. But didn't it? Soraida dared not ask the question. Yet it nagged at her as she watched Estela hurry home to her piñatas and as she lowered and locked the overhead door she had just raised. She returned to her room, kicked off her slip-on flats, undid her apron, pulled off her dress and, still in her slip, climbed into bed. She didn't want to talk to or see anybody. But she couldn't sleep and the longer she lay there, the more she thought about the books that lay right beneath her. *They smashed his face in with a piece of cement.* Soraida's whole body ached. She turned on her side and hugged her pillow to ease the pain but it was no use. So she sat up and got dressed again and tried to think of a chore that would keep her busy.

She left her room and wandered across the courtyard, head down to protect herself from the blast of sunshine overhead, and into her shop. The clothes sat stacked neatly, exactly as she had left them the night before. The air was cool. She stood there in the dim light, letting the chill of the cement floor rise through the soles of her feet, the icy aura of the cement walls surround her, numb her. The muffled fray of voices and vehicles intruded from the street, as if she herself were locked in a tomb while life continued outside. She rubbed her arms, but the skin was tender. The sounds stung but there was no blocking them out. Soraida listened. Somebody was arguing with another whose voice she couldn't hear. Somewhere else, further along the street, were shouts and laughter—a game of soccer or marbles or spinning tops? Children laughing and playing. As they still did. As they always would. The roar of an airplane shook the shop walls. So many sounds.

She thought of her brother. Had he been afraid when he'd come with his wife to see her? Had he known the danger they were in? Had he come anyway, out of love for her? Monsignor Gerardi must have known the risks. Maybe he'd thought his status would protect him. Maybe he thought the war was over. But maybe he knew and had forged ahead anyway, for the sake of his flock, his holy children.

She trudged back to her room, her body heavy with sorrow, leaned down with effort and slid the box that contained the REMHI report from under her bed. *Never Again* was the title. She picked up one of the fat volumes and leafed through it: graphs and tables enumerated the atrocities, a lengthy chapter provided historical context, and then the words of witnesses and victims sought to communicate what words could never fully capture. In print. For all the world to see. No one could erase it, even if they somehow managed to buy up all the copies and burn them. Soraida had planned to show the report to Isabel. To show her what she had told REMHI about Isabel's parents, so that Isabel would know who her father was, what he had fought for and why he had died. So that Isabel could tell Yasmin and Yasmin could tell Leo. So that Hugo would not be forgotten. But Soraida was afraid. She put the book back under her bed and left her room. And as on so many occasions when she knew she must go on, but was unsure which direction to take, she opened her shop.

Isabel heard the news of Monsignor Gerardi's murder on the radio the day after her return from Cuarto Pueblo. She was washing the dishes Yasmin had left in the backyard sink, little Leo asleep in a basket at her feet. She heard the news. She took it in, and as she did the blood left her. Lightheaded and dizzy, she sank to the ground beside Leo and remained there until Yasmin came rushing from wherever she'd been, shouting for her, opening and closing doors, and finally found her.

Yasmin had talked and talked, desperate, breathless, but Isabel could make none of it out. An impenetrable fog surrounded her. The only thing she was aware of was her breath moving in and out. Eventually, Yasmin stopped talking and began to cry, which brought Isabel to. Just. With her daughter's help, she got herself up and as far as the couch they'd finally installed in the living room. She managed to formulate a few words, enough to explain to Yasmin that she wasn't dying. But she needed time. Time and quiet and laurel tea. She slept, for how long she didn't know. Days, possibly. A deep, dreamless sleep. Now and then, Yasmin shook her awake and tried to feed her, but she could only keep her eyes open for a moment or two before she slipped back into an easy oblivion. She knew Yasmin was worried, but she didn't care. No. She did care, somewhere deep inside, but the energy it would take to express it, to squeeze that caring from her innermost self so that Yasmin would feel it was, quite suddenly, beyond her.

"Mami, the funeral's on the news," Yasmin called to her from somewhere in the house.

Isabel opened one eye. Lifted her head. She was facing the couch back. She rolled over, the upholstery scratchy against her skin, and searched the room. An empty mug sat on the floor beside the couch. She couldn't remember how it had got there or whether it had been empty when it arrived.

"Come on. You'll want to see it," Yasmin said as she entered the room, Leo in her arms, and turned on the television. She sat on the couch, nudging herself into the curl of her mother's waist, and put Leo to her breast.

Isabel closed her eyes again. Her eyes hurt. Her body hurt.

"Look at all the people!" Yasmin said.

Isabel squinted at the TV. The warmth of Yasmin's body against her own awoke something in her, a memory, a reassurance. She propped herself on one elbow so she could see what her daughter was talking about.

The enormous plaza in front of the cathedral filled the screen. It was teeming with people. A rainbow quivered faintly over one end of the growing crowd. For two days, the commentator said, mourners had filed in and out of the majestic building, paying their respects at the bishop's coffin, which lay before the altar.

The camera scanned the multitude: a group of novices, dressed in plain blue dresses, black kerchiefs covering their hair, heads bowed;

people weeping openly; others shaking their heads. Some were singing songs from the campesino mass. There were campesinos, too—Indigenous farm workers in their rubber boots and straw hats, women in leather sandals or bare feet, children in the bright weaves of their villages. There were middle-aged and older ladinos and even a few dark-suited businessmen, their auburn- and golden-haired wives and daughters at their sides, teetering on their pumps, clutching leather purses at their waists. You could go your whole life without seeing a daughter or son of the bourgeoisie on the streets of downtown Guatemala City. Yet there they were.

Now and then somebody shouted "Never again!"—the title of the REMHI report—and others echoed the refrain. The crowd stirred. The funeral procession had begun. A double row of prelates in white robes led the way, followed by a young man holding an embroidered banner of purple and gold. Then came the coffin, carried by six clerics. Soon others took over, shouldering the polished wooden casket through the crowd as a group of musicians sang a corrido written in the bishop's honour: "I'm going to tell you the story, brothers and sisters, of a good shepherd . . ."

They circled the plaza, and then, with the television cameras still rolling, went on to Gerardi's parish church—the scene of his murder—and back up another street to the cathedral crypt where his body would be laid to rest. Gerardi's coffin floated in the middle of the television screen, hands from the crowd reaching out to it, people from the crowd relieving the pallbearers and steering it forward. All the while the corrido played, the throng of mourners joining in on the chorus:

Guatemalans, proud of Gerardi,
For truth and for peace
Guatemala never again.

CHAPTER 18

ISABEL IS STRUGGLING up the mountainside, her arms wrapped around the infant at her breast, trying to get away from the men in green who are scaling the slope in columns. Tree branches slap her face as she climbs, their burning scent filling her nostrils. As she advances, they seem to close in on her. Like green men on all sides of her. She increases her pace, holding tight to her daughter. Then the trees themselves are moving. Isabel calls for help but the sound cannot escape her throat. She kicks and pushes with her shoulders and breaks through the branches. On. On. She pushes forward, but the earth at her feet is crumbling, her feet are sinking into it, and the smell, pine mixed with dirt, is everywhere. She hunches over her daughter, trying to preserve a pocket of air around her as the mountain caves in on itself.

Suddenly she is on a trail she recognizes, a dusty footpath that winds past small copses of stunted oak trees and terraced fields aglow with green corn. The green tree-men have vanished. The only mountain in sight is a grey triangle rising from the horizon. She follows the trail eagerly, admiring the blue flowers that dot its borders. Longing and memory are her guide. Blue flowers, blue sky. Green corn. Green for as far as the eye can see. She doesn't question why she is on this path and she dares not ask why she is alone. Or perhaps not alone: something keeps pace with her, something she cannot see. Her fears are gathering. She wipes her face and shakes her head to clear it. The path is right there in front of her. There is no mistaking the direction. No more looking around. She just has to follow it.

Soon the silhouette of a tiny hamlet grows from a brown speck among the cultivated hills. A chalum tree stands like a sentinel at the entrance, its long bean pods rustling gently in the breeze. She approaches, as if to seek permission, searching its branches, which begin to moan and bend. Is it the branches moaning? She lowers her eyes to search the village, but it has disappeared. In its place blazes a dazzling white plain. Isabel's heart lurches. She shields her eyes, but too late. Her eyes burn. Her heart pounds. She struggles to breathe. The thumping within her chest threatens to break her open. The moans have turned to screams that seem to suck her heart from her. One scream. Hers.

Isabel held little Leo in her arms, rocking him and cooing. They'd just got back from his four-month checkup. The doctor, Isabel's boss's brother-in-law, had given him his shot, a prick in the thigh that prompted a few quick tears, then weighed and measured him, rotated his chubby legs in their hip sockets, tapped and pressed his firm belly, and concluded that he was the picture of health. Yasmin hadn't come because—she'd said—she had a job interview. Increasingly, Isabel found she was the one tending to the baby. Yasmin had stopped nursing, so Leo was now on formula and occasional pablums of rice or sweet potato and spoonfuls of banana scraped from the ripe fruit. Isabel often carried him on her back while she worked, the same way her own mother had carried her. She ran errands and cooked with him, travelled back and forth with him on the bus, and sometimes he slept with her at night. Isabel was glad to have this time—Leo's tiny heart beating against her back as she stood over yet another newly excavated grave. His presence on those occasions rooted her to the earth she stood on—kept her, she felt, from falling in. His arrival still struck her as something of a miracle. She pressed her nose to his cheek and whispered into the curl of his ear her favourite line by Guatemala's revolutionary poet, Otto René Castillo: *Nothing can overcome life.*

"He was right," she said. "You're proof of that."

Leo gurgled happily in response.

She took him out to the patio, spread her *peraj* on the ground and laid him on his belly on top of it. He lifted his head, following her movements, as she sat beside him and began to stroke his back. When she made a face, he broke into a smile. It was such a precious age. The smiles, the beginnings of play. Soon he would be rolling over and sitting. All too soon, he would be grown. It pained her that Yasmin was missing these moments. That she was building her life from bricks that would one day—Isabel was sure—crumble and turn to regret. As Isabel herself had done. Like mother, like daughter. Wasn't that what Soraida had said? Perhaps it was inevitable in the world they lived in—a world where even in peacetime speaking the truth could cost you your life. Some peace. Nothing had been resolved. The bones were there in the ground—that fact alone meant this was not over. The pain she felt—all of them felt—was in the very earth they walked on.

Leo had fallen asleep, so Isabel got up to find a trowel and the güisquil clippings Aníbal had given her. She'd taken his advice and started a garden. She'd put in some herbs—oregano, parsley, cilantro, epazote—their green shoots were just beginning to show. If there was room, she hoped to squeeze some corn into the small patch of dirt at the back. After retrieving the trowel from under the sink, she kneeled and dug three small holes in the strip of earth by the patio wall. She placed a clipping in each, and then buried the roots, pressing the earth down with both hands. She brought her hands to her nose and inhaled. Deep, rich, dark. Aníbal called it the smell of life. Death leads to life, then. But not without water. Isabel brushed the dirt from her hands and knees and went to fill a bucket at the backyard sink. On her return, she saw Soraida rounding the corner onto the freshly paved road that led to Isabel's house. That surprised her. Soraida had never visited the house before. In fact, Isabel wasn't sure when Soraida had last ventured outside Guatemala City. A flicker of apprehension leapt in her chest, but she commanded herself not to speculate. Soraida would tell her why she was here.

She lifted Leo gently so he would not wake, carried him into the house and placed him in his Moses basket in the bedroom. Then she ran to meet her aunt.

"What are you doing?" she asked as she relieved Soraida of the woven nylon bag she was carrying.

"Yasmin said you haven't been well. I've come to make you a good hen caldo."

"You've got a hen in here?" Isabel opened the heavy bag but the creature inside was already dead and plucked, the pale body nestled atop a large assortment of vegetables. She glanced back at the long road from the highway. "You didn't have to come all this way," she said. "I'm fine. Really. I don't know what Yasmin's talking about."

Soraida looked her over but kept walking, up the front path, through the front door and to the kitchen. "A good caldo. That's what you need. Look at you." Again Soraida looked her up and down. "You're pale. You're thin."

Isabel placed the bag of groceries on the kitchen table and, after lifting out the hen and setting it aside, drew from it fresh cobs of corn, yucca, a large green squash, a couple of güisquiles, tomatoes, onions. Her aunt's gesture, barging in as if she owned the place, was beginning to annoy her, though she tried not to show it. After all, Soraida had come all that way.

"Where's the pot?" Soraida asked, so Isabel showed her.

Soraida carried it to the backyard sink and filled it partway.

"Do you want me to cut up the hen?" Isabel asked.

"You just sit. You need to rest.'

Isabel remained standing. "What exactly did Yasmin tell you?"

Soraida set the pot on the stove, struck a match from the box on the counter, and lit a flame beneath it.

"She was very worried," Soraida said. "After the bishop—"

"That was over a week ago," Isabel said. "She can't be that worried. Would she have me taking care of Leo if I was in such bad shape?" She sat in one of the kitchen chairs. She was feeling a bit out of breath.

"Leo is here? I didn't know that."

"He's asleep," Isabel said. "In the bedroom."

Soraida studied her as if watching for signs of a relapse.

"I did have a little ... episode," Isabel said. "It was the shock, but really I'm okay now."

Soraida started cutting up the hen. "You don't look okay."

"I'm getting better."

Soraida severed the drumstick from the thigh and the thigh from the hen's rubbery body.

"Of course you are," she said. "Just let your aunt take care of you a little. You're all alone out here. You could use a break."

"I'm not alone. I've got Yasmin. I've got Leo. And I've got a whole organization behind me."

Soraida stopped cutting. She seemed disoriented. Isabel regretted her lack of gratitude.

"I'm glad you came," she said. "It's such a long way. I appreciate the visit."

Her aunt finished up the hen and then quartered an onion and dropped it into the pot. For the first time since she'd entered the house, she turned to take it in.

"It's a very nice place you've got here." The sweep of her gaze stopped at her brother's wedding photo. After a moment, she said, "I'm glad you've got that up."

Then she was back at work, squeezing tomatoes into the water, adding the pieces of hen, husking the corn and breaking the cobs in two. As Isabel watched, she wondered whether she should just get up and finish with the garden. But Soraida seemed to want to wait on her, whether or not Isabel needed it. The panic attack—or whatever it had been—of the previous week had long since subsided. She really was better.

"When did you see Yasmin?" she asked.

"She usually comes by the shop on the way back from the Foundation. Thoughtful child."

It was thoughtful. Why, Isabel wondered, did she so rarely get to see Yasmin's thoughtful side? "I'm glad she's doing that. And you see Leo sometimes, too? I almost never get to town myself. I guess I should try to."

The pot was boiling now, so Soraida lowered the flame: it was full to the brim with large chunks of vegetables. Isabel wondered how she would ever finish it, even with Yasmin's help.

"Now," Soraida said, "let me have a look at my great-great nephew."

Isabel led her to the bedroom. Leo slept soundly, his tiny right hand curling and uncurling.

"I just assumed Yasmin had taken him with her," her aunt whispered.

"She usually does," Isabel said, lying. "But she has a job interview today."

Soraida gazed indulgently at the sleeping child.

"Surely she doesn't need to start work so soon," she said.

"I agree. But she wants to."

Isabel closed the bedroom door and they returned to the kitchen. Soraida removed the lid from the caldo and tested one of the potatoes and a slice of squash with a fork.

"I hope you'll have some with me," Isabel said as she sat again at the kitchen table.

"I'll have a little before I go. I want to get back before dark."

Isabel nodded. "You could stay the night. Yasmin will be back before too long."

She felt uncomfortable with her aunt here. She didn't know what to say to her, what to talk about—not her work, not her time in the mountains, not her childhood, not her parents. Is that what it took to survive in Guatemala? Head down, nose to your own business, never letting anyone or anything lure you from your safe, narrow course? She wished Yasmin would hurry up and get home.

Soraida joined her at the table. "I won't stay," she said. "You're doing much better than Yasmin led me to believe. Poor girl. I think you gave her quite a scare." She looked around the small room again. "I'm glad I got to see where you live. Are you settling in?"

"Yes. It's good here. We're good here."

"Leo looks very well. You're taking good care of him."

"He's a joy."

Her aunt smiled at her and Isabel waited for more questions. But there weren't any. Soraida got up again to check the caldo.

"Auntie, do you mind?" Isabel said. "I've got a bit of gardening to finish up."

"Of course. I'm not here to get in your way. I'll call you when dinner's ready."

When it was time to eat, they barely spoke. But the caldo was good. It warmed Isabel's stomach and body, soothing the tension in her neck, her back, her hands. She remembered the times she fell ill as a child. Her grandmother would kill a hen and serve just such a caldo. She could even remember, just barely, the aroma filling the very first kitchen she knew—her mother ladling the soup into earthenware bowls and placing them on the table, the steam wetting her cheeks and nose as she leaned in to let the warm, comforting smell fill her nostrils.

Soraida was bent over her bowl, sipping at the hot broth. What thoughts or memories ran through *her* head? Out of respect, Isabel didn't ask. But she wondered how Soraida had ended up so different from her brother, why their paths had diverged, why it seemed impossible to bring those paths together again.

Leo woke and started crying just as they were finishing. Soraida, of course, insisted on fetching him.

"I'll prepare a bottle if you'd like to feed him," Isabel said.

It was only fair. Soraida deserved to share in the small miracle, too. Leo watched Soraida intently as he sucked on the rubber nipple. When he was full, Soraida expertly placed him against her shoulder and stroked his back until he burped. Isabel took over when it was time to change his diaper. Soraida watched from the bedroom door.

"I'd better get going," she said.

"You're sure you won't stay? Yasmin will be along soon."

Her aunt shook her head and started gathering her things.

Isabel thanked her again and, with Leo strapped to her waist, walked her to the highway to catch the bus back to the city. The driver's helper gave Soraida his hand and hoisted her up the bus step and into the battered vehicle. As the bus pulled onto the highway, its door remained open, the driver's helper leaning from it, calling out for more passengers.

The visit had been a disappointment, but also a relief. That was Soraida's conclusion as she sat, wedged between two men who smelled of woodsmoke and sweat, unwilling even to turn her head to take in the passing scenery lest she be thought to be seeking conversation. Other passengers stood and sat in the aisle, which was narrow enough to let them prop themselves between the padded cushions on either side. The pack of bodies proved to be a blessing, as it kept them all from bouncing around every time the bus lurched to one side or the other to get past a transport truck.

Clearly, Isabel didn't need Soraida—she was perfectly capable of taking care of herself, just as she'd done for most of her life. Clearly, too, Soraida had no need to worry about unpaid debts, untold secrets. She could make peace with her brother's memory, continue to see Yasmin and Leo, continue to see Isabel, too, from time to time. But nothing more was required of her.

A large transport blasted past them in the oncoming lane, sending a woosh of air through the small openings in the bus's windows. Soraida tried to pull her handkerchief from her pocket without disturbing her neighbours but it was impossible. Any movement caused a ripple of responses. She nodded her apology to the men beside her, and held the handkerchief to her nose.

There'd been something missing, she thought, in Isabel's new house. Perhaps because she'd found Isabel there alone with Leo, or perhaps because it was still so new, but the house struck her as empty. Sterile. The garden was a good idea. And of course, as Isabel got on with her life, maybe she'd find someone to share it with, or maybe Yasmin would settle down and have more children, Leo would grow and start bringing his friends over. Soon there'd be in-laws and cousins, more people than they knew what to do with. Yes, time would fill that house with life. And maybe then, Soraida would feel part of it. Maybe that was all it took. Time.

Isabel spent the evening watching Leo play with her keychain. He'd fuss each time he dropped it until Isabel placed it in his hand again. He'd rattle it and laugh. Then he'd wedge it between his gums and Isabel would have to retrieve it and show him how to shake it. He'd take it and imitate her, and then he'd drop it again. It was almost meditative. "You're better than therapy," Isabel said as she handed him back the keys. Eventually he began to tire. He yawned. The hand that held the keys fell to his side without releasing them. And he was asleep. Yasmin would miss this moment, too: sleep slipping over her bubbly and active son like a blanket drawn across a mattress. She placed him in Yasmin's bed, arranging the pillows around him to keep him from rolling off. And then, so he wouldn't wake alone, she moved him to the wall, changed into the T-shirt she slept in and climbed in next to him. She, too, was soon asleep.

She woke again when she heard somebody unlocking the front door.

"I was trying not to wake you," her daughter whispered when Isabel stumbled into the moonlit living room.

"Is it that late?" Isabel asked, but Yasmin didn't answer. "I have to head out early tomorrow. Do you want me to take Leo with me?"

The moonlight caught the strands of Yasmin's long hair but left her face in shadow. She'd grown up so much in the last months. Still too young to be a mother, but no longer a child.

"I'll watch him," she said. "I should spend more time with him."

"Is anything wrong?" Isabel was more awake now and remembered why she had got up in the first place. "I wanted to ask you something."

Yasmin waited without protest.

"I've got another exhumation, but this one ..." Isabel wasn't sure how to say it. "It's near your great-grandparents' village, where I grew up."

Something seemed to shift in her daughter. She looked confused. "Are they buried there?"

"We don't know yet. That's what we want to find out—what happened there—and recover any remains we can. I was wondering if you would come with me."

"To see a mass grave? To see all the tortured bodies?"

Isabel rubbed her temples. A small pain had begun to radiate from them and was growing. "This is my family," she said. "*Your* family ... I don't want to go alone."

Yasmin stared at her. Isabel felt embarrassed under her scrutiny.

"When?" she said.

"Probably not for another month or two. I wanted to give you some warning."

Yasmin continued to regard her mother, taking in everything she was.

"All right," she said, her face pale in the moonlight. Then she turned and went to the bedroom.

CHAPTER 19

THE FORENSIC ANTHROPOLOGISTS examined the scene from one angle, then another. From the gentle rise that hid the dirt track that had brought them here, from both sides of the grassy area where Isabel stood waiting, from points farther down the slope and along the riverbank. They were reading the earth's surface. Aníbal walked to an area between two shrunken trees, got down on his knees and flattened the river grass with his hand. Behind him the waters of the Pixcayá winked in the pale sunlight.

"There's an impression here," he said. "It's a large area."

Isabel glanced toward her daughter to see whether she'd heard. Yasmin was playing with Leo beneath one of the trees that lined the riverbank, mother and son seated facing each other, legs spread wide, rolling a ball back and forth through the rough grass. The weather was refreshingly cool; the sky, clear. Small puffs of wind rippled the river's surface. Isabel watched their play a moment longer as the anthropologists on either side of her drew spades and stakes and mallets from their gear. Then she turned to Aníbal to await instruction.

The anthropologists set to work, the same methods they'd used in Xesuj, in Chiuleu, in Las Escobas. Again and again and again. The whole country was their graveyard. Measure, mark, dig, photograph, photograph. When they reached bone or clothing, they'd stop, measure again and draw, noting placement of each item and its relationship to others around it, marking it all out on the ground with silver tags, each embossed with a letter: a, b, c, d. And they photographed. They photographed the remains, first with the clothing and belongings in place and then the bones alone. Nothing covering them and nothing, except to a forensic anthropologist, identifying them.

The methods were the same, but for Isabel, this exhumation was not like the others. This was the one she'd been waiting for. The one she'd been dreading. Refugees from hers and other villages had fled to this place after they were driven out by successive attacks on their homes. They'd abandoned their villages and made the long trek here, taking shelter in Estancia de la Virgen and when that became too dangerous, heading toward the river, hoping to cross into San Juan Sacatepéquez and reach the jungle's protective embrace. But the army was on their trail. The refugees were too many to hide. Troops came up behind them and brought in cadets from the military academy on the other side of the river to prevent escape. Some of the soldiers had dressed in Kaqchikel clothing so they could move closer unnoticed before the order to attack was given. When the shooting started, almost three hundred people were camped by the river. Now, fourteen years later, nothing remained but long grasses, smooth river stones and the purring waters of the Pixcayá under the distant sun.

Yasmin was already restless, but she seemed willing to put in the two days Isabel had asked of her. Sometimes she joined her mother at the exhumation area but much of her time was spent bent over Leo, holding him by his hands to keep him upright as they walked around in circles. Leo lifted and placed one foot, then the other, bouncing on his bandied legs between steps, raising his head to find Isabel, his new front teeth gleaming with saliva, so she could applaud his new skills. Over the last several months, he'd started to crawl and point at pictures in books and babble a stream of syllables that before long would become words. Yasmin had grown into her role as mother. In May, she'd taken a secretarial job with an organization that helped migrants, her job, like Isabel's, the fruit of international funding, which at present abounded. Leo would cry when his mother left him to go to work, and he would cry again when Isabel delivered him back to her daughter at the of the day. But when she wasn't at work, Yasmin tended to Leo with more interest and diligence than she'd shown before. She saw Jorge as often as she could. And other than that, Isabel didn't know. Her daughter kept to herself. She did all the things she was supposed to do, but Isabel couldn't really tell whether she enjoyed any of it. Isabel's life had changed, too. As Yasmin saw more of Jorge, Isabel saw more of Max. They were spoken of now as a couple, in her neighbourhood, at the Foundation and here at work. He stayed over sometimes but sleeping arrangements in that small house were anything but straightforward. They'd even started talking about adding a second floor to make room for everybody. Through it all Isabel had waited for this day: from May to September, through the winter rains, through the intervening exhumations and investigations, through joys, through sorrows. Now the waiting was over.

"When is something going to happen?" Yasmin asked Isabel on the morning of the second day, Leo, snug in his rebozo, asleep against her back. The anthropologists had barely got the grasses and the first layers of soil removed.

"It's an exacting process. It takes time," Isabel said. "But once they find what they're looking for, there'll be plenty to see."

Yasmin was about to return with Leo to their spot under the tree, when Fredy, one of the anthropologists, approached, followed by two women with several small children orbiting their feet. The elder of the women, who looked to be in her seventies or eighties, seemed familiar to Isabel.

"This is Eulalia," Fredy said. "I need you to interpret." He gestured to the elderly woman, who came up to Isabel, very close, and touched her arm. The younger woman bent down to let the toddler she was carrying join the other children.

Isabel nodded to Eulalia. She knew her. "Do you remember me?" she asked in Kaqchikel. "I'm Isabel Barrios Cun. Hugo and Rosario were my parents."

The woman examined her. Her irises were murky, almost blind. "I remember every child I delivered." She gripped Isabel's arm now with a trembling hand. "Your dear parents," she said. "They would rejoice to know you have come this far."

Eulalia had delivered countless children from Isabel's village. Renowned for her knowledge of natural medicine, she was also the person Isabel's grandparents would apply to whenever one of their many children or grandchildren fell ill. Isabel remembered the old woman driving away the fright she'd suffered after her parents' death by spraying water over her. She'd cleansed her, too, leading her into the aromatic steam of the *tuj* and whispering to her words Isabel could no longer remember except for the way they lulled and soothed her so she could finally sleep.

"My grandparents?" Isabel asked.

Eulalia turned her nearly sightless eyes toward the men digging.

Isabel felt a sharp pull in her chest.

"We will give them a proper burial," the old woman said. "We have come here to free their spirits so they can finally rest." She pressed her thumb to Isabel's forehead then and Isabel felt returned from a distant place.

"I have a daughter," Isabel said, remembering Yasmin. Eulalia then called over her granddaughter and the various great-grandchildren who had accompanied her, and they all exchanged greetings, Yasmin imitating the handshake, clasping the other's forearm at the elbow, that her mother used with each of the Kaqchikel women. She twisted one shoulder forward to present Leo.

"They are the beginning of a new world," Eulalia said, still in Kaqchikel. "The old world"—she motioned to the anthropologists who bent and lifted, slowly, gently, spadesful of dark earth from the deepening pit —"The old world gives birth to the new. We honour the ones who brought us here." She lifted her hands to Yasmin's face, feeling its shape, stroking her cheeks.

Isabel interpreted for Yasmin, who looked uncomfortable with the woman's touch but afraid to withdraw. "Tell her to stop," she whispered to Isabel. But Eulalia continued to hold her, reaching up to her because she was so small, and spoke again.

"She says she delivered your grandmother, too. That you have her spirit," Isabel said. She put her arm around her daughter's shoulder and gave her a small kiss. "It's her way of blessing you."

Yasmin wriggled free and was about to leave when one of the anthropologists working the dig called out.

"They found something," Fredy said.

It looked like a small moonscape that had somehow appeared in the middle of this verdant field. Devoid of life, a surface of skeletons. They lay twisted together, side by side and on top of each other. Someone had laid them out—they were not simply tossed in. But there were so many packed together in this pit by the river, it was hard for the untrained eye to know where one skeleton ended and another began. The forensic team had worked well past their suppertime and several of them continued even now, under the amber circle of light from a Coleman lamp, to break and brush away the clay that held them, to reveal a shoulder, a ribcage, a child's foot.

Isabel had not left the edge of the site all afternoon, not even for supper. Yasmin, too, Leo now asleep against her chest, had stayed by her side as the bodies were uncovered. They hardly talked, but Isabel held her daughter's hand, squeezing it too hard, involuntarily, whenever an anthropologist exposed something she thought she might recognize. She'd catch her breath and squeeze. In this ground lay her grandparents, aunts, uncles, cousins and who knew how many other people she'd grown up with. She wanted to say something to Yasmin, to talk her through what she was seeing, offer some sort of comfort, but she couldn't speak. She could barely breathe. All she could do was squeeze her daughter's hand.

Isabel had learned about her village's fate when she was still in the mountains, fighting against the army, mere months after she'd delivered Yasmin into her aunt's care. For a time, as she imagined tracking down the patrol responsible and exacting vengeance, the news had fuelled her will to go on. But beneath that angry drive lay something else, a seed of truth that grew in her in time. She had realized they might never win, no matter how just their cause, no matter how strong their conviction, no matter how much the sacrifice. And she'd realized that she might never see Yasmin again, that she'd abandoned her daughter for nothing, for worse than nothing. This moment, this terrible moment with her daughter's hand in hers, was more than she'd ever dared hope for, though she'd continued to declare herself confident of victory.

At almost nine o'clock, the anthropologists climbed out of the pit, the light of their lamps arcing across the night made blacker by their sweep. Then they covered the grave with a large nylon tarp and headed to their tents. Isabel turned to Yasmin. Her child was pale, the shock of what she had seen written across her face.

"I want to go home," Yasmin said.

Isabel tried to embrace her, to apologize. She shouldn't have brought her. Yet she had to. She had to bring her. If this was where Isabel belonged, Yasmin belonged here, too. This was her family, her past, her present, just as much as it was Isabel's. She couldn't just pretend it hadn't happened. That it couldn't happen again.

"Stay," she said. "I know it's hard. But this is important."

Yasmin shook her off. "I hate this place." The tremble had turned to anger. "I hate Guatemala. I want to leave. Now." Leo stirred in her arms.

"Please," Isabel said. "You promised."

"What is wrong with you! I don't want to be here!" Yasmin shouted. Leo began to cry. Yasmin's anger gave way to tears. "Why would you come here?" she said, bouncing Leo and rubbing his back to settle him. "Why do you live this way when you don't have to?"

But Isabel couldn't answer. From somewhere deep inside her grief held her. It was battling to get out and the best she could do was hold it there. Besides, how could she explain? This is what the leaders of this country do to people like me. To indios. She couldn't remember a time when she was innocent enough to be shocked by the violence and brutality. She'd lived with it her whole life. But this ...

Yasmin started walking away, Leo wailing, and Isabel let her go. Before she reached the anthropologists' camp, Yasmin stopped and turned.

Isabel went to her. "Someone is probably returning to the capital," she said. "If not tonight, then tomorrow."

Yasmin held Leo out to her. He squirmed in her daughter's hands, red faced, still crying. Yasmin looked exhausted. "Please," she said, "take him."

So Isabel did, settling him against her. He'd worn himself out with his tears and would soon nod off again.

Yasmin wiped her eyes. "I'm sorry," she said. "I wish I could be more like you, but I can't."

Isabel brushed a lingering tear from her daughter's cheek. "Yasmi, you're just a girl—I was asking too much of you. The whole world has asked too much. I left you alone for so long." With one arm, she pulled her daughter to her and hugged her tightly, Leo, asleep already, nestled between them. "You know, you know I would do anything for you."

"Help me with Leo," Yasmin said.

"Of course." Isabel released her daughter gently and kissed the boy in her arms.

"I love you," Yasmin said, passing Isabel the rebozo. "I don't blame you."

Isabel wasn't exactly sure what Yasmin was forgiving her for, although it could be any number of things. Still, her daughter's words made her feel better. She'd be able to finish the exhumation. She wound the green cloth around her sleeping grandson and tied it off. Having Leo with her would help, too. He was a gift and a blessing.

"I'll find you a ride," she said.

After seeing Yasmin off, Isabel wandered back to the exhumation site. She was still needed here, and even if she wasn't, she didn't want to leave, not now. Eulalia was kneeling down at the edge of the dig, her knees almost touching the taut white string that marked off the spot for exhumation. She was mumbling and moving her hands before her, out over the hollowed piece of earth.

Isabel stepped closer to listen. Eulalia was reciting names, places, relationships.

"Juanito, son of María Albertina Tay Atz and Esmeregildo Balam Sutuj from below the creek in Trapito Viejo. Guisela B'atz Rodríguez and her sisters Justa and Mónica and Esmonda, daughters all of Old Man Jeremías and Vilma, who lie here, too."

Isabel heard names she recognized and ones she didn't. She learned family relationships she hadn't known about. And then she was back there, in the village guarded by the giant chalum tree, following her grandmother along the dirt street that led to the mud brick house where they all lived, several other cousins walking alongside her, and her grandfather pulling up the rear. They'd been gathering pigweed along the riverbank. Her grandmother would boil it up, and they would sit wherever they could find room, crowded together in that tiny house, soaking the tortillas her aunts had prepared in the meatless broth before devouring them. Lifting the earthenware bowls to their lips to drink.

Míriam, Eulalia's granddaughter, placed her hand on Isabel's shoulder. "Grandmother knows all the names," she said. "All of them. The people here"—she jutted her chin toward the pit—"and the survivors. She was here. She came back to help prepare the bodies."

The old woman was rocking back and forth now, her hands at her shoulders, palms facing the grave, bowing, bowing. And still she recited. Finally, she spoke the names Isabel had been waiting to hear, and Isabel closed her eyes. The images of her grandparents had fled. All she saw was black.

Isabel found the note when she got home, propped against a vase of still fresh pink and white gladiolas which she supposed Yasmin had left as a parting gift: "I've gone to USA to see my father. Jorge is with me. Don't worry and please don't be angry. Give Leo a kiss for me. I promise I will send for him as soon as I can. I love you. Y."

She unwrapped Leo from the rebozo where he was sleeping soundly against her chest and placed him in the basket in the bedroom, mechanically, as if she were following orders. As if her will were not her own. Slowly, Yasmin's words took hold. Her daughter had left her. She'd left her infant son. And Isabel had stood by and watched her do it. Maybe Isabel was the reason she'd done it. Because it had been there, this move of Yasmin's, like a storm on the horizon, but Isabel had been so absorbed in her own loss, in her own pain, she hadn't seen it. She hadn't wanted to see it. She'd thought it would just blow over. She'd thought they were actually building something here—a life, a new life. But she'd been wrong. She was always wrong.

Isabel returned to the table, picked up the note and reread it. Would it have made any difference if she *had* paid more attention? if she'd given more? if she'd demanded more? Or would Yasmin have left her anyway? The same way Isabel had when she'd said goodbye to her grandparents and abandoned her village forever. They'd shed tears, her grandmother, her grandfather, but they hadn't stopped her.

Isabel lowered the note to the table, trying to imagine how Yasmin must have felt to take this step, not only away from her mother and son, but all the way to the United States, a long and dangerous pilgrimage across three countries. She couldn't imagine it. She sat there, paralyzed in mind and spirit, a deep sorrow welling up inside her, rising until it all poured out, a flood of bitter tears releasing the ache that for so long had been anchored deep within her. She was not ready to let go. She should have done something to stop her daughter. But who can stop a storm?

CHAPTER 20

"YOU DON'T HAVE to," Soraida said.

Isabel, her face grey, stared at the plate of beans Soraida had placed before her. It was late afternoon, and they were sitting in Soraida's kitchen with the television on. Don Francisco was handing out prizes on *Sábado Gigante*. El Chacal was waving his trumpet. The invisible audience laughed. Somewhere nearby men were unloading a delivery truck. Soraida heard the distant voices, the men shouting instructions to each other as they hurried to finish the job and move on to the next. She'd opened her shop that morning but closed as soon as Isabel had surprised her with a knock at her door, anxious to speak to her. She thought it unlikely she would open tomorrow either.

She repeated herself. "You don't have to do this."

Isabel picked up her fork and moved the beans around her plate before laying it down again.

"She's my daughter," she said finally.

"She chose to go," Soraida said. "She left her son behind. She's counting on you to take care of him."

Isabel struck the tabletop with the heel of her fist, making both Soraida and the fork jump.

"She's only sixteen, for Christ's sake. She doesn't know what she's doing. And Jorge! I never thought he'd do something like this."

Soraida rubbed her chest. "You're right," she said, glimpsing a solution. "Why doesn't Danilo go then."

Isabel said nothing.

"Or at least go with you."

"Danilo's not talking to me. Claudia freaked out. She says this is all my fault. Poison, she called us."

"That's ridiculous," Soraida said. "Yasmin is the victim, if there is any."

"The trip was bound to be her idea."

That's what Soraida thought, too. But why were so many people who should know better letting Yasmin and what she wanted rule the day? Soraida had given up that responsibility, handed it over to Isabel. Yasmin knew where to find her great-aunt if she needed her.

Soraida turned off the television, but Isabel didn't seem to notice. She was holding her head in her hands. She looked in pain.

"Eat something," Soraida said. "You've got to eat."

Isabel lifted her fork again, a few beans balanced on it, but let it drop before it reached her lips. She turned to Soraida, meeting her eyes for the first time.

"Please, Auntie. I will come back. I promise. I won't abandon you or Leo. But I have to make sure she's all right."

She was pale and perspiring. Her hand trembled as it searched again for the fork.

Soraida turned her head, her eyes resting on the blank television screen. Isabel didn't have to promise. Isabel's word was gold—it always had been. But Soraida didn't want Isabel to go.

"By the time you reach her, she'll have already arrived—and sent word. She didn't do this to hurt you. It says so in the note. She'll let you know as soon as she's made it."

Soraida wasn't sure of that, but it made more sense than Isabel's chasing after her daughter.

"I can move quicker," Isabel said. "I've got Mexican ID. I'd be there if they ran into any trouble."

"How would you even—?" But there was no point asking how Isabel could possibly trace her daughter given the many distinct routes that must lead to that massive country, the USA, the dozens, surely, of crossing points. Isabel's eyes had lost their focus again. She wasn't listening. She wouldn't listen. Soraida tried one more tack. "And what will you do when you find her?"

"I'll make sure she's safe."

"And then?"

Isabel shook her head, her lips pressed together. She was on the verge of tears, but she said, "I'll come home." Her eyes were wide, desperate. "I will."

Soraida nodded, a movement so slight it could have been involuntary. But Isabel saw it and relaxed.

"Eat your beans," Soraida said.

This time Isabel obeyed. Soraida pressed her hands together in wordless prayer and waited for her niece to finish.

"Before you go," she said. "I want to show you something."

Isabel raised her eyes in inquiry.

"Not here." She took her niece's empty plate and carried it to the sink. Her heart was thumping against her chest, but she said as steadily as she could, "If you do this for me, I'll take care of Leo until you come home."

Isabel was still chewing. She looked doubtful, but then she swallowed and nodded.

Isabel spent the night at Max's. It would have been a long and lonely ride back to the housing project, and she found it painful to be there now. Max—her waystation. It wasn't fair to him. She knew that. But he didn't turn her away when she asked. He had never turned her away.

She'd left Leo with him while she visited her aunt—in case Soraida had said no, she'd told herself, but really because she wasn't ready to part with her grandson. When she returned to Max's apartment, they were sitting on the bare floor, stacking odd-shaped blocks of wood into towers.

"I raided the carpentry shop," Max said.

Leo had both hands raised above a crooked pillar. He squealed and demolished it with the swipe of one arm.

"I'm the builder and he's the destroyer." Max got to his feet and kissed her. "How'd it go?"

Isabel avoided his gaze. She didn't want those warm brown eyes to reach her. "It went well. She said yes."

She thought Max looked disappointed. Maybe he'd thought she wouldn't go if Soraida had refused. Isabel hadn't even considered it. She knew Soraida would accept.

"We went and got a rotisserie chicken if you're hungry," Max said.

Half a chicken lay on a plate on the ironing board. The room still had no furniture other than the bed. This was Max's waystation, too, she supposed. He must have thought he'd soon be giving up the apartment and moving out to the housing project. Good thing, as it turned out, he hadn't made the change. Perhaps now he never would. Isabel pushed from her mind the thoughts of Max and Leo and the family they might have become. She thought instead about Yasmin, where she might be, what route they'd have taken, how far they'd have travelled. They could still be in Guatemala for all she knew.

"Did Leo eat?" she asked.

Max nodded and then he wrapped his arms around her and kissed the top of her head as Leo started throwing blocks of wood at the wall.

"Are you sure you want to do it?" he said to her. "Are you *sure*?"

Every time she exhaled, she felt she was losing something. But her mind was fixed on Yasmin, honed sharp by the imperative that drew her on.

"I have to," she said.

He released her and squeezed her shoulders. He kissed her lips and then he looked her in the eyes.

"I won't ask you to promise, because I know you can't," he said. "But I want you to know that I want you to come back to me."

Isabel tried to hide it, but she felt rigid in his arms. Surely Max could feel it too. Even now, she was staring past him to Leo, who still sat on the floor, pushing blocks around, making different shapes, different patterns. But she'd heard what Max had said, and she was grateful.

They took the bus together, Isabel and Soraida, to the central plaza, barely a word passing between them. Isabel was quiet, pressing her nose against Leo's back as he slapped his chubby hands against the bus windows, enthralled by the people and cars and buildings speeding past. The sky was grey, a thick haze that promised rain. Maybe it would hold off. Soraida wasn't above thinking the elements took an interest in her tiny human struggle. The sky had given Bishop Gerardi a rainbow. She remembered that now. But Gerardi sat among the saints, and she—she was a sinner of the most common variety.

Mostly, she tried not to think. She was excited, but she was also nervous. After getting off, she led her niece along Seventh Avenue to the wrought iron fence that enclosed the cathedral's front patio. Battered cars and buses churned by, exhaust filling the street like a black cloud fallen to earth. On the central plaza, vendors were drawing tarps over their carts in case of a downpour. The big old building looked unchanged by the events of the past year and a half. But the fence was new. Soraida passed her hand over the face of one of the tan-coloured marble columns that stood at intervals between the railings. "Look," she said to Isabel. She tried to keep the flutter in her chest from infecting her voice.

Isabel, who was jiggling Leo to keep him quiet, did look. Chiselled into the polished stone, in tiny print, were names—hundreds, perhaps thousands of them. Isabel stepped closer, her face now inches from the chiselled letters, and began to scan through the list. She moved from pillar to pillar until she found the Bs. There it was: *Barrios Ibargüen, Hugo, May 12, 1967.*

"How did you know about this?" she asked, shifting Leo to her other hip. The shiny stone surface had caught his eye and he was leaning away from her, trying to touch it.

"Your mother's name is here too," Soraida said, nodding to the column that held surnames beginning with C. Isabel took a deep breath before approaching it. She searched for the name and found it. *Cun B'atz, Rosario, May 12, 1967.* Soraida watched her niece closely. Isabel had tears in her eyes.

"Tell me," she said to Soraida.

So Soraida did. Reaching for Hugo's name, stroking it, the bite of the carved letters under her fingertips, she told Isabel about visiting REMHI and about testifying.

"I was there." She spoke in a whisper. "I saw them die."

Isabel inhaled sharply, but she let Soraida continue.

"I should have told you the first day we met, or the next, or the next. There were so many times I should've spoken up. I knew you were suffering."

Isabel's face was flushed, but still she listened. Leo twisted in the rebozo, his hands seeking the pillar, but she ignored him.

"I was afraid," Soraida said, her voice hoarse.

"Why?" Isabel's eyes narrowed with suspicion. "Why were you afraid?"

Soraida hesitated. It was now or, perhaps, never. She pulled her handkerchief from her apron pocket and wound it through her fingers. "I thought I'd lose you, and Yasmin, too."

"Why?" Isabel repeated, more forcefully this time.

Soraida stuttered when she answered. Her skin was cold. "I sent a note. That's why they came back to the city. To see me." She exhaled, as if she'd been holding her breath for years. Why hadn't she just let Isabel go? This truth-telling would just make Isabel's pain greater. She'd just lost her daughter, for heaven's sake. But for all her fears,

Soraida was more afraid of holding back what was inside her. "Maybe our phones were tapped. Maybe my father ..." She stopped there. She couldn't say it. If she said it, she might have to believe it.

Isabel looked at her for a long time, as if sizing her up, rocking from foot to foot to soothe Leo.

"They didn't need your help or your father's," she said at last. "My parents were already under surveillance. They had my father as a target and they followed his movements—like they did to hundreds and hundreds of other people. Once they'd made their decision, they looked for an opportunity and they took it. My parents shouldn't have come back to the city. But they did."

"Because of me," Soraida said. A sharp pain pierced her chest.

Isabel's expression softened. "They didn't realize any more than you did." She looked at the ground and then at the marble columns covered in names. "None of us knew what we were up against."

"Or they knew and they did it anyway," Soraida said.

Isabel gave her something like a smile, an acknowledgement. "My parents. Did you see who killed them?"

Soraida pulled at her handkerchief. She could see the men as if it were yesterday. The Chevy van. It's door opening. Guns firing. The man who stepped from it, his face, his beret, his eyes. She told Isabel. She recounted every moment, from first catching sight of Hugo to the tiro de gracia that finished him off; every detail, from the blossoming jacarandas to the colour of the killer's eyes. She talked and talked. She couldn't stop talking.

"I told REMHI," she said when she had finished. "I gave them descriptions." Then she straightened, inhaled, and asked what she had wanted to ask all along: "Can you forgive me?"

Isabel looked at her, no longer tense, the lines of her face no longer hard. "You should have told me," she said. "For years, all I had were my own memories to tell me what I knew must be the truth. But it's hard. It's hard not to have doubts when powerful people are telling you different." She touched the column where her mother's name was inscribed, her fingertips barely grazing its surface. "I know you were afraid. I understand that. It was brave of you to go to REMHI. A lot of people are still afraid to speak up—"

Suddenly Soraida was crying. "I'm not brave!" She tried to face Isabel. "There's more," she said.

Isabel stepped away from her. Suspicion had returned to her face.

Soraida brushed the tears away and stood as tall as she could. For courage, she kept her eyes on Hugo's name as she spoke. "When they shot Hugo and your mother, I ran." She wiped her face. "The van and the soldiers were gone, but I ran."

"You were afraid," Isabel said. But she sounded unsure. She sounded hurt.

Soraida shook her head violently. She didn't want to wound Isabel, but she had to confess. "When Hugo fell, I felt it. I felt my heart close. When I turned away, I knew." She was still shaking her head. "I knew what I was doing. I was closing my heart against him, and I was going back home, back to my family and everything that meant. I chose my side."

Isabel's face had clouded over. She wouldn't meet Soraida's eyes. "You were a girl," she said, her voice hollow with defeat. "You were afraid. You wanted to live."

At that moment, Soraida saw in her niece the little girl who had always been hiding there. Vulnerable, afraid, alone. The girl who lost her parents and then lost her grandparents. The girl abandoned by her lover when she became pregnant. The girl nobody came looking for, nobody held out a hand to. Soraida touched Isabel's cheek and gently raised her chin until she could see her niece's eyes.

"It took me years," she said, "to leave that house again. I should have looked for you, but I didn't." She was feeling more sure of herself now. "When you brought me Yasmin, I thought, here's my chance. I can mend what's broken between us, but I stopped short again. I never took the next step, the one that would lead all the way to you." She took Isabel's hand. Her niece looked confused, so Soraida kept talking. She wanted Isabel to know exactly what she had done and what she hadn't. It wasn't forgiveness she sought now or even Isabel's comprehension. She just wanted to understand it herself. "It's like I started out across a bridge but I never made it to the other side. I just stopped halfway, right in Eighteenth Street, set up my shop, lived my life like there was nowhere else to go, nothing else to do. I think I told myself that it was your job to meet me halfway. But it wasn't. It wasn't, Isabel."

She held Isabel's hand in both of hers. And then something broke in her niece; Soraida saw it on her face, in her body. Not a rush of tears or words but something hard and rigid giving way. Isabel leaned forward, rested her head against the crook of Soraida's neck, Leo sound asleep between them, and let herself be held.

CHAPTER 21

THEY SQUATTED IN the metal hold—obediently, silently—backs pressed against the van's panels, eyes focused on the shoe or shirt button or watch of the passenger sitting across from them or on their own hands. They kept that gaze as they bumped against each other, as dark buildings flicked by and disappeared, leaving only, in the square of the van's rear window, a moody grey sky broken now and then by a tree or a water tower or the soft white spray of a passing car's headlights. They kept it as smooth pavement turned to hard rutted dirt below them, as above them, black trees surrounded and then swallowed them. They didn't speak or do anything to draw attention to themselves. They breathed the sour odours of their bodies, felt the jolts of each bump in the road but said nothing. Each mind was fixed, Isabel imagined, as hers was, not on what came next or next or next, but on what lay on the other side. Their goal was everything. This—this cramped and suffocating space, this buried fear, this submission—was but a bad dream from which they would wake. They had no control over it, but soon, they believed, very soon, it would be over. So they sat quietly, each of them holding tight to the core of themselves as though it were a gold nugget.

The van jerked to a halt and the driver's door opened. Inside its hold, the migrants inhaled in unison and turned toward the shaft of light that bounced across the twilit sky. They heard the van's rear door handle rattle, the door crack open. Isabel shielded her eyes as the beam of the pollero's flashlight swept over her and they crept, one by one, out of the vehicle.

"Move it," the pollero commanded, holding the flashlight near his head so that it lit only his leather boots, his pot-belly and the hand, etched black with grease, that held the van's door open. Once they had all tumbled out, he hauled a sack full of plastic bags from the back of the van and handed a bag to each of the migrants.

"Put your shoes and your clothes plus any belongings in the bag."

They obeyed without a word. Nothing the pollero said or did would break the spell. A wide, grey river stretched before them, the far side dark and foreboding. The Río Grande. On the opposite shore, the United States of America. They lined up along the riverbank—tall, short, young, old, thin, stout, healthy, frail—their eyes now searching not the far bank but the water's opaque surface. Water, the idea of it, flooded their minds. They were already drowning. Isabel fingered the Mexican voter's card that sat in her shirt pocket and gave her hometown as somewhere in Chiapas—the most Guatemalan of the Mexican states. She wouldn't need the card or the name on it when she reached the other side. One false identity would replace another. The most intrepid of the migrants had already stripped to their underwear and were starting to cross. She watched a young man stride easily through the sluggish water. In his wake, an older man, fearful of stones and holes hidden in the grey river, poked the water with a tree branch, looking for solid ground, before placing one foot in front of the other. Beside him, the moon's reflection floated like a tarnished silver bowl. Isabel pried off her runners and bent to remove her socks and jeans and then her shirt. She rolled them up, lay them on top of her shoes and her other belongings and slid all of it into the bag the pollero had given her. Hugging the bag to her chest, she stepped into the river.

It had taken Isabel two days to get this far. From Eighteenth Street, she'd caught the bus to Tapachula, Mexico, crossing the bridge from Tecún Umán to Ciudad Hidalgo over the first of the two international borders she would face, yellow bicycle taxis weaving through the traffic, migrants wading through the water below, Guatemala receding. As Mexico drew closer, she'd remembered her aunt's words, about crossing a bridge and stopping halfway. Soraida's confession outside the cathedral, every painful word of it, had given Isabel the strength she'd needed to make this journey. She'd felt supported. Loved. As they crossed the border bridge, the image came to her again, her aunt's running her finger over the names chiselled into the cathedral's polished stone pillars, stopping when she reached the name of Isabel's father, her finger lingering there. Yes, for half her life, Soraida had marked time in Eighteenth Street, but now, mentally at least, she was moving on. Yasmin, in contrast, had started running even before Isabel's return and perhaps would never stop. Isabel had returned and now she was leaving. They'd been, all of them, wandering in circles. Wandering the turning world. Doing their best. Yet there on the border bridge, feeling Guatemala slip away once more, failure coloured everything Isabel saw. Her fellow passengers. The muddy Suchiate River. The migrants. Her failure. Her country's. So she'd turned again toward the front of the bus and concentrated on what lay ahead. Yasmin lay ahead.

From Tapachula, Isabel had travelled inland and north on overnights to Mexico City and then Monterrey. When questioned she'd told people she was going to see her sister who was studying at the university in Puebla. Farther north she'd said she had work at a maquila in Ciudad Juárez. They were stories as true as anything else she could say out loud about herself. Mexican police and soldiers made regular checks, ordering anybody without papers, anybody who looked Central American, off the buses. Isabel watched in dismay as another Guatemalan was plucked from his seat, dragged down the bus aisle, baseball cap on his head, a small backpack slung over one shoulder—dead giveaways. Isabel had left her backpack behind. Her scant belongings were crammed into a new canvas satchel. She thought of Yasmin, facing the same trials and the same threats, but without the false ID and practised covers eighteen years of underground life had given Isabel. Forced, perhaps, to ride the rails north on the notorious

Beast. Her Yasmin—ignorant of the wider world. A child still. Isabel's imaginings never made room for Jorge, who had grown up in Mexico, who probably carried Mexican ID, and who was undoubtedly at Yasmin's side. She could only imagine Yasmin as small and alone.

In Miguel Alemán, a border town backing onto the Río Grande, Isabel looked up the pollero, paid him and joined a dozen weary-looking Guatemalans, Salvadorans and Mexicans as they packed into the back of the tiny white van that brought them to the river whose waters now lapped gently at her thighs. The water was cool, almost comforting, after the heat of the van; the current, slight but insistent; the ground beneath her feet, sandy but firm. Isabel eased forward. The water grew deeper. As it reached her waist, she lifted the bag containing her clothes and shoes to her head and balanced it there. She took another step. Another. The pollero had remained on the bank behind them, aiming his flashlight at the far shore to help them locate their target. He wouldn't be trying his luck on the other side. He had a booming and lucrative business right where he was. He'd told them, though, where to pick their way up the opposite bank and find the dirt trail to the right that would lead them to his American partner.

Isabel heard something overhead and looked up to see, silhouetted against the darkening sky, a long V of geese flying southward. North to south as she moved south to north. Like her, always moving. She watched a straggler, the last bird in the V, beat its long thin wings to catch up with the others. Even the birds knew, instinctively, which direction to take, who to follow. As a child, she'd often dreamed of soaring like a bird, gliding along a current of air that lifted her high above all danger. Perhaps it was dreams like these that propelled her daughter. Nowadays Isabel dreamed about walking. She'd grown to prefer life close to the earth—this dark, fertile earth that spoke to her through the soles of her feet, that kept her upright, stable, even here in the middle of this river, that sustained villages, towns and massive cities, this powerful earth that stretched up the far bank, beyond the horizon, through jungles and forests, over mountains, under lakes and oceans, uniting the entire globe. She remembered talking to Guatemalans who'd fled their native lands during the army offensive and made their way through the jungle to Mexico, learning of their amazement at having encountered a land that produced exactly the same plants and animals as the Guatemalan side of the border, that looked and smelled in the thick jungle of the region very much like home. And they found people on the other side, Indigenous campesinos, who saw them, the Guatemalans, as people just like themselves and brought them food and gave them shelter and gave them land.

Isabel searched the sky, but the geese were already out of sight. Ahead of her, several migrants were nearing the other side. Just a few more metres to go. Like her, Isabel imagined, most of them thought they'd soon be back home. And many, of course, would be. But not so soon as they'd thought and not without the strains and scars the time away would leave. Some of them would never make it back. They'd get lost in the North, never quite earning enough money to end their pilgrimage, seeking solace in that strange land, slowly integrating, eventually starting a new life, a new family.

Something like that must have happened to Luís.

The opposite bank rose before her like a heaping mound of garbage, and as Isabel got closer she realized it *was* a mound of garbage, a massive wall of discarded plastic. The first migrants were already there, peeling the bags from their belongings and tossing them onto the heap. Isabel stared at the wall. She was a couple of metres from shore, but her feet refused to take another step. She thought of Yasmin, beautiful Yasmin. Wouldn't she give her life for Yasmin? Hadn't she already? She thought about little Leo, motherless already, in the care of a devoted but aging aunt. And she thought about Soraida and all the things Isabel had asked of her. An invisible chorus waited on the bank behind her: her mother, her father, her grandparents, her ancestors. Her fallen comrades. Thousands of murdered non-combatants: students, union leaders, teachers, catechists, children. Ixil, Mam, K'iche', Kaqchikel. Each of the transvestites shot down in Eighteenth Street. Byron, bleeding into the dust of La Limonada. Guatemala and all its ghosts. Still wounded, still haunting her.

A breeze moved along the river, raising goosebumps on her arms and shoulders. The water had turned cold, the night air brisk. She didn't want to disappear into this river or on the other side, in the imperial North. She still had a life to give her people. There was still so much work to be done. Her parents had known that. That's why they'd left her behind when they went to the city. It wasn't only to keep her safe. They'd known that whatever happened to them, she would go on to live her own life. Make her own choices. She remembered her father tossing her skyward and catching her. She heard her mother whispering to her, *chi, chi, chi, little bird*. They'd made themselves let go.

"Yasmin, I love you," she said to the chill night air, as if the waters or the wind would carry the message.

CHAPTER 22

ACROSS THE CITY, raindrops slid to earth in straight unbroken lines. For two days they'd fallen in an unceasing patter too gentle, so it looked at first, to harm anybody or anything. But the rain had saturated the city's ground soil, filled gutters and drains to overflowing, loosened mortar, weakened foundations, upended trees and brought down bridges. Soraida watched the scenes on television. In Izabal, where the winds had been violent, whole families awaited rescue on their rooftops in the middle of a mud-coloured sea. In Sololá, the downpour had wiped a village off the side of a mountain. *Mitch*, the news anchors called it, and from tropical storm to hurricane to tropical storm again Mitch's blade of water and air had ploughed through the isthmus. Soraida checked the newscast during each meal and before she turned in for the night. She watched when she fed Leo his bottle or soothed him into sleep. The damage, it seemed, was confined to Central America. Yasmin and Isabel would be well beyond its reach by now. But it was hard not to wonder and worry.

Leo had just started on his morning ration of Incaparina mixed with powdered milk, pulling at the bottle's rubber nipple with his new front teeth, when the knock came. Soraida plopped him into the baby walker she'd borrowed from a neighbour and went to answer. It was Isabel.

"Oh!" Soraida said, at a loss momentarily for any other word. She recovered herself and waved Isabel indoors, out of the rain. "You must be soaked," she said.

Beads of water fell from the tips of Isabel's hair and nose and from the satchel that hung from her shoulder. Her face was red and drawn. She wiped it with the back of her arm and shook the water from her hands before kissing Soraida's cheek.

"I need to change," she said. "I'll just be a minute."

Soraida followed her, down the corridor, across the courtyard, to the bathroom, where Isabel entered and shut the door. And then she waited, questions sprouting and growing in her mind like mushrooms. Her niece emerged a few minutes later in a dry T-shirt and jeans, rubbing her head with a towel. The sodden jeans and T-shirt she'd arrived in dripped from the shower rod behind her.

"Well, did you find her?" Soraida asked. "Is she all right?"

Isabel had caught sight of Leo, who was banging his bottle against the plastic tray that encircled him.

"Can I?" she asked.

He must have recognized her voice, because he lifted his eyes to her, dropped the bottle and started to squirm, waving his outstretched arms.

When Soraida nodded, Isabel rescued the bottle from the floor and plucked her grandson from the walker. She nuzzled his belly.

"Hello, little man," she said.

Soraida repeated her question. "Well? What happened?"

Isabel turned to her, her lips pressed tight. She had tears in her eyes.

"What's wrong?"

"I failed," she said. "I turned back."

"And Yasmin?"

"I don't know." Leo rested his head against her shoulder. Isabel stroked his back. "Give me a moment," she said. "Please."

So Soraida sat at the kitchen table and waited. Sometimes no news was good news, she told herself, turning from Isabel to the television, which was retransmitting yesterday's footage. Isabel, too, raised her eyes now and then to the screen as she circled the table, rocking Leo, until he fell asleep.

"Do you want him in your bedroom?" she asked.

Again, Soraida nodded. She wasn't sure what else to do. She was thinking about Yasmin. Yasmin out there alone in a big unfriendly land. She'd been sure Isabel would find her. Isabel always did what she said she would. When her niece returned from the bedroom, she took a seat beside Soraida and watched the newscast as Soraida watched her.

"I couldn't do it," she said at last. "I got all the way to the river and I couldn't do it." She turned from the newscast. "How many times have I told Yasmin I would do anything for her? But it was a lie. I'm no mother. I've never been a mother. I used to tell myself that everything I did was for Yasmin. But that's a lie, too. It was all for me. And it still is. Is it any wonder I've been alone my whole life?"

On the screen, a tree slid from a riverbank into the tumultuous current.

"Of course you're a good mother," Soraida said.

Isabel didn't respond.

"Yasmin will be okay. She will. When she finds her father, she'll get in touch."

Isabel had turned back to the newscast, so Soraida left her there, staring at the screen, and went to fix her something to eat. She took a blackened plantain from the fruit basket and sliced it into four pieces. Isabel was home. That was important for Soraida and for Leo. Soraida prayed that Yasmin would see sense and turn around, too. But if she refused, Soraida was prepared. She placed the plantain pieces in a small saucepan, added a stick of cinnamon and water from the jug and put the saucepan on the stove. It surprised her that she was able to let go of Yasmin after acting as mother and father to her for most of her life. But she was. She lit the stove and went to check on Leo.

He had rolled onto his back, one chubby arm flung against the pillow Isabel had placed beside him to prevent a fall. His mouth formed soundless words as he slept. Soraida rolled him onto his side again, toward the wall, and moved the pillow snugly against his back.

She heard Isabel enter.

"How's he been?" Isabel whispered.

"Perfectly fine—as you can see." Soraida pulled the woven blanket over his legs and tucked it around him. "I don't know that he really noticed the change. Yasmin was already away so much. And you—." She straightened and smoothed her apron. "He's used to being with different people, and you're back sooner than we thought."

Isabel smiled down at the sleeping boy and brushed a lock of sweat-soaked hair from his forehead.

"And how have you been?" she asked.

"Let's go to the kitchen, where we can talk properly," Soraida said.

Isabel turned to go, looking back once more at her grandson before she left the room.

"It's been terrible here," Soraida said once they were seated. "How on earth did you get through the storm? There's damage in Petén and Izabal, in Sololá, and here in the city, too." She dabbed her face with her handkerchief. It was warm despite the rain. "There were mudslides in La Limonada.'

"Byron's family?" Isabel asked.

"They're safe. They're at a shelter for now, but then what?"

Isabel shook her head. "It didn't start until I was on the bus headed back. I wondered whether I'd have to hole up somewhere and wait it out, but our driver just kept on driving. Taking his chances. Maybe he wanted to get home. He kept the radio tuned to Radio Sonora the whole way, I suppose to hear where the weather was headed or just to get the news. And we were lucky. We got through. No checkpoints either with so much rain." She looked around the small kitchen. "I couldn't see out of the bus at all."

Soraida reached for Isabel's hand, which was cold despite the room's heat. She rubbed it between her palms to warm it.

"Your friend—Danilo—he came by. People at the Foundation have set up shelters. They've been collecting things for the victims. So I told him to take what he needed."

Isabel continued to scan the kitchen, her eyes resting on the dish rack, the alarm clock, and again on the television.

"And Max, too," Soraida said. Something like a small electrical current moved through her niece. "He came by, I suppose because he wanted to know if I'd heard anything."

Isabel turned to Soraida. She lowered her eyes.

"So now he's helping Danilo pack up things from the shop. In fact, he's supposed to come by this morning."

A smile lighted her niece's face. "Haven't *you* been busy," she said. "Careful, or they'll try to recruit you."

Soraida laughed and waved the joke away with her handkerchief. She patted Isabel's hand. It was good to see her niece smile.

"What can I do to help?" Isabel said.

Soraida showed her the bags of clothing stacked in a corner of her shop and Isabel set to work, filling more bags and stacking them with the others. The air was thick and close, the light dim. Outside and above them, the rain drummed lightly against the rooftops, the street, the market canopies. It felt good to be doing something. Anything. The trip north had emptied Isabel out. She'd come back, but she wasn't sure what she had come back to do. To care for Leo? To mark time until Yasmin's return? Maybe that was enough.

A number of the shop's wooden stands were bare.

"Are you getting another bale soon?" Isabel said. "To replace all this?"

Soraida shrugged and kept working.

Nearing ten, they heard a knock and Isabel went to answer. It was Claudia. She held a plastic bag over her head against the rain. Behind her Max stood dripping.

Isabel backed up so they could both squeeze inside. She greeted Claudia first. "I don't know anything," Isabel said. "I'm sorry."

Claudia hugged her. "We were so worried about you."

"You haven't had word either?"

Claudia shook her head. "They'll get in touch when they can. We've just got to be patient." She moved aside so Isabel could greet Max. "And right now, we've got work to do. I guess your aunt has told you. Funny how things work out."

Isabel pressed her face to Max's chest. He smelled like damp wood.

"I failed them," she said.

As he'd done when they'd parted the week before, Max wrapped his arms around her and kissed the top of her head. She felt for a moment as though she were nestled within a warm, moist cocoon. Then Claudia slapped his shoulder and he released her.

"C'mon," Claudia said. "We need to get everything ready before Danilo gets back." She took Isabel's arm and started down the corridor. "You did the right thing. We need you here. Remember when we left our parents? We were barely older than they were. And we weren't leaving for love but to go to war. Our parents were proud—they let us go."

Isabel glanced back at Max, who smiled at her as he dripped.

"I'd better dry off," he said.

There would be time, Isabel told herself. There would be time for everything. It sounded in her mind more like a prayer than a certainty.

The stands along one wall of Soraida's shop already stood empty and the rest soon would. Soraida caught Isabel staring.

"They might as well take it all if there's a need," she said.

"And what'll *you* do?" Isabel said.

Her aunt beckoned her to follow, back to the house and into Soraida's bedroom, where she ushered Isabel in and shut the door. Isabel hadn't set foot in the room in more than a year. They sat on the bed.

"What?" Isabel said.

Soraida didn't reply right away. She eyed the wardrobe door before she turned her gaze on her niece.

"I want to give the shop to Byron's family—to Élida, her mother, little Soraida. I don't . . ." She said no more.

Isabel studied her aunt. The past year had taken its toll. Soraida looked older, but also more at ease, free of the strain Isabel had always observed in her. A long time ago, as a young woman, Soraida had abandoned safety and comfort for the sake of the people she loved, and now she was ready to do it again.

"You really have been busy," Isabel said.

"I've had it mind for some time—even before." She gestured to the barred window above the bed. The sky was blue again, as if there'd never been a storm. "You wouldn't mind?"

"Why would I mind?" Isabel said.

Soraida had taken her handkerchief from her apron pocket and was pulling at it, her brow knitted. When she realized Isabel was watching her, she lay the handkerchief open on her lap, smoothed it out, folded it into a small square and returned it to her pocket.

"Your house at the housing project," she said. "Is it still yours? They haven't given it to somebody else?"

"No. It's mine. I've got title."

Soraida was pulling at her fingers now.

"Auntie," Isabel said. "Do you want to come live with me?"

There were tears in Soraida's eyes.

"You won't miss it here?" Isabel said, just to be sure.

Soraida shook her head. "I really won't," she said.

With Claudia, Isabel made arrangements to accompany Danilo on his trip back to Sololá. They had a shelter set up in San Lucas Tolimán, where a massive mudslide had obliterated an entire village. It was Kaqchikel territory. Isabel could serve as interpreter. Danilo pulled up around eight the next morning and they packed the pickup with the remainder of Soraida's stock. Soraida had gone to help Élida move her mother and daughter from the shelter. As soon as Isabel hopped into the truck cab, Danilo started talking, as if he'd been saving every detail of the last week just for her.

"I went by on a whim," he said. "I really didn't think Soraida would offer more than a bag of clothing—businesswomen that she is. But she went all in. *All* in. Because of you, you know. It's like command central now. Not really, but she's been great. Claudia loves her. Really. They're practically best friends. It's like Mitch just washed away everything that didn't matter. Clean slate. I don't mean that, of course. People have lost everything. People who hardly had anything to begin with. But for us—it's brought us closer to our own people again. I'm feeling better, I know that. I feel like I'm actually doing something worthwhile."

Isabel was happy to listen. She was feeling better, too. Maybe it was an illusion—the emergency had forced them into action and action always felt productive even when it wasn't. But we are the things we do. She'd long believed that. It was up to her to make what she did now count for something, something that would take root and grow. Grow slowly, perhaps, perhaps quietly, but grow, nonetheless. She was beginning to glimpse a future.

The rain, despite the destruction in so many parts of the country, had left the fields they passed through green and sparkling. They headed south, the volcanoes Pacaya and Agua towering above the jagged hills on either side of the highway. As the road veered to the west, the landscape flattened into a wide fertile plain. At Cocales, they turned north again, toward Lake Atitlán and its ring of guardian volcanoes.

About fifteen minutes outside San Lucas, where the highway descended slightly between scrubby fields, Danilo slowed the pickup. It was an unremarkable stretch: squat green bushes dotted the sides of the road, green crops lay beyond them. "You've got to see this," he said, checking the road behind him before he killed the motor.

Isabel twisted to look out the cab's back window. There were no other cars. On the shoulder stood a bent and faded metal sign. The only word Isabel could make out was *mysterious*.

The pickup started to move, backward. It was rolling uphill.

"What on earth?" she said, turning back to Danilo. "What is this?"

"A mystery."

The pickup continued to roll, against gravity, to the top of the knoll.

"This is amazing," Isabel said. "How did you find it?"

"People know about it. There's a sign." He pointed to the sign Isabel had tried to read. "I don't know why more people don't know. It blows my mind every time."

"You do this every trip?"

He grinned. "Almost every trip."

"It's amazing," she repeated. "Does anybody know why?"

"Oh, probably. But it doesn't really matter why. Does it?"

Isabel scanned the landscape, bubbling with new growth. There was a whole world out there to discover. She would do what she could do to help Guatemala heal, to restore balance. Doing so would help her heal, as well. But some mysteries would be forever beyond her. That, too, was life. She squeezed his hand. "Thank you," she said.

Danilo turned the key and started the engine. "We'd better be going," he said.

As they pulled away, his pager buzzed. Keeping one hand on the wheel, he removed it from his shirt pocket, read the number and shut it off.

"There's a municipal phone centre not far from the shelter," he said. "We can stop there."

He didn't say another word until they got there, and neither did she. But he held her hand as he drove. Isabel watched the road. Her heart was pounding. Fifteen minutes seemed a very long time.

At the phone centre, a one-storey cement building in horizontal blue and white stripes, they were assigned a booth. Danilo sat on a stool between its Plexiglas walls and dialled as Isabel stood behind him and looked on. He listened to the message and signalled to Isabel to open the pocket directory he'd handed to her.

"They made it," he said. "Write this down."

Into the receiver, he said, "Can you say that again?"

Isabel wrote down the ten digits Danilo repeated to her and gave him back his phone book. He dialled again.

Before the first ring had finished, she heard the click, a distant hello.

"Jorge!" Danilo shouted into the receiver. "Jorgito!"

Then he was listening, his head twisted toward Isabel and his mouth open somewhere between a smile and the words he was trying to form either for Isabel or for his son. "Hold on a second," he said. "Isabel's here too." He clasped his palm over the receiver.

"*They* were worried about *us!*" he said, winded already. "They heard the news about Mitch and they didn't know where exactly it'd hit. And then right away they were taking up collections to send down. All of them. Jorge, Yasmin. Luís too." He caught his breath. "You can wire it," he said into the receiver. "The money—you can wire it to the Foundation or to Soraida. Doesn't really matter. We're all working together. I'll find out where and let you know. I wish your mother was here. She's been desperate. No, no. She's fine. You know how strong she is. As soon as we get back to the capital, I'll get her to call. Erika misses you, too. So much."

He was wiping tears from his eyes. He seemed to have forgotten Isabel was standing there. Waiting.

"Okay," he said finally. "Good. Yes. I'll put her on."

He got up and passed the phone to Isabel. Every cell in her body quivered. She took a deep breath and exhaled slowly before she took Danilo's place in the booth and spoke into the receiver. "Hello?"

The voice on the other end reached her, as weightless and airy as a spring breeze. The words, as soothing.

"Hello? Mami? Is that you?"

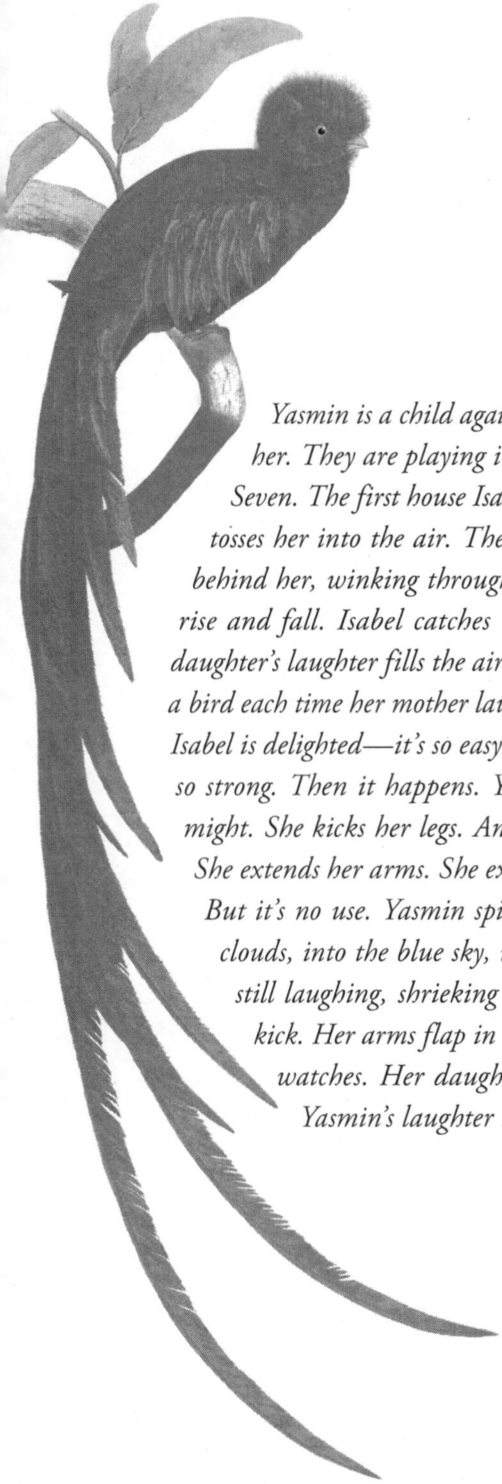

PART IV

kaq'ïq' (air)

Yasmin is a child again, three years old, and Isabel is with her. They are playing in the patio of the old house in Zone Seven. The first house Isabel knew. She lifts her daughter and tosses her into the air. The girl is laughing. The sun is bright behind her, winking through strands of smooth black hair that rise and fall. Isabel catches Yasmin and tosses her again. Her daughter's laughter fills the air, she spreads her arms and flaps like a bird each time her mother launches her skyward. Higher. Higher. Isabel is delighted—it's so easy. Yasmin weighs so little. Isabel feels so strong. Then it happens. Yasmin flaps her arms with all her might. She kicks her legs. And she is out of reach. Isabel jumps. She extends her arms. She extends her fingers. She jumps again. But it's no use. Yasmin spirals upward, past the round white clouds, into the blue sky, up, up, until she is circling the sun, still laughing, shrieking from the thrill of it. Her bare feet kick. Her arms flap in a ridiculous, beautiful dance. Isabel watches. Her daughter is a speck against the blue sky. Yasmin's laughter reaches her still.

ACKNOWLEDGEMENTS

Although I built this novel around certain historical events (the end of the internal armed conflict in Guatemala, presentation of REMHI's report on wartime atrocities, the assassination two days later of Monsignor Juan José Gerardi Conedera, Hurricane Mitch), it is a work of fiction. I encourage readers who are interested in learning more about the war and its costs to seek out both *Guatemala: Never Again!* by the Recuperation of Historical Memory Project (REMHI) and *Memory of Silence: Report of the Commission of Historical Clarification* (the Truth Commission mandated by the peace accords).

I drew on the latter for my description of the massacre beside the Pixcayá River and on publications by the Guatemalan Forensic Anthropology Foundation (FAFG) for descriptions of the exhumations. An important source for better understanding the history of San Martín Jilotepeque and the war's impact there was *San Martín Jilotepeque: Memoria, Conflicto y Reconciliación, 1950–2008*, by Glenda García García and Emiliano Armira Atz. I relied on the article "Survivors, Victims Return to Guatemalan Villages," written for the *National Catholic Reporter* by Lorraine Orlandi, for my depiction of the ceremony and reburial of victims in Cuarto Pueblo. The epigraph is my translation into English of an excerpt from Sam Colop's 2012 translation into Spanish of the *Popol Wuj*. Beyond these publications, I am obliged to the hundreds of people I spoke with while I lived in Guatemala during those years. Thank you for sharing your experiences, your views, and your aspirations with me.

I am grateful to the Canada Council of the Arts and the Ontario Arts Council for the grant support I received while writing this book. Heartfelt thanks also to the team at Guernica Editions: to Michael Mirolla for his guidance and sharp editor's eye, to Marisa Jorgensen for promoting the novel, and to David Moratto for its gorgeous cover. Thank you to Leslie Shimotakahara for choosing *Even the Birds* for the Guernica Prize for Literary Fiction and for suggesting several revisions to improve it. Thank you to Joy Kogawa, Carmen Aguirre and Rajinderpal Pal for your endorsements.

I am indebted to Juan Everardo Chuc Xum for his expertise in the Kaqchikel language and his knowledge of Kaqchikel culture and worldview and to Karina Siguil for her close read of the manuscript as a Guatemalan who lived through her country's transition from war to peace.

Many other people helped at earlier stages. Participants in the Long Stuff office of the now defunct Zoetrope Virtual Studio, in particular Marko Fong, read early chapters, offering encouragement and insights. Members of my in-person writing group (especially Laura Wythe, Sue Brown and Mary Lou McRae) read every chapter that followed and helped get them ready for submission. During a wonderful retreat on Pelee Island, Heather O'Neill gave new direction to the first chapter. Daniel McIvor, when he was writer-in-residence at Western University, did his best to get the manuscript into an agent's hands. That vote of confidence meant the world. A course taught by Jennifer Manuel helped greatly with revisions. Editors Matthew Godden and Allister Thompson also supplied thoughtful feedback. Thank you, thank you to each of you.

More recently, in the School of Creative Writing at University of Toronto Continuing Studies, I have found a supportive and accessible (online!) environment where I can continue to develop my craft. I am grateful for the learning and the connections made.

Finally, thank you to José Juan, Nohemí and Nelson for the joy you bring me every day, and to Enedelio, my biggest cheerleader. *Los quiero.*

ABOUT THE AUTHOR

Ruth Taylor worked as a journalist in Guatemala from 1994 to 2003, before returning to Canada and taking up fiction. Her short stories have appeared in *The Massachusetts Review*, *The Dalhousie Review*, *Potomac Review*, and *This Magazine*, among other journals. In 2024, she won the Penguin Random House Canada Student Award for Fiction, and in 2025, the Guernica Prize for Literary Fiction. *Even the Birds* is her first novel. Ruth lives and writes in London, Ontario.

MIX
Paper
FSC® C100212

Printed by Imprimerie Gauvin
Gatineau, Québec